BLAME

PAUL READ

Legend Press Ltd, 107-111 Fleet Street, London, EC4A 2AB
info@legend-paperbooks.co.uk | www.legendpress.co.uk

Print ISBN 978-1-7850792-1-4
Ebook ISBN 978-1-7850792-0-7
Set in Times. Printed in the United Kingdom by TJ International.
Cover design by Simon Levy www.simonlevyassociates.co.uk

After gaining a first in Fine Art at the Kent Institute of Art and Design at Canterbury, **Paul Read** moved to London, finding employment at Foyles bookshop before becoming a teacher, an experience he drew on for his debut novel, *The Art Teacher*. Paul received a distinction from City University London for his Creative Writing MA. He currently lives in Italy with Patricia and their two children.

Follow Paul on Twitter
@paulreadauthor

For my parents,
for not being the ones in this book.

PROLOGUE

The three of us trudge to the summit with heads bowed, the north wind twisting the long grass flat under our feet. Our midday sun is a ghost behind clouds pregnant with snow, and nothing in this beautiful, hostile place has a shadow.

Mum holds the box. It's made of thick purple cardboard, about the same shape and size as a child's shoebox, and is bound by an unpretentious elastic band. Suddenly, she slows.

'Here. This is the place.'

The view – all jutting piers, undulating shores and wind-lashed hawthorns – rises to meet us as we scale the crown, and fifty unspoilt miles of the south coast unfurl before us. At the horizon, the sky becomes the land becomes the sea. My eyes smart with the cold.

'He loved this place,' Mum affirms for the hundredth time, this recently retired woman who used to dress for any occasion but today wears tired jeans and a shapeless brown jumper. The weather has made an unruly thatch of her hair.

She slides the lid off and the three of us peer inside.

My brother's reaction is as I'd expected, but I take no pleasure from the vaguely harrowed expression he wears. He's not a man of science and had been expecting the grey ashes of television drama. What he sees instead is an exercise in simple physics: the pulverised dry bone fragments from a cremulator risen, via convection, through the lighter granules after ten years of sitting in the corner of Mum's bedroom.

'It looks like…' he begins.

9

'I know,' Mum says.

A middle-aged man approaches from a path below, his waterproofs vacuum-sealed against his torso by the swirling wind. A black Labrador leads the way, sniffing at the sparse hedgerows. I look to the others.

'Shall we wait?'

They both nod. We've waited a decade; another two minutes won't hurt.

'We should turn our backs,' my brother suggests, pointing across the green-grey, 'so he's taken across the Downs, that way.'

He's.

We turn away from the wind, though it seems to make little difference.

The approaching man quickens, as if he knows we're waiting for him. His eyes are apologetic. In his wake, clouds break and snow begins to spiral in small flakes, black against the white sky. They settle on the frozen ground.

So, this is the day it has to happen. My brother's right: those fragile, shell-like bone particles are *him*. This is more than a gesture. This is goodbye.

We have arrived at an ending.

Mum begins to pour as she walks along the brow of the hill, leaving a little trail of fragments behind her. As the larger granules run out, the smaller particles are released, catch the wind and disperse in a thousand different directions. My brother reels, having caught some in the eye. We laugh. My mother hands the box to me and I empty a little more. The ash diffuses through the wind in a spectral curtain of swirls and eddies. I can taste it on my teeth. Mum stands back at some distance, lost in thought. I hand the box to my brother and he shakes out the remainder, his eyes red from the cold and the ash.

Then, it is over.

We stand there, cinders in our mouths, our hair, upon our coats, watching the snow mingle with the dust, float back down to Earth a part of it, and with every blink I see a fresh tableau within the churning sky. Candlelit lovers caught unaware through a thin gap in a door. A coffin-shaped Nokia ringing to announce a murder. The beginning of love above New York as a semi-naked silhouette hurries back to bed. Blood leading to the closed doors of an ambulance. All times are here and now and one and the same, condensed, with this moment, into a single journey. And it all seems like yesterday.

We fall into a group hug and stare out over the whitening view. I'm the first to speak.

'Bye Dad.'

Time travel. It's an easy, forgiving process. It takes nothing to go back, to rewrite.

It's often said that history is scripted by the winners. Personally, I think 'survivors' would be a better word. I've been several people in my time, and my return visits to those others' pasts are unreliable at best and complete fabrications at worst. I have survived myself, but only just.

Don't believe a word I tell you. Take it from me.

We return to the car park, our shoes creaking across the compacting snow.

I can see my wife reading a book in the back of the Cherokee. Our son is upright in his car seat beside her, in a sleep which could, and does, survive fireworks and thunderstorms but cannot cope with the imperceptible tread of a parent's footstep. Sure enough, he stirs, then turns a slow, accusatory head towards me. This extrasensory perception alerts his mother to my presence. She checks her smile immediately, assuming it's inappropriate. I beam back, but this only serves to make her uneasy. She knows the full range of my smiles, and this one didn't fool her at all.

She stuffs her book out of sight and winds the window down. Her eyes, pink and watery, focus on the empty box Mum carries.

We all get in without another word. My brother in the back. My mother next to me. I know it's just my imagination, but the snow slowing the wipers seems grittier than usual. The analogue clock mounted to the Jeep's dashboard shows it's much later than I realised. Once again, time ran away from us.

Mum asks if the snow will cause problems for the car. I reassure her that it won't.

On the way to the restaurant, I attempt to close my mind around the memories and feelings we've just thrown into the air. I can't rationalise or order those lonely fragments of time. All I can do, as the chatter around me grows in its geniality and my son steals the conversation away from the darkness, is watch the narrow roads unlace in the rear-view mirror, my thoughts whirling with the bone particles, hunting for answers, for chronology, trying to get back, right back, to a beginning of sorts.

And then I hit the ice. The Jeep bucks, jolts out of my control. I try to do as you're told to do in the circumstances and steer into the skid but the steering locks beneath my hands and we glide, in slow motion yet at thirty miles an hour, into an oncoming van, its driver's horrified face nothing but an open mouth screaming towards us.

PART ONE

CHAPTER ONE

My father died today, around mid-afternoon I'm told.

I hadn't seen much of him during his latter years, his years of letters, though I'd heard from plenty of his bank managers. So strained had our relationship become we could only communicate through financiers, like a divorcing couple. To tell the truth, I didn't mind bailing him out from time to time; it kept his literary ambitions ticking, it kept him busy. And it kept him the hell away from me.

'Was your father a religious man?' she asks, blonde, one gene shy of albino, a figure at odds with the mahogany and brass splendour of the rest of Kirkby Funeral Consultants. She's about thirty, not unattractive, and sports no wedding ring on the petite hand fondling a St. Christopher against a salient, chenille-clad bosom.

'Religion wasn't a big part of his life. At least, it never used to be.'

She ticks a box with an exaggerated flourish. 'Okay. Did he make any arrangements himself about how he'd have liked things to go from here?'

It takes me a few seconds to comprehend the essence of this question. 'A Will hasn't been found yet. It was... sudden. I only heard he died a couple of hours ago.'

The pencil hovers, snatches at another box.

I practise my shrug in response to queries about coroners and death certificates and my apathy is taken as the cue to broach the issue of prices. A white hand passes me a pamphlet of funeral options while the other gestures towards a vinyl-smooth headstone, the word 'exemplar' carved into its marble.

'Anything that suits?' A patient voice, traipsing through the routine. I picture her at customs, in stiff blue polyester: *Did you pack these bags yourself, sir?*

'Perhaps.' I'm still directing my breath away from her. My 'family circumstances' granted me early leave of work and, though this is debatably not a joyful occasion, it was happy hour at The King's Arms.

'Forgive me for asking… You weren't particularly *close* to your father, were you, Mr Marr?'

When I shake my head, tiny lines of tension around her eyes relax. Grief, it seems, puts even funeral arrangers off.

'Please call me Lucas. Sorry, what was your name again?'

'Anna,' she says, or perhaps 'Tanya,' standing and crossing the room to unearth another brochure from a cabinet by the window. Outside, London's summer sky has bruised and the sun cuts like a hole punch through the fumes.

I realise too late that I'm staring at her reflection. A smile sputters briefly in the crescent dimples of her cheeks as she hands over a booklet entitled *When Someone Dies*. Our fingers graze.

'Will your father's service be a local one?'

'He lived on the south coast. My mother's dealing with most of the immediate formalities, but she asked me to find out some details.'

'Not a problem. Kirkby Funeral Consultants have branches all over the country. We can liaise with our people down there.' She taps at the keyboard on her desk and a printout eases from the LaserJet behind her. I'm passed the sheet, which breaks down the costs of several funeral alternatives, and my eyes are drawn to the date in the top right corner. Thursday, 30 June, 2005. Forever consigned to history as the day my father died.

Collecting my modest pile of leaflets together, I rise. She

lingers by the desk, silent and somewhat expectant, refusing to offer her hand.

'He can't have been very old, your father. After all, you're not... Well, you're quite...'

'You're kind of young to be doing this gig yourself.'

She announces it's only her second week without supervision. Before this she was a PA for a minor Tory MP. There's probably a joke here somewhere. After a while, I realise I'm no longer listening to a word she's saying. *Executor. Indemnity. Disbursement.* Out of habit, I lean in for the flirt, drop my eyes and gaze at the plump, yielding aperture of her mouth for a deliberately uncomfortable amount of time. *Testator. Crematoria. Probate.* She begins to lose the thread of her sentences, stumbles over words.

'You do realise your company's acronym is KFC, don't you?'

She finds this far funnier than she ought to.

'I better be off,' I announce. 'It's gone six and I'm probably making you late for something, aren't I?'

Her eyes don't leave mine. 'There's no real hurry.'

'In that case... what would you say if I asked you out for a quick drink?'

Those modest dimples betray the choking of her smile, a moment's hesitation, perhaps calculation. 'I'd probably say, "That would be nice, thank you," but I guess you won't know until you ask.'

'Would you like a quick drink?'

'Wait here. I won't be long.' She disappears behind a blue velveteen curtain, into the main part of the parlour.

I take the opportunity to siphon a cup of water from the gurgling cooler by her desk, then prowl the reception area to stomp some feeling back into my legs. It must be a depressing place to work. Pictures of white doves and lilies adorn the walls, John Donne poems, haloed cherubs. Bored of waiting, I poke my head through the back curtain and find a low-lit corridor, half a dozen doors leading off it. She's in a cramped, untidy office to the right, her back to me, applying make-up by use of a small handheld mirror. I'm spotted in its reflective surface and she spins round, surprised.

'Sorry,' I say. 'I was looking for the… bathroom.'

She acknowledges the creaking euphemism with a cute smirk, then nods down the corridor.

I push open the door to 'The Chapel of Rest'. At the rear of the room an open bible rests on a low lectern, flanked by candelabra and a gold-framed painting of a mournful Virgin Mary. Ornate floral displays bloom pinks and yellows from all four corners and in the centre stand two mahogany trestles, presumably the catafalque on which coffins are to rest. A broad, wooden crucifix hangs over all.

I discern a light sighing. Anna-or-Tanya's behind me, her eyes painted that little bit darker, her mouth showing a touch more rouge. The jumper has gone, replaced by a flimsy yellow vest.

That tangled liaison between sex and death – a promise of immortality on the stroke of *la petit mort* – spares her decision to beautify herself, renders it no less appropriate than my present grubby fantasies. Ejaculation and expiration are bedfellows, for sure, but here, in this room, the notion is so… temptingly wrong. The bible, splayed on its lectern, petitions us with notions of resurrection through incorruption yet the blunt fact is that modern humans have lasted two hundred thousand years thanks to back-alley quickies and after-hours congress in boardrooms. In order to eschew mortality, I must be haunted by desire.

I take the step that separates us and kiss her. My heel strikes a trestle and we sink to the carpet, against the lectern. The bible falls, Deuteronomy-side up, as I slide off her vest to reveal the soft pout of her belly, a constellation of tiny moles.

And then she stops, holds up her hands.

We sit avoiding each other's eyes. 'This is… Your poor father…'

From the depths of some hitherto uncharted realm of patience comes, 'You're right. You're quite right. I'm sorry.'

'No, no. It's my fault. I don't know what I was thinking...'

Firm avowals to meet up for a drink at a later date follow, but we now speak to each other in the voices of amateur dramatic performers and both know I'll head straight to another funeral directors' in the morning.

Once passion's gone, guilt revisits the scene of the crime. Did I lead her on? Misread the situation? Only when my eyes rest on the picture of the Virgin behind her do I recall the cross which hung like a razorblade round Anna-or-Tanya's neck, now discarded under her crumpled vest. She desperately wanted to live for the moment but eternal life got the better of her.

A bell tinkles.

'Bloody hell, I never locked the door.' Panic laces her voice and a look of infinite culpability spoils her face, as though she's about to cry.

I gather my clothes. 'I better go.'

In the reception, a middle-aged man of repentant demeanour is waiting, grasping the hand of a young boy. The man's sorrowful jowls and drooping eyes give the impression he's suffered terribly at the hands of gravity.

'Hello?' he calls. 'Are you still open?'

I brush past and escape into the early evening. Behind me, a flushed and backwards-vested Anna-or-Tanya greets the visitors. She's not even looking as I press a fist to my ear, with pinkie and thumb extended in an approximation of a telephone, and mouth 'I'll call you,' through the glass.

CHAPTER TWO

'And did you?'

My right shoulder presses the mobile phone to my ear while both hands refocus the microscope. An image hardens into clarity through the eyepieces: a yellowish nebula swimming with insect-like hieroglyphs which I translate into the relevant column in my notebook. I unclip the Petri slide and insert another.

'Sorry. Did I what?'

'*Call* her?' Aaron repeats.

I only mentioned yesterday evening's shameful encounter to Aaron, I think, in an attempt to harvest a degree of comedy, but somewhere along the line I can't help but feel my anecdote veered towards bragging.

'No chance.'

'Bit grim, if you ask me. At the funeral parlour.'

'It wasn't like we did it on a coffin,' I tell him, pandering to the unspoken assumption that I slept with… whatever her name was. Machismo fills in the dots, the implications.

But I've misjudged the tone. I can hear it in my old friend's voice. 'So, anyway. Um, point of the call: are we still up for later?'

'Sure. I'll see you at eight.'

'Cool. And, Lucas, you're… y'know… okay, yeah?'

'Why wouldn't I be?'

I end the call, put the phone down and bend my eyes to the next slide. Through the eyepieces, the clustering of enzymes resembles the drifting continents of foam atop a pint of bitter. At least, when I'm able to focus properly they do; tiredness increases the depth of field to a point where reality smudges and several times I zoom the lens in to find it's my own eyes that fail me. Twice my phone hops and burrs on the polished slate of the bench. It's a hometown dialling code. I let it ring.

'Come in!' I shout, in response to a firm, familiar knock on the lab door.

A slender woman, about thirty, enters and clomps in the direction of my PC with a flat-footed gait. She wears a grey pullover, blue jeans, and in the light from the window her dancing brown hair sports a dash of red. There's a touch of fire in those dark eyes, too.

'Afternoon, honey,' Mariana says, before pulling up a stool and opening a bag of vinegar-doused chips. Sterility, hygiene, contamination: these words mean little to our IT department.

She stabs a sausage towards my computer. 'What's the problem with it this time?'

'It's slow, and I don't trust the rattlesnake noises it makes when I turn it on.'

'Syngestia must've given you the worst computer in the building, Lucas. I've been working here six months and I reckon you've called on me every week.'

I shrug. 'What can I say? A man gets lonely dabbling in Pharmacogenomics all day.'

After she's checked the connections, Mariana wriggles herself into a comfortable position on the stool then starts clicking through a list of on-screen protocols. 'So what's Pharmo-kacko-thingamabob when it's at home?' she asks in her not-quite-American, not-quite-English accent, the drawl of a New York émigré.

'It's the study of genetic inheritance, essentially. It's possible, one day, that medicine will be tailor-made to each person's own makeup. Imagine that. *Personalised* drugs will be safer and more efficient than today's catch-all remedies, with their side effects and...'

I distinguish the lack of interest in her eyes. The top lip sheathes her large front teeth in a mocking semi-pout. Heaven knows why I'm so attracted to these oversized incisors.

'...It's not the most interesting research I've ever done, I admit. At the moment, I'm looking for DNA variations that occur when a single nucleotide in the genetic sequence is altered, every 100 to 300 bases along the 3-billion-base human genome.'

Mariana licks a finger, wipes her hand down the outer thigh of her jeans. 'Wow,' she intones, then informs me the IT department's rebooting all servers for an hour at around five o'clock, and that I'll need a new firewall. We'll never fully understand each other's sciences.

Perhaps sensing my ignorance, she changes the subject. 'Doing anything exciting tonight?'

'Just meeting someone for a drink.'

She splays unpainted fingertips against her heart. 'Not another woman, Lucas?'

God, she's wonderful.

'An old friend,' I tell her. We're meeting in the West End. What you up to?'

'Not much.'

Maybe it's time I took a chance with Mariana. For all I know there are others at Syngestia who ring the IT office on a weekly basis to announce they've virused their laptops to death. Maybe, given time, one of them will capitalise on their mutual flirting and innuendo. The building's hardly overburdened with women under forty, let alone attractive brunettes with the physiognomy of Colgate models.

'Why don't you come with us?' I ask. 'We're just having a few at The Phoenix. Bring a friend if you like.'

I perceive a momentary flicker of surprise cross her face. She drags her stool closer to mine and ducks her eyes to the microscope. 'Well, per*haps*. If it won't be spoiling a boys' night or anything.'

Having succeeded in placing Mariana's hand on the fine adjustment knob, I encourage her to focus the microscope, referring her to the black rings of Golgi apparatus, the circular vesicles and the eyeball-like reticulum, glowing a strange, luminous green.

'It's like a little solar system,' she says.

The laboratory door flies open.

'Heard the latest?' Mumbling Frank asks, in a voice shriller than usual, hands worming restlessly around lab-coat pockets as though hunting greasy change.

Mumbling Frank's in his early forties, but is already somewhat hunched and his stubble's a permanent smear of grey on the lower half of his face, made all the greyer by the contrasting pallor of his skin. He's dullness incarnate, and the kind of jobsworth you usually find only in state-sector officialdom. This, pharmacology, is his life.

I indicate I've no idea what he's talking about.

'… EasyBreathe patent's … withdrawn,' he explains. '… lab-rats … long-term gastric problems … impurities … so close to manufacture … a damn fine pickle …'

I attempt to translate for Mariana. Apparently one of our new asthma analgesics has developed adverse side effects in test patients.

'Oh, *shit*.' The way Mariana casually picks through her bag of chips reveals she neither understands the magnitude of the problem, nor remotely cares, but the urge to bully this officious white-coat with a clipboard is too strong for most to resist.

Mumbling Frank looks from one of us to the other, faintly hurt, and announces, 'You know … not supposed … eat in the labs,' before moving to his side of the bench and the cytochrome enzymes that'll take his gossip seriously.

'Calm down, Frankie. Are you sure about this? Last month you suspected you'd found the cure for *ageing*.' Poor Frank; I'm aware I'm playing him now, purely for the thrill of seeing Mariana smile. The EasyBreathe rights are worth a fortune and, if he's right, Syngestia could be forced to instigate sizable job cuts.

'Trust me… stem cell therapies… eliminate pathogenicity…' he sulks, warming up his fingers with a pipette.

My phone rings again. I ignore it.

Mariana scrunches up her paper bag and arcs it towards the bin by the door; it misses by a respectable foot and a half. She follows it to the exit with a sardonic saunter. 'I'll come back and fix that firewall later, boys. I simply can't bear all this *excitement*.'

Aaron ducks forward and states the obvious the moment Mariana slips off to the toilets. 'She's… amazing.'

I should've seen this coming. Mariana didn't bring a friend after all.

Prominent cheekbones become knifelike as Aaron sucks at his pint. He's dark-haired, densely-browed and boyband-attractive; a scenario he frequently takes advantage of. Aaron means business this evening: he's wearing that hideous red and blue leather jacket with the white piping, the one he mistakenly believes enhances his sexual allure.

We've met at The Phoenix Bar, a windowless cellar under the eponymous Charing Cross Road theatre. Pretentious, thirsty types lounge on a long bar and groups of jobbing actors cluster in low-lit booths. Two half-cut women descend the stairs from the street above, the burn lines of early summer recklessness exposed by unfeasibly short skirts, and smile in our direction.

'It's this jacket, man,' Aaron proclaims as the flesh-flaunters side-saddle their way onto barstools. 'The birds love this jacket.'

'Your jacket sucks. You look like a pit-stop girl.'

'Stop ogling, boys.' Mariana returns to her seat opposite us. She's chosen not to change, still wears her workday jeans-pullover combo.

Obliged to talk like adults again, I enquire about Aaron's latest writing project.

He corrals the objects on the table between us with a familiarly compulsive obsession, aligning ashtray, cigarette packet and lighter with the mathematics of his universe, while outlining the plot of a hostage drama based loosely on Graham Greene's *The Honorary Consul*.

'Is it a novel?' Mariana enquires.

'No. No one writes novels. Except in novels. This is a screenplay. It's been green lit, actually.' After three pints every artist inside The Phoenix tells you they've got a film green lit, or a book on an agent's desk, or a role in the new Spielberg. 'It's on its seventeenth draft,' he informs us.

'Christ,' Mariana laughs. 'I never realised writing was such a waste of time.'

In my experience, actors, writers and artists seldom tell the truth about their careers. And seldom spend any time working. Aaron squanders much of his day bemoaning the fact he didn't follow me into the pharmaceutical industry. I envy his spare time. He envies the salary provided by an industry which coughs up roughly nine million pounds on research *every day*.

'And how's it going at Pizza Hut in the meantime?' I ask.

Aaron shoots me a charming sneer then turns, fully, to Mariana. 'So you're from America?' He already employs the faux-fascinated, brow-knitted look he's been successfully withering girls with since the turn of the millennium.

'*South* America,' she replies. 'Venezuela. But I did live in New York from like the age of three. I came over to England five years back. I *love* New York, but… you run from where you were brought up, don't you? Plus, people there can be so damn rude.'

'There are rude people here too,' I offer.

'Some, sure, but rudeness is worse than dullness. And that's what England's produced *a lot* of: dull people, Mumbling Franks who quietly get on with their jobs for fifty years without once going, "Hey, goddammit, I'm worth more *than this*!" and then rushing out to shoot people dead in shopping malls. Dull is good. Dull is unthreatening. Dull is existential angst reduced to playing hooky a couple times and a brief sob over a soccer team's relegation.'

Possibly in an attempt to exclude himself from the rest of us 'dull' Brits, Aaron snatches a tenner from his pocket and shunts it across the table towards me. 'Get the next round will you, mate.'

Mariana announces a penchant for Margaux. Whether Aaron's aware of the cost of the wine I don't know, but he nods and says, 'Fine with me,' purely because he wants to impress her. I slide his tenner back across the table.

'And when you return,' he says, 'you can tell us about this bird at the funeral par…'

I deliver a sharp kick to his ankle.

'You guys,' Mariana says, smirking. 'I don't want to hear any of your filthy college stories.'

The bar is barnacled with thespians. British drink-buying etiquette dictates old-fashioned stoicism, but I chance my arm and flutter some currency at the nearest barboy. He ignores me, of course, so I regard the signed images of long-dead matinee idols behind him until a stoned bargirl, serving drinks under a screwed hive of ginger hair, finally asks, 'What'll it be, handsome?' She wears the name of the theatre's latest production across her chest.

I buy the drinks and steel myself before my return to the table, assuming Aaron to already be in full-on flirt mode. Evidence of broken collusion is palpable in the atmosphere as I approach.

Neither of them can look the other in the eye. Neither of them can look me in the eye. Over the three of us hangs a morbid, heavy sheet of disquiet.

I take no notice of the mobile yelling in my pocket as Aaron produces a colourful flyer from his. It's a postcard for a new club on Brewer Street. The photo shows a posse of happy, toned, scantily-clad lightweights. 'Three quid off with this. Anyone fancy it? It's called Hell, of all things.'

'What do *you* feel like doing, Lucas?' Mariana asks in a voice tinged with the higher octaves of sympathy, a pitch that tells me my father's inconsiderate death is now public knowledge. Her Bournville eyes are full of pity as she places a warm hand over mine. Impulsively, one of my fingers links with one of hers, which curls its tiny, reciprocal grip. Aaron pretends he hasn't noticed and patiently swallows another glass of vino, his expression cool, free of discouragement. This is a man who's been polishing the same movie script for four years.

'Disgusting,' he announces, staring aghast at the wine.

Mariana oxygenates hers in the glass, sips at it. 'Full-bodied. Buoyant. A hint of lavender, cherry, with a... yes, an aftertaste of tobacco. Let's call it eight out of ten.'

Aaron furrows his brow, for once without affectation, then sips again. 'Yeah. Lavender. Cherry. Definitely. I mean, it grows on you.'

Mariana nods at the Coke in my glass. 'You never struck me as a teetotaller, Lucas.'

'Over a year now,' I lie.

'And well done, you.' Aaron says, raising his glass.

Mindful of my lapse yesterday – the first drink in thirteen months – and the appalling behaviour it engendered, I can only look downwards as he toasts me.

'One day at a time,' I inform them.

The mood has long been killed and we stare in brittle silence at the table. At the back of my being, somewhere, somewhere, sorrow searches desperately for an outlet. Nostalgia, perhaps nothing more than a cicatrice on the mind, lashes out on behalf of old feelings and, rather abruptly according to the startled reactions of my drinking companions, I stand.

'I'm going to Hell,' I announce.

CHAPTER THREE

The rain grows confident, slicing at the night like scratches on film print. Nevertheless, I'm overdressed, judging from the rest of Hell's queue. A Goth girl in front of us wears black hotpants and those big Herman Munster shoes. Two queens behind expose a collective four nipples and ten inches of underpants.

'I'm not sure it's my kind of place,' Mariana confesses.

'No?' It hardly looks like my kind of place either.

It's just the two of us at the moment. Aaron's meeting his contact, Big Ralph, in the pool hall under Centre Point and will join us once he's scored some ecstasy made with ninety-eight percent talcum powder. He'll then spend the next two hours telling me he loves me and chewing his tongue into new shapes.

'I don't know. Look, Lucas, I'm in New York next week so I won't see you at Syngestia but maybe we could do something this weekend? A coffee? How about it?' Mariana's near-permanent look of satirical disinterest has slackened from her features, replaced by something unreadable, expectant.

My phone bleeps another voicemail reminder. I haven't listened to the backlog of messages yet, but I can imagine the gist. My father's still dead.

'Who keeps calling you?'

'It might be my mother, wanting to know when I'm going down to Becksmouth.'

She takes my arm and pulls herself against me with unladylike strength. 'Why don't you go see her tomorrow? We can have that coffee another time.'

The queue jerks forward as Hell's doors digest another reveller. A pair of self-conscious bouncers, incongruously attired with toy tridents and little red horns atop bald pates, still manage to be intimidating and look upon us all as potential terrorists.

'Honey,' she says, 'why didn't you tell me your father died?'

I don my griever's hat. 'I don't like to talk about it.'

'I don't wish to pry Lucas, but…' Her hands rest on my hips. 'Look, everyone has their ways of coping, I understand that, it's just … maybe your mom needs some comforting. She obviously wants you to go back home. Why *on earth* did you come into work today?'

When I fail to come up with an answer she cups my chin – for a moment I think she's about to kiss me – before asking, 'Are you alright, Lucas?'

'Of course.'

Her mouth hardens. Such indifference over familial death, Mariana's thinking, can't be real. Such shameless apathy. It must be a front.

She just asks me, straight off. 'How did he die?'

I tell her the truth.

Even under the glare of Hell's neon lettering, I see her face blanch. She stumbles slightly, stepping back from me, and her stilettos lose the kerb. A taxi slices past, fractionally missing her faltering frame, and the driver hollers an expletive through his yawning window. 'Right, well, I'll, um, see you Sunday then. Maybe?' Over her shoulder, Aaron splashes towards us.

'Hey! You can't go!' he tells Mariana. 'It's gonna be an awesome night!'

She stiffly puts out her hand. 'It was nice to meet you,' she says.

Aaron adopts the stoop of an Edwardian gent, plucks up her fingers with his right hand, his left hooked behind his back, and gives her hand a valedictory lick from fingertip to wrist, cackling roguishly. Mariana doesn't even pretend to be charmed.

'Look after Lucas,' she whispers, within my earshot.

She waves a flustered adieu to the pair of us and evaporates into the night as our queue moves forward. Aaron and I both try to pick her out amongst the tumbling, wankered strides of Soho's fashionistas, but she's gone.

'You alright?' he asks.

I really wish people would stop asking me that.

The underworld's not so bad once you're in. Hell's owners have realised that the gimmicky, Dante-esque theme can only be stretched so far and, apart from the red, oesophageal entrance corridor and the trident-bearing bouncers, the nightclub's relatively pretension-free. More than a few clubbers have come, perhaps naturally enough, in fetish gear and are standing with their backs to the wall, looking at the rest of us as though we're the ones in the wrong place.

Aaron weaves back from the bar with two bottles of water. He claps an arm around my neck to support himself and I can almost see the possessive entity that is MDMA threatening to bulge out through his eyes, his hungry hands, his clenching jaw.

'Great, aren't they?' he gurns.

I nod, stick my thumbs up, and when he palms me another pill I conceal it in my back pocket with the others.

In his defence, he thinks he's taking care of me, that he's lightening my night. He assumes going chemically and loudly off the rails would be anyone's normal reaction to the death of a parent. I swim with him to the toilets.

Another rush hits Aaron and he retches in the sink before presenting his parboiled face to the mirror. He laughs when he sees his reflection, which takes some doing now his eyes no longer follow a conventional, united trajectory. He sports the pinpricked pupils of a bilious crack-whore.

'God, I'm beautiful,' Aaron humbly announces.

I find nothing so entertaining about my countenance: it's exactly the same mug I see each time I look, showing more stubble than usual, looking slightly less fresh. My hair's as blonde as it was when I last looked, my irises as green. Few laughter lines are evident at the squint of my eyes; I haven't laughed this evening.

Aaron lunges at me. 'My bestest, bestest friend… Who'd have thought it, eh? How far we've come since those old days.' Hands cup the back of my head, Mafioso-style. 'You and me have been through some crazy shit, haven't we? I still remember that night, like it was yesterday, mopping up the blood as your dad waited for the ambulance, helping him to…'

'You're wasted,' I tell him.

Some bloke with flinted eyes and sliced brows enters the toilet. He's balding, wears a Ben Sherman he probably bought a decade ago and has an overloaded parsnip of cannabis clamped in his crooked sneer. I wish the government would hurry up and introduce this smoking ban they've been talking about for years.

I take my cue to duck into a cubicle and drop the three pills Aaron's now given me down the toilet then, just to confirm my mother's number, access my missed calls list. She's there, but she's not the most recent caller.

Maybe it's Mariana. She did look extraordinarily flustered when she left. Maybe I shouldn't have told her the truth: that I've absolutely no idea how my own father died. Perhaps that is a bit odd.

Suddenly I'm curious. How did my father – hardly an old man and, it would seem, in rude health – come to breathe his last? My mother, her usual non-communicative self, didn't even mention a cause of death. And I was too fazed to ask.

I ring the number. It tolls once then an automated response kicks in.

31

'Welcome to Sinton Hospital. Our offices are open between nine am and eight pm, seven days a week. Please call back during those times and quote the extension you require.'

None the wiser, I hang up.

I find Aaron on the dance floor, wetting a teenage girl's tongue with his own. Presumably she gave him permission. Here we are again. Another Friday night.

When I was Aaron's girl's age, dancing like I hadn't yet worked out the jut of my own elbows, I assumed older people were jealous of my youth. Only recently, having discovered *everybody* looks down on those younger than themselves, have I been able to regard my own spotty adolescence as one might watch the growth of an unremarkable biological specimen. I developed as expected, the usual spurts and inflammations of commonplace experience. A confidence the older generation knew as arrogance, a fast-honed sarcasm masquerading as intellect, an indolence borne out of having the rest of time itself in which to graze.

From time to time I wonder about those acquaintances from my college years. Do they spend their weekends like this? Is Marcus in The Two Sawyers, still trying to drink that yard of ale? Does Sarah trawl summer seafronts in search of French exchange students for her 'snogathon'? It's possible. Two generations ago, almost everybody had children by the time they were my age, but this hedonism seems to be how people are expected to spend their extra years of teenagehood.

Staring at the forest of spasmodically bobbing dancers, it occurs to me that I used to enjoy nights like this. Tonight, my bones swell with something that might be longing, or grief, or both. Shot through with fatigue, the vision of an innocent Petri slide-cum-pint of bitter floats back to me. My hands shake. My eyes feel dry. The autonomic defence mechanism we've labelled pain, without which no species on Earth could survive, is trying to tell me something.

Will this Cold Turkey never leave me?

Pressing through the smoking jailbaits and gimps, the slurred and swinging lights, I wonder about Mariana. By my estimation, she's only a year or two older than me. Where is she? In the bath with a book? At a sensible friend's house, watching a movie?

As I make to head for the exit, someone tugs at my sleeve.

'My jaw hurts and my throat tastes like an ashtray.' Aaron's wobbling, staring at me as though I might be someone he knows. I watch him fish a receipt out of his back pocket, Hell the headline, for an undetermined sum that causes him to wince. He stows it in his wallet and wanders off to join the cloakroom crocodile for the jacket he's still wearing.

I steer him towards street level, arm firmly around lean and leathered shoulders.

'Come on, Casanova. I'm putting you on the night bus.'

'Where are you going?'

Outside, it no longer rains, but neon is reflected in deep and shuddering puddles as we squelch our way to the nearest stop.

'A place I used to call home.'

CHAPTER FOUR

The strange, foreign country that is England begins once London's behind you: the low-rise in the shadow of church spires; crows perched on telegraph poles above livestock grazing in oceans of green. From the train, each windmill, every bale of hay, is an archaic shock to the system. And as a tunnel ends, revealing the grey sea sidling alongside our sleepers, I get a taste of silence.

I take another look at the gold medallion set into my key fob. *To thine own self be true*, it says, the words spaced around an alarmingly illuminati-style triangle and the number 12, to denote the passing of the final month of my recovery year. I try to tell myself it's only me I've let down, but I didn't make it through that year on my own. For giving into cravings I genuinely thought were behind me, I feel the disgrace of the whole fellowship.

I pocket the fob as the train pulls in.

After walking the length of Maudlin Road, I turn into the drive of a modest, detached residence, the roof gutter of which drips sporadically onto a crew-cut front lawn. Twenty seconds after the bell, my mother answers and pulls me in for a terse but welcoming hug. She reeks of Elizabeth Arden.

'Your phone not working?'

'How are you, Mum?'

A nod. 'I'm fine.' She's wearing a blue silk sari she bought the last time she and Clint went to Delhi, and a pair of desperately unfashionable black jeans she considers 'slimming', despite being the slightest fifty-year-old I know. She jerks her head towards the dining room, as though announcing pleasantries are over and business should begin, and as she does so her dark hair comes loose at the back.

The dining room table is awash with papers. We sit down. 'I found a nice local place that's going to organise it,' she says, almost smiling. 'They've got a lovely Chapel of Rest.'

'But I found a place in London which has an office near here too. I took the afternoon off work on Thursday, and I can't begin to tell you how difficult things have been there lately.'

I begin to tell her how difficult things have been there lately. She's not interested.

'Lucas, you haven't exactly been forthcoming with information and there's only so long one can wait with a Death Certificate rattling round in one's handbag. Besides, this place releases doves. He'd probably have liked that.'

Clint bumbles into the dining room, slightly heavier set than I remember him and dressed in a sagging T-shirt that proclaims *I'm Not as Think as You Pissed I Am*. I stand for the flaccid handshake. He pulls up a chair next to my mother and we both sit down. It's like Christmas Day again, round the bone-dry turkey. Clint and I make the effort, try to appear at ease. It must hurt his face, smiling like that.

'Okay. So what do we need to do?' I ask.

'Everything,' my mother replies. 'We need to sort out his bills, insurance, credit cards. We should make some phone calls and send letters out as soon as possible. He's got relatives in Scotland, a cousin and an elderly aunt.'

'And we're telling them the burial's next week sometime?'

'Cremation. Next Saturday.'

'Is there money in the estate to pay for everything?'

My mother and Clint exchange glances. The divorce cleaned my father out convincingly, as the extension to the back of my mother's house testifies. Once sleek and unblemished, its UPVC looks cheap and tacky now, having aged as ruinously as everything in this sleepy, seaside town: the same old festive lights outside the station every year; the peeling paint on the Channel-whipped colonnade.

'There will be,' she says. 'Once his flat's been sold.'

'What about the Will? I mean, what did *he* want done?'

'Well, we found one but it doesn't say much. He obviously wasn't expecting his heart to give out on him. He thought he had more time. Who doesn't?'

So then, a heart attack. I picture his last moments and try to feel compassion: he's at his desk, writing, when his heart twists and fails. He manages to ring 999 from a desk phone but is dead seconds later, pitched forward on his papers.

'What does the Will say?' I ask.

'It wasn't much of one to be honest. A piece of paper with a choice of song for the service, that's pretty much all.'

'And what does he want played?'

'*Flowers Never Bend in the Rainfall* by Simon and Garfunkel. The rest of it's up to us. The hearse, the coffin, a route for the cortège. I thought it would be nice if his ashes were scattered in the memorial gardens in Sinton, where his father is... Or on the Downs – he loved that place. What do you think?'

I don't mean to sound as bored as I do when I reply, 'Whatever'. I'm willing to go along with my mother's suggestions but her mention of a nearby area has prompted a fuggy memory from last night. Didn't I receive a missed call from Sinton Hospital?

'You can stop the act now, Lucas. It's not 1989 any longer.' My mother directs this under her breath and it hisses out like a slow puncture. 'May I remind you that he was your *father*? You didn't like him, fair enough, and I don't blame you. I know he did some bad things but, God knows, we both made him suffer for it. I... loved him once, just as you did, so the least we can do is see him off with a modicum of dignity. We all deserve that.'

Clint coughs, as though to draw attention to his own nervousness, then says, 'Hey, Lucas, my old man died five years back. It hit me hard but... we go on, don't we? I mean, we have to. Once we've learned we're not in control of our lives, don't own them, what is there left to do but live them well?'

I stare at his impassive, weathered face, a face so grey it might've been cut from basalt. What's he talking about? It hasn't *hit me hard*. Has my mother not talked to him at all in the time they've been together? Has she not told him *what happened*?

My mother shoots him one of her glares. He gets up. 'The kettle's boiled. Anyone for a cup of...'

'No thanks,' my mother tells him as he recoils towards the kitchen.

I sit and stare at the table. The weekly applications of wax can't disguise its age, the chipping to the fold-out leaf.

'How long are you here for?' she asks.

'Um... Not sure. Maybe only...'

'And will you see Granny and Granddad while you're down?'

'Perhaps next week might be easier, before the funeral. How are they?'

'You know them. They'll survive us all.' She's talking to the view out the window. 'Granddad often asks after you. They got your card for their anniversary, eventually.'

The sound of a cup rattling in its saucer re-announces Clint's uncomfortable presence. He passes my mother a set of keys which she then hands over to me.

'What's this?' I ask.

'The keys for your father's flat. I assume you'll want to have a look around. It's yours now after all.'

I'm glad I'm sitting. 'What? I thought you said he left it to you and that's how you were paying the remaining funeral costs?'

'No, it's how *you're* paying the remaining costs.'

I grab the keys and motor to the door. Behind me, my mother calls, 'And I think you should see your brother, since you've *finally* deigned to grace us with your presence.'

My father lived in a top-floor flat at the sea end of the high street. I step into a hallway redolent of coffee and rising damp. His shoes and coats are still by the door.

The first room on the left is small, a converted study with a desk in front of bay windows, through which I glimpse a slice of the Channel between the rowing club and long-derelict amusement arcades. Last week's *Saturday Guardian* sits on a low coffee table next to a faux-crystal decanter of scotch. Several Lever Arch files line the shelves.

A computer's tower is flashing under the desk. I slap the keyboard's space bar and the ageing Compaq wheezes to life, its unwieldy monitor whiting to reveal a Word document, disclosing the last, unfinished line my father wrote: *She ran to the window, and through the falling snow she*

Maybe my prognosis was correct. Maybe he *did* die at his desk, in this very room, though there's no evidence of disturbance, nothing to indicate the fate that befell him. In fact, his death, now I'm at the scene itself, strikes me as odd. He had, to my knowledge, no history of heart problems. I wonder if my mother's even heard any confirmation from a coroner. Was there an autopsy? Who found him?

I save the file, directed to a folder entitled *Untitled Draft7*, then turn the computer off.

There are a few objects in the unfamiliar room I remember from my childhood, such as the five-balled Newton's Cradle, whose smooth silver orbs swung backwards and forwards in perpetuity when clacked together, and the pink quartz chunk that hunkered on our dining room mantelpiece. My father's homes during his last decade were like Russian dolls, each smaller than the one preceding it.

I take down a file entitled *Your Blue Room* and scan the opening lines.

Three girls raced, an arrow, through Lisbon's *Praça do Comércio*, holding clammy hands in the last of the day's heat. A flapping, purple-silver cloud of pigeons evaded the charge by bursting to the sky and, amongst little showers of spiralling feathers, glided to rest on the equestrian statue of José I. It was late September.

And another, called *November Spawned a Monster*,

It doesn't really matter where it all started, just as it's equally irrelevant to mention the nature of the weather at the time, the season concerned, the wax of the moon. However, because I'm a romantic, I should mention that I was in the Tate Gallery hiding from an early summer downpour under a sky that would host, rather earlier than usual that evening, a satellite two days new. I was neither drunk nor sober.

At the rear of both files are dozens of polite rejection slips from various literary agencies, apologising that they're not taking on new authors at present, suggesting he try elsewhere. I don't claim to be an expert in literary criticism but his books' openings seem heavy with adjectives and unnecessarily wordy. He'd had few readers: a couple of short stories in freebie magazines, a scattering of journalism, a self-published dyad of novellas. He probably wasn't as good as he thought he was but, like many people digging a life for themselves within his trade, he was undoubtedly better than the world will remember him being.

My father started writing soon after the family fell apart and, from the look of his shelves, did so prolifically. Success eluded him nevertheless. Maybe he would've struck upon something in a few years' time, if his heart had been stronger. I replace the files, an unexpected and unwelcome sadness beginning its dull, toothache creep within me. Such dedication certainly wasn't evident during my upbringing. And he failed at that too.

Under a set of shelving lies a battered, dusty black briefcase, very similar to one my grandparents bought me for my sixteenth birthday in the desperate hope that I'd choose a career in which such a noble item would be indispensable. Closer inspection reveals the case to indeed be mine. It's sitting atop various old comics I used to enjoy, beside a shoebox containing action figures and die-cast cars, and some school exercise books. This is where I've been relegated to, this dusty shrine on the floor, buried under my father's unread manuscripts.

A slow shiver burns up my spine. The emotion the sight of this case has inspired is tied to a memory I can't place, don't want to place. I fear this object. I recall my mother's voice telling me to stop the act, that *this isn't 1989 anymore*.

Moving back, I knock the decanter off the table and it thuds to the floor, the stopper coming loose and releasing the rusted, paint-stripper aroma of my father's whiskey of choice. Immediately, as I bend to replace the bottle, a metallic scratching from somewhere within the flat echoes this thud. I'm not alone.

With the decanter held like a weapon before me, I follow the sound to what I presume is the living room. Taking a slow, deep breath, I toe open the door, then feel unaccountably foolish when I discover a green and yellow budgerigar gnawing frantically at the steel of his cage. Maybe he's missing company, pining for the freedom of the lounge's high Edwardian ceiling. He stops when he sees me approach and regards me with dumb eyes.

The living room is tidy. All the books are alphabetised, his DVDs clustered by genre. A solitary VHS case, faux-leather designed to mimic a hardback book, lies on the television; yet another tacky artefact from my childhood. There's a photo of me in an oval mount on the mantelpiece, one half of a hinged frame I share with my brother. I'm dressed in the colours of my junior school, my smile impressing no lines upon my cheeks. My brother's photo is new, taken within the last year.

The room smells faintly of terpenoids – no doubt skunk was a self-medicated antidote for his failed literary career – though I find nothing but a few strands of tobacco in an otherwise spotless ashtray. My father either tidied up thoroughly hours before his death, perhaps anticipating a visitor, or someone aired and cleaned this place after he died. I wonder who.

I quickly survey the rest of flat. The bedroom is strewn with clothes – a pair of jeans lie discarded as though recently stepped out of, the waist still holding a yawning memory of his body. The novel by the unmade single bed is the latest Booker winner. In the kitchen, I discover a small mountain of washing up and, in bathroom cabinets, little evidence of mindfulness towards coronary thrombosis. No antiplatelet drugs, not even aspirin. Everything confirms, like those shoes sleeping by the doormat, that the owner of this flat wasn't planning to go anywhere anytime soon.

I walk back into the lounge, unhook the budgie's cage from the wall and march with it towards the front door. To my shame, it takes a superhuman effort not to run. This eerie, silent, spotless home has got me spooked. I don't believe in ghosts – I don't believe in very much at all – but I sense an unwelcome presence here. I sense something's wrong. And I sense that something highly suspicious happened here the day my father died.

CHAPTER FIVE

The funfair comes to Becksmouth every summer. It's exactly as I remember it, right down to the bad paintings of Eighties horror-movie characters decorating the ghost train. I don't recall quite so many young gangs patrolling the place, mind you; it always seemed a family-friendly fair. The sedate Merry-go-round and Teacups are all but empty, whereas The Gravitron's host to plenty of teenage screamers.

I'm by the hoopla stall when I spot my brother loping towards me. He's seventeen or eighteen now and, unusually for a teen his age, looks neither twelve nor thirty; he looks seventeen or eighteen.

'Hey there, Ryan.'

'Hi.' We shake dry hands as his eyes slide towards the birdcage at my shoes. The creature chirps, as if in recognition.

Part of the reason Ryan looks that rare thing – his age – is down to his choice in clothes. He isn't wearing the latest fashions of his generation, nor is he trying to dress older than his years. Instead he wears a hodgepodge of charity shop apparel and clothes he's had for eons. His jacket fits him, but is clearly second-hand, while his trousers are too small and expose two ankles' worth of mauve sock.

Or maybe this *is* the latest look. I'm out of the loop, I guess.

'Fancy a go?'

He scratches the fuzz on his chin, squints at the stall, its cuddly toy prizes. 'Yeah ok.'

The attendant hands him five hoops and takes my pound. Ryan ruffles his big, electric-shock hair, then hurls the first hoop at a wooden block. He lands all five, winning a toy fire engine, which he refuses. We both try our hands at a similar game, in which balls are flung into small baskets. Again, Ryan wins.

'Been practising?' I ask.

'I bowl yorkers,' he explains, whatever that means.

Bored with the sidestalls, we head to a burger van. Ryan asks if he's got any drinks and the vendor admits that he lacks the licence to sell alcohol but claims to have got round this legal loophole by giving out raffle tickets for one pound fifty, upon the purchase of which he hands out 'complimentary' cans of Stella. Ryan wants a Coke anyway, having never touched alcohol in his life. I get the impression, since he's failed so far to develop a liking for the hard stuff, even in the wake of our father's death, that it's unlikely he ever will. At least, I hope that's the case.

'So, how you doing?' he asks me for what might be the third time, his gaze glued to the screen of his phone.

This is how it's going to be; skirting around the reason for my visit, making small talk like strangers until we recall our blood bond and end up sniping and argumentative. I wonder how long we'll hold out for, who'll crack and fire first.

'I told you, I'm fine. Can't we go elsewhere?'

'Meeting people, aren't I?'

'Right. How's college?'

'Shit.'

'Favourite subject?'

'Dunno. Maybe PE?'

Our conversation remains trite: the opening of a new restaurant on the high street; the speed of mobility scooters; a recent beach party. 'Man,' he says, 'they had a DJ and everything. Mum told me, about Dad, when I got home. I was on the stairs.' I don't know why he adds this detail, perhaps to emphasise that he was around and I wasn't. I wonder how often he used to see our father. Once a fortnight? Twice a week? Every day?

We walk as we talk, hollered at by the salesmen through the tinny, squealing sound of the fair. The air is, in turns, sugary with the sickly scent of ice cream and perfumed with the smoke and oil used to fry hot dogs and onion. I let a little while pass before asking, 'So where did it happen? Where did Dad…?'

'At his flat.'

'And who actually found him? The body?'

'His tart.'

'His what?'

'Didn't you know? Dad was doing some twenty-year-old. Sophia. They weren't living together but she was round there a lot. They met while he was guest-tutoring at Brighton Uni. He was a bit old for a midlife crisis if you ask me.'

'He was only… *how* old was he?'

'Forty-eight.' He speaks down to me, in that quick, offhand way teenagers tend to do when riled, but I wonder what else he knows that I don't, about the circumstances behind our father's death, about his life. Those sharp, frozen eyes of his might not necessarily contain wisdom, but they doubtless harbour secrets. When Ryan looks into mine does he perceive, in some way, my recollection of the blood which dripped from our father's hands? Can he see the red prints up the wallpaper, on the cutlery drawer, the hall carpet? Can he see 1989 as lucidly as he can the morning he heard his father was dead?

'And this Sophia, she found him *soon* after he died?'

'We think so.'

'You *think* so?'

'Well she called us straightaway. After the ambulance, I mean.'

'Did you ever meet her?'

'Never.'

We stop beside a shooting range. I notice Ryan's eyes have reddened, but he sniffs away the moment, defiant, as though presenting grief might insult either of us. He's obviously not the person I should be grilling, under the circumstances.

It wasn't the same for Ryan, back then. He wasn't lied to like I was, and he knows that. He had nothing to take as personally as me, even if he'd been old enough to understand what was going on. But he still blames me for my anger, rather than our father for planting it there. Ryan remained unchanged by the events of that summer, and in many ways is nothing like me. Maybe he will be, one day. After all, I was nothing like me at his age.

'For the record,' he says, without a hint of emotion. 'I don't want to go over "it". It's in the past.' His tone is resolute, final. 'Give us a quid.'

Ryan seems on edge now, aggressively jabbing his rifle towards the targets as he stabs the trigger, as though this momentum will give the shells extra power. Still, he's not bad, but not quite accurate enough to win a prize this time. I know I won't get any closer to the bull's-eye so I don't even try.

Afterwards, Ryan and I walk to 'The Eggs', a kind of Ferris wheel with freewheeling ovoid compartments replacing the more traditional cars. 'I'm meeting them here,' Ryan says, looking at his watch. While we wait, I talk about the minor crisis at work and Ryan listens, sarcastically, somehow inflecting the silence with a well-practised adolescent cynicism. *Working for a living? What a fucking sell-out!* It occurs to me that he's being disparaging about what I do because I did the same to him, patronisingly asking after his favourite college subject as soon as we met. We both consider the other to have a chip on his shoulder.

His friends turn up, threatening in their gawky, sulky way, the brooding presence of those who feel perennially hard done by. There are three boys and two girls, one of whom, a slender thing with a ring skewering her lip, immediately attaches herself to Ryan's side. She smiles back at me, smug and closed. The boys sip furtively at cans of raffle-ticket Stella.

'You coming on The Eggs?' Ryan asks me.

'I've got the budgie to look after.'

'I'll look after him,' the kid in charge of the ride offers, already unhooking the bird from my grasp. Disconcertingly, he appears drunk as he mimics the budgerigar's every shrill chirp and curious tilt of its head. The bird executes what seems to be his favourite trick in response, clawing his way along a wire bridge between two steel platforms before performing a mid-air shit. 'Pulled a bird?' is wisecracked by someone in Ryan's posse as I'm ushered into a sick-smelling cage with my brother and locked into a seat. The large wheel rotates, slowly, and we rise towards the sky.

'Been on this before?' I ask.

'Yeah.' His friends are waving at us from the cage below. We sail higher.

At the very top, Becksmouth looks preposterously small. My school, Mum's church, a lone wetsuit agitating the shimmering glass of the Channel with a circling jet ski, all linked by a stone's throw. Below me is The Harp, an Irish-themed pub. I wonder if its walls are still adorned with pre-war Guinness posters and sepia photos of Joyce, Yeats and the craggy-faced Beckett; I wonder if Beverly, with her generous measures, still serves there. I wonder if the stout still tastes like a bottomless, creamy embrace.

Our cage screams.

I'm upside down, hurtling over and over. A sock in a washing machine. For an eternity.

I feel the need to sound thrilled, for some reason, so emit a ludicrous 'woo' and then a shrill 'yeah'. Ryan's silent beside me. Eventually, I recover a semblance of equilibrium, only to notice how extremely rusty our main axle appears.

Just as I think I'm about to be sick, the torture ends.

'You alright?' Ryan asks as I clamber from the cell, planting a tentative foot on solid ground. For once, the question isn't an allusion to our father's death.

I can't reply.

His friends pay to go on again as I stagger to collect the budgie. The group didn't seem to expect me to stay this long, so my geriatric performance hardly disappoints them.

'He's yours if you want him,' I declare, nodding at the bird being passed back to me by the snickering attendant.

Ryan presses his lips into a ball, scowls, then jumps into the next cage. 'I'll see you at the funeral,' he monotones.

I head back to my mother's house. Ryan was energyless, grieving, and the encounter was an empty one. Entering the high street, it occurs to me why.

I was the one my father offended. *I* was the one he lied to. And *I* was the one who rejected him afterwards, refusing to acknowledge his very existence for a decade.

So why, Ryan must be wondering, am *I* the one who gets his flat?

Down Coleridge Road, I approach an establishment called 'Becksmouth Superstore'. In the old days, before it started buying up its neighbours and expanding in my absence, it was a tiny old newsagent called Candy Corner. I catch sight of a shift worker as I pass. The figure prowls an aisle, replenishing stock after the day's sales, arms laden with cheap home accessories. When I realise who it is, I reel from the window, paving slabs beneath my feet pitching at forty-five degrees. Time has left this lonely phantom gaunt and despondent, hunched into a form twice his natural age as he meanders off between toasters and cut-price clip frames.

And now I remember.

My heart pounds at my temples. I watch my tired, unshaven reflection peel from the glass. And then I'm running, the budgie flying beside me, back to my father's flat.

Inside, I breathlessly grab the briefcase and tear it from under the shelving in a shower of dust. Unable to recall the correct combination number, I hurl it against the wall then prise it apart with a letter opener. School exercise books spill out, as do several scrawled essays on ghosts and outer space, their titles constructed from Letraset. There are several drawings, too, rendered by a young hand showing an early predilection for sfumato in the guise of big, grey fingerprint smudges. Buried amongst all this, I find something of far greater significance.

It's not that I'd forgotten this object existed, but that I'd long ago blanked where I concealed it. And what perfect timing: in the wake of my father's death, I almost feel the need to justify hating him. I know this artefact will provide ample validation.

The doorbell rings.

I walk to the hall, reluctantly shifting my face into an expression jovial enough, I hope, to deflect the staves of suspicious neighbours who've seen lights ablaze in a dead man's home. I pull the door back.

'Moved in already?' my mother asks.

'I... What? No... Can I help?'

'You okay, Lucas?'

'Bloody hell. Yes, I'm fine! Why's everyone always asking me this?'

The brutality of the hall light above my mother deepens the lines around her mouth, thins and stretches the skin of her cheeks. Even her hair has lost its lustre, preparing itself for greyness. Only the eyes remain young; darkly emerald, almost blue towards the pupil.

'There's no need to shout, Lucas. I was just seeing how you're doing, whether you're coming back to the house anytime soon.' She touches two fingers against my elbow.

'I'm alright, honestly. I'll be along in a bit.'

'You've been here *ages*.'

'Not really. I met Ryan at the fair.'

'Oh. Right.' She starts to back away from the flat, into the dark communal corridor. Her wary demeanour alerts me to the fact that this is possibly the first time she's visited her ex-husband's home. 'There's steak and kidney pie waiting, if you're interested,' she imparts on the turn. Despite having handed me the keys in the first place she now seems keen to remove me from my father's territory, as though revisiting that parental tug-of-war she won long ago.

'No. Thanks anyway. But, before you go… Tell me about this girl Dad was seeing.'

My mother shrugs, takes a slow step back towards me. 'I know very little about her. His first lady friend for some time from what I can gather. Her name's…'

'Sophia. She found his body.'

'That's right. She contacted me the same day, barely able to speak. You'll meet her at the funeral I expect. If she turns up.'

'Why wouldn't she?'

'I haven't heard from her since. Don't know how to contact her. I'm the one sorting this whole bloody mess out. Me, of all people! The woman who left him over fifteen years ago!'

'And what about the cause of death: it was definitely a myocardial infarction, was it?'

'A what?'

'A heart attack.'

Her deportment speaks of the utmost secrecy, as though information's not to be trusted in my hands. But the truth seems to want to unveil itself, through the sighing and rising of her chest, the tremulous swinging of a handbag against her side. 'They're not *sure* about that. The post-mortem results aren't available yet.' She talks slowly, reluctantly, addressing the corridor over my shoulder, the lamp burning in the living room.

'So there *was* a post-mortem?'

'Don't act so alarmed. He was perfectly fit and the death was sudden. It's normal procedure.'

'I'm not alarmed. Why didn't you tell me?'

'What's to tell? Anyway, I only got the call confirming the autopsy this afternoon. We're awaiting results. Although the guy from the hospital did say something about an inquest.'

'An inquest? Mum, you *do* know what that means don't you? He definitely said "inquest"?'

'I think so.'

'But you told me you had a Death Certificate.'

'Oh, that was, you know, rhetoric.'

My mother's imprecision with the facts probably has more to do with the coroner's own ambiguity – and death's protracted bureaucracy – than my ignoring of the Becksmouth clan. But her reticence to divulge much is down to a simple truth: I'm not really part of the family anymore.

'So his death's suspicious? But... I'm here. I mean, I've been *touching* stuff. I knocked his whiskey over. Will that be a problem?'

'The police have looked round already, when the death was reported.' She says this more as a statement of fact than as reassurance they won't want to look around again. 'We'll know the situation soon enough.'

I nod, utterly confused. A metallic ache returns to my bones, my tendons, the back of my throat. Not now. *Not now*.

'What do you think the coroner discovered?'

'I've no idea,' she says with an old parental stab of finality, the direct eye contact that acts like a full stop. 'It's not bloody *CSI*, is it? What do you think happened? He choked on his own ego? Don't worry about it. Look, I've got to go. I'll see you later.'

I close the door and head back to the study. *An inquest*? My mother's been playing mind games for quite a while now and she's become irritatingly good at it. And my father was no better: he couldn't even die in clear-cut circumstances.

I again pick up the long-misplaced relic from the briefcase.

Onto its milky coffee-coloured façade, are dry-transferred the words,

LUCAS MARR (11¼)
A DAILY DIARY
TOP SECRET!

I can't help smiling at the last line, the magnificent sense of my own importance. I suddenly recall how, at the sundown to each day, I made sure the diary was securely tied around its middle with a grey lace from an old school shoe and secreted between the springs of my bed frame and mattress, lest another member of my family should try to read it. Laughably pointless paranoia, looking back, considering the weight of the secrets others were keeping from me.

I walk through to my father's lounge. The sun's faded outside the curtains and street lamps shine puddles of fake dawn across the coffee table, silhouetting parched plants on the windowsill. The leaves of a bromeliad droop like straw fingers. I pull the curtains together and sink into an armchair with the childhood memoir I'd forgotten for over fifteen years. I'm shocked at how slim the volume is, that a lifetime's enmity could be substantiated by such slender means.

Did I suspect, as an eleven-year-old, that my unruffled, sheltered way of life was soon to come crashing to its end? That a close family member would become, forever, a rival, a stranger? Perhaps so. Is that why, on some unconscious, prepubescent level, I felt the need to chronicle the summer of 1989? Or was I simply trying to recount the good times while they lasted? Whatever the reasons, I never dared write a diary again.

The diary's still in pretty good condition – as a child, I was as fastidious as I was bookish and remote – and the only obvious evidence of wear and tear comes in the form of a slight kinking to the wire-spiralled spine, undoubtedly inflicted when I flung the briefcase into the wall. I can't stop my hands from trembling as I open the diary.

My ordered, legible, pre-Bachelor of Medicine handwriting is executed entirely in pencil, unjoined and rounded where deference was shown to a dictionary. Pages creak softly, complaining about this sudden attention after so long pressed against their brothers, and, as I flick the slide switch on a tall floor lamp, the orange-yellow blush scatters itself over the diary causing the blue veins of handwriting to rise from the cheap paper.

I lie back in my father's chair and begin.

THE FIRST PART OF
THE DIARY

Sunday 25th June 1989

Dad gave me this diary for Christmas but nothing exciting happened so I didn't write anything yet.

Today Mrs Smithson died.

Me and my best friend Julian who lives next door saw her body carried into an ambulance by 2 hairy paramedics and she was covered in a sheet and her arm bounced out all bony and with bulging knuckles. Mrs Smithson smelled of dusty farts but Dad says she had 'a good innings'.

Here is a map of the area around my house

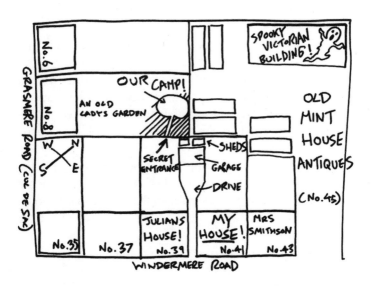

After Mrs Smithson was driven off me and Julian ran to our secret camp. Our camp can be reached through a crack in the fence behind Julians shed and is big enough for 2 people and is covered by a jungle of brambleweeds and Death Star dandelions. Me and Julian are the only ones who know about the camp and we swore never to tell anyone else. Ever.

Julian said that he bet Mrs Smithson fell over because most old people die when they fall over, but I said that most of them die of shock when burglars break in and he went 'sometimes they get cerebral meningitis' which is what his gran died of. Julians face was red like always. Some people call him fat but he is just big for his age and he has black hair and his dad is a policeman.

I will put this diary somewhere safe so I can write down all the other wicked things that happen this summer.

Thursday 24th August 1989

I found the diary again. It was under the bed like Mum said it probably was.

Julian and I went on a special mission at The Old Mint House today. The Old Mint has lots of metal storing crates and a peeling sign at the end of its driveway saying 'Money paid for old valuables'. Our mission was a complete success because we found the skeleton of an umbrella that we used as a bayonet and a dead pigeon that was a quality hand grenade until its head fell off.

We went back to the camp and made a wood sign at the entrance that says 'KEEP OUT! DO NOT ENTER'. I thought this might draw attention to the camp but Julian said it would make people think twice. Also our mums know about the camp now anyway.

Mrs Smithsons ghost has been quiet today.

Friday 25th August 1989

This evening I went with Dad to the park over the road to look at stars. He pointed out Betelgeuse and I told him its a red supergiant.

He was well impressed.

I imagined all the stars exploding and going supernova at the same time and what it would look like if they did. The sky would light up but because theres no atmosphere in space the explosions would be silent. Dad bought me books on space for my birthday and I always try to quote them so he knows I've read them properly.

The sign with the green horse in 43s front garden was changed to SOLD ages ago. I asked Dad what he thinks our new neighbours will be like and he said 'No idea champ.' I said they'll have to exorcise Mrs Smithson with thermometers and holy water and Dad smiled and asked if the 'old cow' was still knocking on my wall at night. I told him she is but that nothing scares me anymore.

He lit a cigarette and winked at me and told me not to tell Mum.

Saturday 26th August 1989

Massive news. The King family have moved into 43 and the father has a Captain Haddock beard and his wife has short hair like women did in the war and they have 1 son and 1 daughter.

Dad pretended not to be spying on the Kings as he cut the front lawn with those big scissors that look like a pelicans beak. When he came back inside he said our new neighbours were 'ruddy unfriendly'. Mum made her telling off face at him and nodded at Ryan who's only 2 and isn't allowed to hear swearwords so he suggested we go and play football in the garden.

Dad is super skill at football. If he didn't have to work in a bank he would have played at Mexico 86 and then I could of had a sticker of him. The other boys from the school team liked it when Dad came along on Sunday mornings to cheer me on because he used to bring mini Mars bars at half time, but he didn't do much cheering because I didn't do much scoring. My team all called him The Wookie because he won't cut off his sideburns or long curly brown hair, even though it hasn't been the 70s for 10 years. They used to ask me 'Is the Wookie coming?' and if he wasn't I was put in defence or substituted for Gary Goalhanger Baker. I think I was only in the team because of Dad's Mars bars.

Dad said 'Come on champ' as he walked up the garden, and told me to give it a really GOOD kick.

I did but the ball whooshed over the fence into 43s garden.

Dad sighed and went in to watch *Grandstand*. I was following him into the house when the ball came back over the fence with a thud.

I went down into the vegetable patch where Keegans buried under a cross made from 2 lollipop sticks and saw a boy at the wire fence. He was wearing a Tshirt with a tank on it and his hair was blonde. You can spell that with or without an e. My hair is also blonde or blond. The boy said his name was Daniel and he was 12. Because light travels 6.2 million million miles in 1 Earth year I told him he is 6.2 million million miles older than me. He looked at me and went 'your well shit at football.'

I asked if he liked his new house and he said 'Theres funny wallpaper. It stinks of wee' and I told him 'An old person died there. Her ghost haunts that room' and pointed up to Mrs Smithsons old bedroom, which was next to mine.

Daniel stroked his chin and said 'Chinny reckon.'

Then his mum called him for tea and I went to the secret camp with Julian and told him about Daniels tank Tshirt and his blond or blonde hair. We decided we'll call for Daniel tomorrow.

Sunday 27th August 1989

We interrogated Daniel while we sat on the swings in Sinton Woods and ate liquorice allsorts. We discovered he is going to Blackheath School and doesn't know the furthest thing you can see with naked eyes is the Andromeda galaxy (he guessed and said Uranus). He knows more about dinosaurs than me because I don't find dinosaurs interesting because Dad once told me they had brains the size of tinned potatoes.

Then there was danger. 2 bigger boys came over all serious looking.

'What you doing here? This is our park' one of them said. He wore jeans and had a beard made of spots.

Daniel said 'I don't see your names on any signs, unless your names are 'Public' and 'Playground.''

Julian and I laughed and the other boy went 'Look at Skinny and Fatty laughing at Dickheads shit jokes.' He was taller and had a shaved head and had a white vest on that showed hair under his armpits. Then the boy with the spotty beard gave Daniel a duff on his lip and shook him by the neck. Daniel just kept staring at the bigger boy like he didn't even feel it so the boy gave him another good hard duff.

'We'll let you 2 off this time' the boy said to me and Julian. 'But if we EVER see you here again we'll break off your fingers and cut your throats.' He flobbed on my shoe and walked off. The boy with the shaved head kicked Daniels bike then followed his friend.

'See you around' Daniel said all cheerful and with blood over his teeth and chin.

I will now draw evidence of the bigger boys.

59

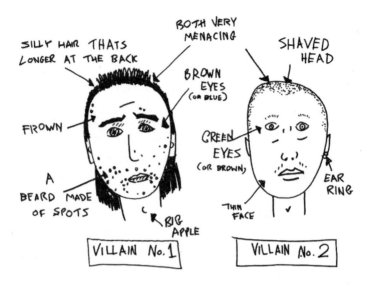

SILLY HAIR THATS LONGER AT THE BACK

BOTH VERY MENACING

BROWN EYES (OR BLUE)

SHAVED HEAD

FROWN

GREEN EYES (OR BROWN)

A BEARD MADE OF SPOTS

BIG APPLE

THIN FACE

EAR RING

VILLAIN No. 1

VILLAIN No. 2

Once I'd wiped the flob off my shoe with grass we picked up our bikes and rode back. Julian was saying things like 'You showed em' to Daniel, or 'We'll get em next time.'

Later, Granny and Granddad came round and Granddad ate 2 Battenberg slices and Granny told him off because he's supposed to be watching his cholesterols. Everyone detected I was quiet and thought I was being moody and Mum said I was doing an impression of Dad. She was the only person who laughed and she still had her church clothes on to show off to Granny and Granddad.

Dad went 'You alright champ?' and I told him bigger boys threatened to cut my throat with my own finger bones and he said boys like that have low esteem and no intelligence and thats why they go round in big gangs, because they haven't got any identity on their own. I said there were 3 of us and 2 of them so we actually outnumbered them and he looked at me all disappointed before going out for a sneaky cigarette at the bottom of the garden all orangeade in the sunset.

Sunday evening

After Granny and Granddad left, Mum and Dad were brave
enough to shout at each other again so I went upstairs
and heard Dad slam the front door and go and see Uncle
Jeffrey, who has hair like someone Scottish and Mum says
is drinking himself to death. Suddenly scary wailing and
knocking came from the wall next to my bed and this was
followed by clanging on my window. I opened it and saw
Daniels head sticking out of his window. He was holding a
load of small stones.

He asked if I thought he was a ghost and his lip was all
curled and smirky. Then he pointed across our gardens at The
Old Mint and asked if I think that place is haunted.

I've never seen lights on in the Victorian building at the
back but tonight it was flickering as spooky red shadows
moved inside.

He asked me what that 'dumb thing' was on my wrist and
I said it was Julians friendship band. He told me I was king
of the gaylords and slammed his window.

I bet Daniel doesn't know that the sun will grow up into a
red giant and swallow the earth in 5 billion years. Then *he'd*
be king of the gaylords because he'd have to sleep with the
light on, like I had to when I first read about that.

Monday 28th August 1989

Today was a bank holiday. Me and Dad flied an eagle kite
at the park over the road and afterwards he bought me a
Desperate Dan bar and some chocolate sticks that come in
cigarette packets from Candy Corner and he said (I think)
'I don't condone the practice of selling chocolate in this
fashion,' but bought me them anyway.

When we got back I went to see if Julian wanted to play
but his mum said he wasn't in.

Tuesday 29th August 1989

Today I had to be fitted for a uniform for High School. The old lady in the shop had mega cold hands and made me jump. Mum said I was in a silly mood and the old lady went 'The worst years are to come' which made me want to throw crayons at her. Ryan ran around the shop then did a poo by the Hush Puppies. He gets away with everything.

Mum and Dad had their loudest argument EVER this evening and it ended with Mum storming up the stairs shouting 'Don't ever call me THAT in front of the children again.' I don't like it when Mum cries but I don't know how to make her stop. Dad went to the pub with Uncle Jeffrey and didn't come back until it was dark, singing *Ladies in Red*.

Wednesday 30th August 1989

Fantastic news! Granddad isn't dead.

He is in hospital though, getting 'the best possible care'. Mum said he'll be fine as she left for the hospital, but this is also what she said when Keegan started looking grumpy because of rabbit cancer.

Now I am lying in bed and thinking about ways to cheat death like sucking out the snakes poison or having a bulletproof car. You can probably survive a plane crash by jumping from its wing just before it hits the ground. I've tried this before by jumping from my bed but I guess the bed would have to be falling through the sky for the experiment to be proper scientific. Anyway by the time I'm old I'll be able to replace parts of myself with robotic bits and hearts and lungs will be fuses and chips and when a liver blows up I'll be able to go to the doctor or B&Q and get it replaced.

Dad has just walked past my door and said '10 minutes then light off champ.' Adults always budget time because they are scared of it I reckon.

Thursday 31st August 1989

Mum made me go with her and Ryan to church today even though its not Sunday and she got on her knees under Jesus to pray for Granddad.

I pretended I was praying too but really I was thinking about how I don't want to go to church anymore and would rather stay at home like Dad does and watch horrors. One Sunday when I had a runny nose I stayed at home and Dad was watching *Night of the Demon*. I do want Granddad to get better but praying is well dull and also last month I prayed I wouldn't have to go to church but I still had to today so praying is pointless.

I called for Julian this evening but he wasn't in AGAIN.

Friday 1st September 1989

Granddad was at the end of a ward of 6 beds with a wire running like snot from his nose. I kissed him on the cheek. It had lots of white stubble on it. Most of his hair is grey even though it was black when he was young and Mum has dark hair too. Apparently I get my blonde or blond hair from 'my fathers side'.

Me and Mum and Dad and Ryan listened while Granddad told us about his heart attack and how he knew it was trouble. He said it was like 'cramp in the old ticker'.

I asked him if he was scared of dying and he said he was terrified, so I asked him why as he goes to church and should get into heaven easy.

Everyone looked at me the same way Julian looked at me when I got Megatron for Christmas. Then a nurse with a trolley of food came along and Granddad asked if he was allowed anything and while the nurse was checking his chart at the end of the bed Mum went 'Yes that'll be the best thing for you I reckon. A good hearty meal.'

Granddad asked if she was being funny and everyone laughed. Then Dad asked the nurse if she had 'Tumour sandwiches' or 'Steak and kidney stones pie' and the whole ward laughed and even Mum looked happy. Then Dad thought for a while and nodded at Granddad and went 'Chicken dodgy ticker masala?'

People were groaning because the jokes were bad I think but then Granddad grabbed his heart and shouted 'You bloody bugger!' and everyone stopped laughing and thats when the doctors came along with the oxygen masks.

Afterwards even though Granddad was going 'I'm fine, I'm fine,' we were told to leave. Mum didn't speak to Dad the whole way home.

Friday evening

I can hardly write straight because my hands are shaking.

Daniel clanged my window. He said there was an 'emergency' and started climbing out the window. I was amazed when he put his hands on the big drainpipe between our rooms and shuffled down before jumping into his garden. I opened my window. It was a long way down. If I fell I would have definitely died. I climbed onto the ledge and grabbed the drainpipe and started to slide down but jumped too early. I didn't show Daniel that it hurt and limped down to the bottom of the pitch dark garden.

A figure in black appeared and it was Daniel in a balaclava with only his eyes showing like an Irish bomber and he whispered 'Follow me' and I followed him behind the sheds and when I realised he was leading me to the secret camp I started to hear my blood beating in my brain. 'We shouldn't be here' I said 'this is Julians garden.' But Daniel just laughed and crawled on his knees through the hedge.

Julian was already inside with a torch. I checked for the Keep Out sign and it was STILL THERE so I asked Julian what he thought he was up to but my question came out too friendly and highpitched, like 'Hey, what you up to Julian?' and he said we were going to get back at the bigger boys and that Daniel knew where one lived. He shined the torch on a Sainsburys bag with 3 bricks in it and Daniel threw me a balaclava and Julian put one on too. It was too cramped with 3 of us.

I was so angry that Julian had showed Daniel the camp I thought I was going to cry so I let them walk in front of me up the drive. Mum and Dad were watching TV in the living room and the light was on. We climbed the front gate so it wouldn't squeak and walked to the other end of Becksmouth. We must have looked well suspicious with our disguises.

'Its number 12' Daniel said and explained the plan: we had to throw our bricks through the bigger boys front window then run back to the camp through a footpath escape route behind Sinton Woods. We took a brick each.

'Now!' Daniel shouted.

CRASH! The window exploded! I dropped my brick and followed them towards the footpath and I don't know if it was my feet or my heart but there was this boom boom all around me and angry voices. Daniel and Julian must have gone a different way back because they both disappeared and I'm definitely faster than Julian.

I was out of breath when I got back home and started climbing the drainpipe. I'd managed to get on my window ledge when the back door flew open. I tried to get my leg up but slipped and had to hold extra tight to the drainpipe to stop myself falling and bits of the ledge sprayed off under my foot.

That was when I heard Dad say 'And just what do you think your up to young man?'

I wasn't fast enough to come up with anything decent so I just explained I was practising 'army manoeuvres' and scrambled inside my room. Dad said 'I'll manoeuvre you in a minute' and ran inside to shout at me until Ryan started crying.

Saturday 2nd September 1989

Dad came up to see how bored I was but I like being grounded because I get to read my books. He had a can of beer in his hand and made me swear I wouldn't climb out the window again and I told him I wouldn't and he let me have a sip of beer. 'Now you're a man champ' he joked. I think hes growing a moustache because his top lip was darker than normal. He sat on my bed and talked about the responsibilities that come with growing up and how I should remember that whatever happens he and Mum love me very much. I thought this was an odd thing to say. He'd been drinking a lot of beer.

I have a full size plastic skeleton hanging on the back of my door that I bought last Halloween and Dad took it down and started to dance with it and went 'This reminds me of my wedding night' and I asked him why he danced with a skeleton on his wedding night and he sighed and said he hoped I'd never understand. After he left I drew a moustache on my lip with a felt tip to see what I would look like if I could grow one but rubbed it off with flem when I heard Mum and Dad screaming at each other about the price of window locks.

I washed the friendship band Julian gave me because it had been getting dirty, which is maybe definitely why Julian doesn't like me as much as he used to.

~~Sunday 3rd September 1989~~
THE WORST DAY OF MY LIFE EVER

I didn't want to go to church so refused to get out of bed and Mum said 'Blow this for a game of soldiers' and went without me.

Dad had stayed behind to look after Ryan and was pleased I was home because I could babysit while he 'popped out for something'. Dad is definitely growing a moustache. He told me not to let Ryan out of my sight and left saying 'I'll be back in an hour.'

The horrors are kept under the TV in video boxes that look like hardback books and I found one with a label on it saying *The Omen* so put it in the video player and sat on the sofa. I was 'the man of the house'.

Ryan started booing when the music started so I told him to go and play in the hall and I got as far as a brill bit where the nanny hangs herself before I had to put the video back. Unfortunately Ryan scribbled over the hall wallpaper in marker pen so I probably won't get an opportunity to watch the rest because when Dad came back he said 'Babysitting isn't really one of your talents is it Lucas?'

When Mum got back she kept talking about how school starts tomorrow. I told her that because I will be at a different school to Julian and Daniel they will start to like each other even more and me less. This is why when Mum saw Julian in the driveway on his skateboard after tea she suggested I go and talk to him. I reminded her I was supposed to be grounded and Mum looked at Dad for advice but Dad shrugged and said he was off to Uncle Jeffreys house. He had a video box with him and I thought this was strange because there weren't any cases missing in the living room and wondered whether he and Uncle Jeffrey were going to watch a horror that was too scary to keep by the TV. He rolled his eyes when Mum made him do the washing up and I sneaked out the house.

We went to the camp and I was on lookout near the entrance. The camp is browner now and most of the blackberries at the back have been eaten and Julian was wearing an orange jumper that hes had for years and is really tight around his tummy. He was still all excited about Fridays mission and when I told him about being caught climbing back in my window he found it so funny his face went red.

'But why did you show Daniel the camp?' I asked. 'I thought it was OUR secret.'

Julian just looked at the ants crawling between us so I asked 'Have you been seeing Daniel a lot?' and he went 'I called for you loads too. You haven't been in' and I told him I went to the park with Dad and church with Mum and the hospital to see Granddad.

I told Julian about the video Dad took round to Uncle Jeffrey but he didn't seem very interested in this mystery so I told him about the ghostly red lights Daniel pointed out at The Old Mint. This made him want to investigate.

We walked down the drive to the Victorian building as our giant shadows stretched ahead of us and we found a broken window round the back and carefully climbed inside and began to do some detecting.

This is what we saw

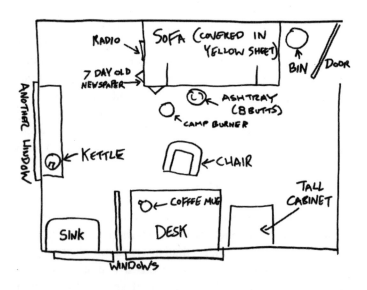

There was a desk next to a tall rusty cabinet with 2 strips of film hanging in it like the ones Dad gets back with his photos. There was a chipped blue mug on the desk with mouldy coffee in and a sink in the corner with 2 white trays inside and small candles floating in them. On the other side of the room was an old sofa covered in a yellow sheet and in the middle of the room was a glass ashtray with 8 cigarette butts that smelled all soily like the camp and some butts had lipstick on them. Underneath the sofa we found a radio and a newspaper from last Sunday.

Julian pointed to footprints by the door and said 'Someone was here today. That footprints wet' and I had to admit this was good detecting. Then he walked over to the bin and went 'Eurgh! Look at this!'

Inside the bin was a thin see-through balloon with some white liquid inside tied in a knot at the end. I picked it up but Julian hit my hand and made me throw it back all disgusted. He was trying to do the curling lip thing that Daniel does.

Then we heard footsteps.

Julian jumped inside the tall cabinet and I looked around for somewhere else to hide but there wasn't anywhere so I squeezed in too and swinged the door closed. It was cramped with us both in so I crouched on the floor and Julian stood at the back. I was scared we were going to be caught but I was even more scared in case it was those bigger boys. I didn't tell Julian that though.

There was the scraping of a window being lifted and then shoes went click click and a light came on and the room went red. I could see through the crack in the door as a woman pulled some thick black curtains together then went to the sofa and folded the cover all neat then lit the candles.

When she started to take off her clothes I was worried she would hear Julians breathing.

Then there was another window scrape followed by more clicking feet and the woman walked out of sight and I heard the smooching sounds from the boring bits of James Bond films. Julian was struggling behind me, trying to see through the crack above my head.

The woman went 'Your late. I thought you weren't coming.'

There was the clunk of a box opening and then more

smooching and the woman moved into the middle of the room and lit a mega long cigarette and it smelled like burning dirt. She was holding one of our fake book video boxes! Then a man without his top pushed her onto the sofa but I still couldn't see him properly because they were moving too fast and she kept holding his face against hers with a hand that had black fingernails. They were doing some very sloppy kissing.

Julian was fidgeting about behind me and the cabinet door started to slowly slowly slowly open.

They carried on kissing and I didn't know where to look because it was the most horrible thing I have ever seen EVER. Our cabinet door bounced on its hinge and the man stopped and turned towards us.

He had large sideburns, curly brown hair and was growing a moustache on his top lip.

I legged it from the room and the cabinet went bang really loudly like it toppled over with Julian in it but by then I was already at the window and cutting my hands on the broken glass. I didn't feel any pain or the blood dripping down my wrists until I stopped running to let the sick out and I realised I was in a strange part of town and the sun had set and I was able to see Cassiopeia and I think Pegasus.

PART TWO

CHAPTER SIX

Half-numb, as if after waking, my body rises to pace the alien room. The thermostat is set to twenty-three but no heat emanates from the radiators. The frames hung with fishing twine from picture rails are all slightly out of place, as though dusted in a hurry. I have no idea how long I've been reading for; I might well have been here the entire length of the period the diary covers.

I'm unable to avoid holding the diary under my nose and breathing in.

The release of acetylcholine brings back snapshots of an old world: a smattering of brown, picked woodchip pocks on the wallpaper next to the bed; the nutrient-rich musk of football boots, topsoil still clinging to the studs; a background whirl from the plastic vent cut into the single pane of my window, through which bleeds an evening scent of thunderstorms and the mint growing in the garden beneath my window. The olfactory senses are more powerful than my old self's writing skills, but I deliberately painted my days with broad strokes.

I try to slide the diary into my pocket but it won't quite fit. Out of respect for my old self, I don't force it in and instead hunt through my father's kitchen for a bag. I find a collection of plastic carriers in a small larder containing a washing machine with an open, mouldy detergent tray. After wrapping the diary in one, I slide it through the budgie cage and head to the front door.

I've read roughly a third of the diary's length, but feel no need to continue just yet. I know worse is to come.

So, yes, I was right. Adults *are* scared of time. Of course we are. Unlike children, who appear the very luminous embodiment of immortality, we're its victims, its ultimate joke. And I don't think you even need to be particularly old to appreciate that. Reading something like this, I realise just how far down the road I've walked.

Poker and I have never had a mutually beneficial relationship, ill fortune having dogged me since our first date, when I lost seven pounds to tight-faced rivals at Aaron's kitchen table. Since then, the stakes raised, my losses increasing accordingly, the prudish chaperone known to players as 'running cold' has recurrently come between me and any genuine love of Texas Hold 'Em.

This evening is no different.

The tipsy novice opposite, smirking behind what seems to be a perennial cigarillo habit, raises me to the limit then demolishes my pair of nines with four jacks. The following hand, a hard-faced pro wades all-in and forces me to fold when I harbour a higher straight. The kick of my body's natural fight-or-flight stress hormone, noradrenaline, has been slowly boosting the heart rate and triggering the release of glucose from energy stores in an attempt to sharpen my mind against nervous tension, but all it's really done is cause me to haemorrhage nine hundred pounds in ten minutes.

I stopped gambling at roughly the same time I gave up the drink and... Well, it seems all my poisons are returning.

Stop here, I tell myself. *For everyone's sake, stop here.*

I mutter my apologies and escort my father's budgie to the bar.

I'm holding on. I can do this.

'What'll it be, sir?' the barman asks, with a perceptible caution. The sweat must be visible. My shaking hands.

'Just a lemonade please.'

The tiny Royal Flush Casino is decorated in the colours of faux-luxury chocolate wrappers. The ceilings are golden, the carpets royal purple. Fear and sweat have commingled with a library's hush to produce a simmering electrical storm of greedy, fanatical meditation, a high-stakes beehive of anxiety.

Orgiastic cries of disbelief shriek from the other table. A white-haired woman wrapped inside absurdly large cataract glasses sweeps a mountain of chips towards her as a well-dressed young man hurls his cards to the baize after a tense showdown. There's a smattering of envious applause and then a cathedral murmur washes back over the room, the clacking of the roulette tables. Not long after, their croupier, a long-legged brunette in a low-cut gold dress, slides over to the bar and asks 'Michael' for her 'usual'.

'Rough night, babe?' She nods at my lemonade.

Is it tonight? I consult my watch. Seven o'clock. Sunday. I need to catch that train.

'This place is too noisy. I found it distracting.'

She smiles without humour. Addicts are experts at making excuses. 'What's with the bird?' she asks.

'Lucky charm.'

When asked, I divulge my losses. 'Some charm,' she says in a voice betraying no surprise.

She casts languorous eyes over the tables, the rigid faces of the players, and tells me her name's Laura. She's as composed and indifferent as a femme fatale and the scent of rosewater snakes around her exposed neck like the wisping curlicues from a *Loony Tunes* cartoon. The thin but clear nasolabial folds either side of her mouth mark her out as older than she first appeared.

'I'm not really allowed to fraternise with the customers, you know. You'll get kicked out if my bosses think we're socialising. Look up there. Eye in the sky.' She nods towards a ceiling-mounted camera blatantly ignoring us.

'So why are you talking to me?'

75

'You're kind of handsome.' Employing a man's cheap flirting tactics, she slowly looks me up and down.

Her paranoia isn't completely unjustified; a security guard by the blackjack tables is squinting our way. Not wanting to get the woman sacked, I finish my drink.

Just before Laura sashays off to set up the next game, I feel a gentle tugging near my groin. When security's looking in the opposite direction I investigate my pocket and pull out a queen of hearts with a phone number scribbled across it.

For a brief moment, I'm taken aback, but the depositing of the card was far too practised, far too cool, to feel sincere. We exchanged but a handful of sentences; this is, surely, nothing more than a tart card, a souvenir for the loss of nearly a grand. Perhaps it's even company policy, to ensure a bankrupt loser's return. Crude tactics notwithstanding, Laura's gorgeous and most men would give her a call, but I know she only considers me a catch because I can afford to run cold once in a while.

Stepping from the casino, it takes me a moment to remember where I am. Becksmouth wears the approach of her evening in the fizzing, stuttering neon of fish and chip shop signage, the sparkle of emerging stars. I'm heading to the station when my phone rings.

'Hello? Lucas?'

Most people sound different through a microphone, the bandwidth of telephones being much narrower than the human ear, but this voice is clearly identifiable; warm, unhurried, and ambivalent about which side of the Atlantic it heralds from. I do my best to keep the delight and surprise from my reply.

I fail. 'Mariana... Hi.' The last person I was expecting to hear from.

'Hey, honey. So, did you go see your mom in the end? I know we talked about meeting this weekend but... I got kind of busy myself. You know what it's like.' Her vagueness is refreshing. She's keen but not desperate, and excuses are beyond her.

'How did you track me down?' I ask. 'I never gave you my number.'

'I got it off Aaron while you were at the bar the other night. At least I thought I did. I called it just now and got...'

'Aaron?'

'Yep. He's cunning. He gave me this number eventually, but only on the condition I meet him for a drink "sometime". He kept going on about his film script and how it needed, like, a second pair of eyes, and how I may be able to "help" because there's Venezuelan blood in me and *The Honorary Consul* was set in South America... Pretty tenuous... Look, I'm sorry I gave you a hard time Friday. I don't know the first thing about your family and I really shouldn't be judging you. It was none of my business. Sorry.' This tiny soliloquy comes out almost in one breath.

'You've nothing to apologise for, Mariana. I shouldn't have tried dragging you to that awful club. Anyway...' I change the subject, not wishing to prolong her obvious embarrassment. 'Looking forward to your trip to New York and escaping us "dull" Brits?'

She sighs, tells me Syngestia have reneged on her week off and require her to come in to help sort out 'the problem' at the labs. Her voice tightens again.

'So Mumbling Frank *was* right. The EasyBreathe patent's in jeopardy.'

'Looks like it,' she laments. 'But why pull *my* vacation? How shitty is that? I mean, what use am I going to be?'

Mariana, on top of ensuring Syngestia's PCs run properly and our network remains secure, is also charged with checking and fixing the robots that screen hundreds of thousands of compounds every day. Those little machines are going to be put through their paces in the next few weeks but, even so, they haven't broken down in the two years I've been working for the company. Paranoia must be flying around the place.

'I've had the flight booked for months. My mom's expecting me at JFK Tuesday morning.' She either shifts the receiver to her other ear or exhales at length; all I discern is a brief spike of static followed by a sniff. 'Shall I just tell work where to go?'

'Please don't. They'll never find another computer expert as beautiful as you.'

'Hmm. *Slightly* smoother than the lines your friend tried on me.' Her voice has temporarily returned to its regular, unstressed pitch. She subtly presses the subject of my grief once more: 'How's your weekend been?'

I consider telling Mariana the gory details. Irregularities behind my father's death meant, thankfully, that the offer to visit him 'in state' (that is, pumped full of formaldehyde and ethanol to sustain a corporeal shell in the absence of his soul), wasn't made. His flat contained no clues as to the whereabouts of 'Sophia', no phone number or address, not even a surname. She's nothing but a ghost who informed my mother of her ex-husband's death, a young woman my father proudly mentioned, but never introduced, to his youngest son.

'I did come down to Becksmouth, in the end. My weekend wasn't too bad. I lost a bit of money but won a budgie.'

'Sounds… good. Well I guess I'll be seeing you.'

'Tomorrow.'

'You coming back to London so soon?'

'Yeah. There's no point me being down here at the moment.' I helped my mother out this morning with notifications about the death but it's all up in the air while we wait for the outcomes of the coroner's knife work.

'Okay. I'll see you tomorrow then.' She sounds unsure, or unconcerned. I wish I knew which.

'Bye, Mariana.'

After I switch off my phone, there's a sharp jangling of coins. A tramp appears to half-heartedly toast me with a Styrofoam cup. I don't recognise the area, having managed to turn the wrong way after leaving the casino, so I stick a fiver in his cup, as though to make amends for throwing nine hundred pounds away, and ask him the way to the station.

A short walk later, it's obvious he had no idea where the station is. I've missed my train and my arm aches from lugging this damn birdcage through town.

I find myself in a residential square, its lawn scarred by the purplish shadows cast by surrounding horse chestnuts. A jogger fizzes past me before fading into the darkness ahead, reappearing every time she passes under one of the ancient street lamps which showcase the five-storeyed, dark-bricked terraces to my right. Brass door knockers gleam behind black iron railings and, through the windows, disapproving and long-dead relatives glower at Neoexpressionist works of art above heirloom grand pianos half-covered in bowls of potpourri. The posh part of town. Now I'm really lost.

At the far end of the square, a belly dancer dances in a pub window, her naked stomach gyrating in a sequined bedlah as bass-heavy hip-hop reverberates through shisha-pipe smoke. The clientele – mainly women, expensively dressed – are transfixed. I consider entering, but remain outside, indecisive.

I've been experiencing similar hesitation lately. Tiredness, discontent, I don't know what it is. Maybe I just crave an alternative to the pubs, clubs and after-club clubs which have filled my third decade on Earth. After all, the pleasures within could so easily be found elsewhere, and the draught chemicals their customers guzzle aren't hard to come by either; I can attest to this only too well.

Behind the square, looms a four-storey Victorian building in blood-coloured brick. Atop the roof sits a squat dome with a nippled cupola, and the near side of the building swells out in a high porch. In it I glimpse the rich, polished woods of a reception and the coronae of soft lighting through clean glass. Strangely, all the side windows have thick security bars across them.

I step closer. The sign reads 'Sinton Hospital'. I've walked farther than I realised.

The budgie trills as an incomplete memory struggles to assert itself. Why is this place significant? I peer over my shoulder, hunting through the jagged trees twisting from the square, as though looking back the way I've come will solidify the asked-for recollection, and my eyes are drawn to a poster behind Perspex, just outside the hospital grounds.

The advert shows a young family on a stony, British beach, daughter on her father's shoulders, son wrestling an ice cream from the hands of a smiling mother, all improbably unaware of the cameraman who's snapped them in their moment of windswept bliss. Underneath runs a caption: *Syngestia, working towards a safer tomorrow.* It's a new ad, to get our company name out there, to bolster public trust. For some reason the decision was made to compare our work ethic to that of a contented family unit.

It seems pretty far off the mark to me. Archaic in choice of the locals' holiday location, it almost predates an age in which forty percent of marriages end in divorce. The children are cherubic and smartly dressed, the mother impossibly attractive, but it's the father's face I'm drawn to: skin lined but healthy, hair greying, he waits on the threshold of old age. Since I can't remember his exact appearance after ten years, this man easily takes on my own father's attributes. This is who I see when I recall the head which turned towards me in The Old Mint House, his lover's fingernails black against his bare skin. Overlong hair only a man in the early stages of male-pattern baldness knows the preciousness of. Ocean-green eyes which don't, or can't, look directly into his son's.

My father was easily distracted. Always looking out windows at the stars when he should've been listening. Even in photos, he's failing to eyeball the camera. His parents were both shopkeepers and could speak to anyone; being brought up amid chatter he took to saying little at a young age. This wouldn't have got him far socially so I expect he developed his rather abstract sense of humour as a bridge between his own world and everyone else's, but he remained perfectly at ease with silence. He just couldn't bear fidelity, felicity or the truth.

The poster has been defaced. An animal rights activist – persistent but trivial thorns in the side of science – has appended to the top of the boy's head two blood-red devil horns and a speech bubble from his beatific lips announcing, simply, 'Butcher'.

The budgie flaps in his cage, little wings a sudden and terrible ricochet in the darkness, and my heart stops for a moment. The bird hops onto his perch, fixes his black eyes upon me, and chirps a sound I can only describe as mocking laughter.

CHAPTER SEVEN

Before I can turn to lock my front door behind me, I connect with a huddled mass on my doorstep and almost lose balance. A body stirs beneath my size tens.

'What the...?'

A confusion of black hair appears from under a gaudily coloured leather jacket. Aaron looks at me with dead eyes, a fleeting uncertainty growing into recognition as his brain engages. He staggers to his feet.

'I was ringing the bell but you didn't answer.'

I test my buzzer. It works fine. Aaron was probably ringing the downstairs flat; the Polish couple moved out a month ago.

'What are you doing here? Did you sleep on my doorstep?'

He sheepishly lowers his gaze, then rotates his shoulder and cricks his neck.

Under the morning sun, I evaluate Aaron scientifically. His bottom teeth are faintly yellowed by the tetracycline he was prescribed to combat his teenage acne, the only remaining traces of which are marginally oversized pores between his temples and quizzical brown eyes. He could do with some more of this sun's ultraviolet, a week's sleep, a haircut.

'So, what's up?' I ask.

'This is pretty embarrassing. I don't really remember why I came here. I think I was, you know... I wanted to check how you were. Your dad and everything...' He's hungover. The way he checks his watch tells me he wishes he'd woken earlier and hightailed it long before I left for work.

This is hardly a recurrent problem, but Aaron does seem to have issues with the fact that I no longer drink. He respects the fact that I'm teetotal, and doesn't attempt – too often – to coerce me into joining him, but old habits are harder to break for him than they were for me. And that's what I am to him: a habit. Neither of us wants to admit that alcohol was a major thing binding our friendship together and so we carry on as we did, with me holding a lemonade. I've been told that the abstainer represents enlightenment to the alcoholic – and if Aaron got so drunk on a Sunday night he thought sleeping on my doorstep was a good idea, that's probably what he is – the proof that it can be done. But a part of him thinks I've let him down and, even if he doesn't know it himself, he's hanging around to see when – and how hard – I fall off the wagon.

'Hey, I forgot to mention,' he announces, rooting around for conversation. 'That tasty creature you work with called me yesterday. I tried to put her off you but...'

'Her *name* is Mariana,' I snap back.

Aaron wears his shock like a handprint upon the cheek. My taxi to work arrives.

'I'm only joking,' he says. 'Look, I promise to back off if you like her.'

My hand is on the front passenger door when Aaron jumps, uninvited, into the rear of the cab. By way of apology, I get in the back alongside him. Though we've occasionally fought, in that cagey, territorial way men do over male friends, we've never quarrelled over a woman.

'I'm sorry, Aaron. I'm not feeling myself today.'

'It's okay,' he replies, over-casually, yawning. He smells of smoke and a kind of campsite mustiness.

Aaron details his night as we swing our way into the Crouch End traffic. The school run has clogged every inch of asphalt and white van drivers holler their irritation over muffled breakbeats and organ-quaking basslines.

I'm less eager to start the day, but this is more than Monday-morningitis; all I'm bound to be doing for the foreseeable future is rooting around for solutions to the EasyBreathe debacle.

We drop Aaron off at Turnpike Lane. 'Fancy doing something next weekend?' he asks. I notice he's peeled off the No Smoking window sticker and re-adhered it in a right-angled fashion. I'm used to this sort of Obsessive-Compulsive behaviour but the driver looks at him as he might regard someone who's defecated on his back seat.

'Yeah. I'll call you.'

As I watch him mooch off from the kerb my words retain a defensive knell, like I'm killing off a bad date. He's a good man, Aaron, and though I'm a little embarrassed about the manner in which I confessed to liking a certain work colleague, I'm glad I bumped into him: I won't forget his promise to back off from Mariana.

The taxi jettisons me outside Syngestia's new £7m laboratory and headquarters, a vast aircraft hangar of glass, and I scurry through the main foyer to the lifts, flashing my badge at the security behind the curved chrome reception desk. The scrubbed and watered rubber plants, parlour palms and ficus trees glisten in the air-conditioned foyer.

'Meeting's just about to start, Mr Marr,' a semi-attractive woman I don't recognise informs me, her headset's thin black microphone hovering two inches in front of a plastic smile. Her words don't register until I've arrived at my empty lab.

I slip on my white coat and catch the lift to the next floor, where the large assembly hall echoes with the murmuring of over a hundred scientists. Panic has stretched itself into most voices, creating a confederacy of sopranos. A frowning Mumbling Frank, by design or accident, has an empty seat next to him. I pretend I haven't seen it and look around for Mariana.

She's sitting over on the left-hand side, but the neighbouring seats are taken. I wave at her then sit two rows in front, where a number of places are still empty. A few seconds later, she joins me.

'You're late,' she says, half-smiling. She's without make-up as usual.

'So you decided to stay with us, after all?'

'Obviously.' The jokey dig she bestows my ribs is probably an afterthought, designed to mask the displeasure inherent in her rejoinder.

When the bigwigs take to the stage a hush falls over the room. We're told what most of us already know, that a new asthma drug by the name of EasyBreathe was ready, sold, that everything was done that, we thought, possibly could be in laboratory conditions but long-term reactions are now being exposed. Five years on, many test patients are developing gastric problems and our patent has been withdrawn until we can find out why. The tone of the meeting is grave; the corporate heads can't understand how such a massive and potentially litigious side-effect has slipped through, how initial research was approved. It's simply *unheard of* that a chemical compound, proven to be stable after years of research and with impurities already controlled to very low levels, is halted so close to manufacture. It's not as if we don't have other contracts going on, but this is a big one, what with the number of asthma and allergy sufferers increasing at their current rate.

We're told we've got a month at best to work out the reason for the problem and the expression 'All hands on deck' ends the briefing. We shuffle off to our departments.

Mariana walks with me as far as my laboratory, leisurely spanking her thigh with a rolled-up wad of IT directives. We don't talk. The loss of her week's holiday has clearly pissed her off and I'm finding myself irrationally tongue-tied.

'Do you want to do lunch later?' she asks. Her lips are parted, inviting. Her eyes are curious dark slits.

'Nice idea,' I say, pressing my back against the wall to

allow a couple of frowning technicians past. 'I'll come and find you later.'

She strolls off unhurriedly up the corridor, and I slide backwards through my laboratory door.

I welcome the air-conditioned peace of the lab, if not the crystal purity of the daylight skewering through the windows. There are five of us in here, including a mumbling Mumbling Frank.

Tired, I do what everybody's probably doing. I procrastinate.

What a truly horrific, wondrous invention the internet is. A million ways to ignore your talents. According to a national news website, for instance, a forty-foot-wide asteroid by some drearily acronymous name has just missed our planet by 400,000 miles, passing through the exact position Earth was in only five hours before. If the asteroid had impacted it would have created an explosion twelve times as powerful as Hiroshima.

I can't believe nobody's making a bigger deal about this. Syngestia's profit margins would look a lot less worrisome if one of those smashed into us. Some of the asteroids orbiting out there are so large they even have their own moons.

Somewhere in my childhood, an interest in astronomy clearly segued into a love of the behaviours of structures, of naming stuff, of evidence based on experiment and, sometimes, when I'm engaged in research the normal flow of time seems to accelerate. Lunch comes and goes and I don't hear from Mariana.

She's done a good job on my computer – indeed, the EasyBreathe product database powered up in less than half an hour – so it would be churlish not to thoroughly investigate the ingredients our failing medicine contains. I scroll through the computer looking for a particular microbiology paper, published when subcellular studies were first made in the fields of allergy and immunology. I find it and print it out.

Though the lab's airy breeze and cheap coffee has cleared my mind somewhat, I notice that my hands tremble, causing the paper to jump about so much that at one point I leave the world of metalloprotease and pylori to spin round with the intention of turning off a non-existent fan.

Syngestia have a vast number of medical articles in their databank and I read all day, sustaining myself with yet more vending machine cappuccinos. Throwing myself into this, hopefully lengthy, problem suddenly seems like the appropriate distraction from everything else in my life right now.

It's therefore somewhat disappointing when, long after everyone else in the lab has gone home, I solve it.

I ring Phil, my department head, and, rather arrogantly, I'll admit, tell him of my findings. He laughs. And it's not a disbelieving, indulgent chuckle either. It's a full-on, 'That's a good one,' belly laugh. Yet another scientist with sense-of-humour issues. But I like Phil. He was on the interview panel when I auditioned for this gig and his warm, matter-of-fact attitude helped put this nervous upstart at ease.

'Okay,' I tell him, 'in layman's terms, I reckon the problem is down to a bacterium found in the intestines of thirty-five-percent of the population reacting to one of the ingredients in our new drug. We thought we'd countered any adverse reactions through the use of an inhibitor; however, this inhibition was itself stimulating an enzyme which we then had to add another inhibitor to inhibit. The side effect of *this* is a quasi-quiescent infection of the intestines in said thirty-five-percent of the population.'

'Oh, you're not joking.' He sounds rejected.

'It should be stabilised by bovine serum albumin.'

There's a long silence from the other end of the line, before he demands to see me in his office.

'It's Lucien, isn't it?' The managing director wearily rises from his leather armchair to shake my hand.

'Lucas,' I correct.

Besides Phil, there are two bigwigs in the office, called back in to work at short notice to speak to me, peering over spectacles with fingers locked into mini pagodas. I doubt either of them have any more idea what goes on in the pharmacology labs these days than a meat-eater does about the true contents of his sausages.

'We'll look into it,' Phil says, handing the microbiology paper to the third suit, who hurries out of the office with it as though it's a cipher for a wartime decoder. Although, to be fair, it's likely someone in government is watching the events at Syngestia closely.

'Tell me what you do here,' the nameless director says to me.

'I'm on the second floor,' I explain. 'Pharmacogenomics.'

A blank face, like he hasn't heard.

I attempt to elaborate and end up doing my finest impression yet of Mumbling Frank. '...more powerful medicines, better, safer ... dramatically reduce the number of deaths and hospitalisations that occur each year as the result of adverse drug response ... more accurate methods of determining appropriate dosages ... a decrease in the overall cost of health care...' His face, halitosis-close, is as red as a sergeant major's. '...family DNA ... genetic qualities passed down ... always endangered by the things that kill our parents...'

He's still staring at me. I finish my speech, more through having run out of confidence in it than by arrival at any kind of conclusion. It's damn bright in here. Sunspots march across my cornea, making the walls appear to be sprayed with blood.

'Do you know what fascinates me about medicine, Lucien?' the red face says, finally relaxing back into its leather chair, the only vaguely imperial touch to an otherwise sterile and minimalist office. 'Why I get out of bed, day after day, and walk these corridors? Medicine makes our lives longer, easier. But it will never end. We will never find a cure for finding a cure. We're looking to defeat cancer, for example, and yet we're spreading that very disease, propagating it through technology, microwaves, supermarket bacon. We keeping ourselves busy by chasing our tails, expensively inventing ways to counterbalance our lifestyles and mop up after society's ills. Promiscuity... binge drinking... drug abuse.'

'You've been here how long, Lucas?' Phil cuts in. He's obviously heard it all before. He has a kinder face than the other man, but is no less rotund. Funny how obesity wasn't mentioned in his colleague's list of modern sins. He moves, with the slow awkwardness of sciatica, to the window and perches uncomfortably on the ledge. 'Two years, isn't it?' He knows how long I've been here.

'Something like that, sir,' I say, aware that sounds like no time at all. In fact, my route here, my entire *history* – the Chemistry, Biology and Physics A-Levels taken in a backlash against the arts; my doctorate graduation ceremony at Oxford; the fast-track fellowship at a rival company; arriving at Syngestia to find I was a full ten years younger than my immediate colleagues – now seems little more than phases from a dream.

Phil's looking at me with his head on one side, like my father's budgie. 'You know your stuff, I'll give you that. It could well be this... enzyme you've mentioned that's at the root of our problem. We'll investigate. On another matter entirely, though... How are you coping?'

'Sorry?'

'You've recently had a family bereavement, have you not?'

'Oh... Well, we're awaiting confirmation of an inquest. No one quite knows what happened. I mean, my mother *thought* he'd had a heart attack but...'

The sergeant major's attitude towards me doesn't change. He turns to the window, sighs. 'Philip, give this fellow two weeks' leave if you think he needs it.'

Phil assures me, in the fawning manner of a poll-battered

public servant, that he'd be only too happy to grant me time off.

'On that subject,' I say. 'I've got a friend in IT who's had her holiday withdrawn. Now, I'm fairly sure my theory about EasyBreathe will be proved correct. You won't sort the problem out overnight but the boys in Pharmacokinetics can narrow the field off the back of my data, I'm sure. She's not *essential* to the programme at this stage.'

'No?'

Phil looks for help from his superior, who wafts the air with a loose wrist in what strikes me as a very Italian gesture and, after a scornful clearing of his throat, enquires, 'Do I sense a conspiracy here? What is this? Are you two *doing it*, Lucien?'

I chuckle, sympathetically; the managing director's clumsy attempt to wield the lingua franca of a subsequent generation has somehow made him appear a monstrous pervert.

Acknowledging this, a blushing Phil leads me to the door. 'I'll see what I can do, Lucas,' he says in a whisper.

'I'm sorry. I don't understand. Where's the "conspiracy"?'

'Mariana was the one who informed us about your father. I guess it looks a bit... I don't know. Strategic, shall we say? Anyway, leave it with me.' He all but winks. 'And, Lucas...? Sorry again to hear about your old man.'

CHAPTER EIGHT

'Have you always been an arrogant smart-ass?' Mariana asks.

We're in the Tama restaurant in Mayfair, amid a sea of white tablecloths and sparkling, upturned wine glasses. It's almost empty but we've been asked three times if the too light, too delicate food is to our satisfaction. Personally, I only wanted your common curry house, a place where I could break naan with my bare hands and drip chutney without being gastronomically pilloried, but she deems the occasion worthy of Michelin stars.

'I only said EasyBreathe was simple to fix. Which it is. Humans aren't *that* complicated. Did you know that one of the largest known genomes belongs to a single-celled amoeba, with over six-hundred-and-seventy billion base pairs, some *two-hundred times larger* than the human?'

'Yeah well, I'm sure I'd be impressed if I knew what half those words meant.' She thrusts another forkful into her smile. 'What are genomes?'

'Seriously?'

'Seriously.'

'Okay, imagine your body is a computer. It needs lots of bits to make it work, circuits, chips, wires, whatever, but most importantly it needs a computer programme, which runs because of a code. Deoxyribonucleic acid, DNA, is that code, containing the instructions which allow a living thing to grow and survive. An organism's genome is basically a complete DNA sequence of…'

'What's that?' She looks bored. 'Little helixes and stuff? All I know about DNA is that it's used to trap killers.'

'It *is* used to trap killers. You can't escape your genetic makeup. Entire hereditary information is encoded in our DNA and many human characteristics are determined by it.'

'Which is why I take after my mum in looks and my dad in personality,' I'm informed.

'There is such a thing as *behavioural genomics* but that's one for the psychologists to ponder. It's got nothing to do with my work at the labs. Certainly, all *physical* traits are defined by our DNA.'

'I think there's a lot to be said for this behavioural genetics thing.'

'I don't.' Perhaps this comes out too tetchily. 'You might pick things up from your parents in your formative years but nothing's innate within us. No one's born with a latent desire to be a mechanic or a ballerina. You're a product of your surroundings. We're born blank slates.'

'I don't believe you. My little nephew, he was born with his personality, he just *was*. I've always seen it. There's no way he was going to be anyone other than him. He was a yahoo from day one.'

'Yes, well, maybe he's an outlier.'

'A what?'

'An outlier. A measurement that doesn't fit the pattern of other data. Most of us are just born as crying little shitbags.'

'Some of us *still are* crying little shitbags.' She smirks.

Is this flirting? It's so much easier when women just give you their numbers on the back of playing cards in casinos, or get their maternal instincts and sexual frustration confused in funeral parlours.

'Anyway,' she continues, 'I guess this is science versus… What shall we call my world view? The flat earth theory?'

'Next you'll be telling me you're against animal testing.'

'I am.'

'You are? You work for…'

'I know who I work for.' She frowns, chews. 'Animals have an intrinsic right not be used for experimentation. It's unethical, simple as that. I know you *scientists* will say that human lives are saved as a result...'

'Why do you say "scientists" like that?'

'Like what?'

'Like it's a dirty word?'

'Did I?'

'Mariana, my job is mainly spent conducting screening experiments, the splicing and scraping of molecules into an infinity of possible results. You wouldn't believe how dull it is. Yes, the consequences of my data *are* tested on animals – and the law dictates this must happen before any clinical trials are conducted on humans, by the way – but I don't perform that role any more than you do. We both walk the same corridors though. We both know what goes on. Your hands are no cleaner than mine, just because you don't support the testing...'

This must be the worst date in recorded history. She sits back and crosses her arms.

I can't bear the silence, so go on. 'Computers alone can't interpret metabolic and toxicology tests, or the subsequent efficacy studies that are needed. For that, we require at the very least, fruit flies and transgenic mice, animals with the lowest degree of neurophysiological sensitivity. You know, I would go so far as to say that *every* major medical achievement has relied on animals in some way. Insulin, which revolutionised the treatment of diabetes, was isolated from dogs, and leprosy vaccines were developed using armadillos... Incidentally, how's your lamb?'

She picks up her fork, as though to stab it between my eyes. 'Alright, I get it. I'm a hypocrite. You practice that speech a lot?'

'A few times.'

To my surprise, she's smiling. Wisely, she changes the subject. 'I didn't see this coming, I must admit.' Perhaps she means our dinner. Perhaps she means the resurrection of her holiday. 'I mean, that you were able to fix anything in the state you were in this morning; I thought you had a hangover.'

'I don't dr...'

'I know.' She squints, as though trying to X-ray me. 'So what's the matter? Not sleeping well?'

'Not really.' I nod cautiously at her champagne flute. 'What's it like?'

She takes another sip. 'Peachy. Biscuity. A blend of... Pinot and Chardonnay. A hard-to-criticise choice.'

'You know your wines.'

'What made you stop drinking?'

'I... there wasn't one particular event. I'd... had enough.'

'It must have gotten bad.'

'It's more that it became boring, I suppose...'

'Have I said something I shouldn't have?'

'No, not at all. Why?'

She excuses herself from the table and I watch her roll her derriere to the toilets. Aaron once told me, during one of our more intellectual conversations, that 'arse men' are cowards compared to 'breast men' since they steal their fleeting glimpses whilst women aren't even facing them. I replied that it was hardly gentlemanly to do otherwise. I look at the kitchen staff. Cowards, the lot of them.

When she glides back, she picks at her food without speaking.

'So...' I ask. 'You always been obsessed with computers?'

'Not exactly.' I sense evasiveness.

'Where were you working before you started at Syngestia?'

She sighs. 'I did a number of things, in a number of places, none of them very exciting. Lucas, when you said we're born blank slates... Do you honestly mean that there are no naturally gifted musicians or artists or sportspeople? That they're just better because they've practised more?'

'I guess I do.'

'So anyone could have written the music of Mozart? Or painted like Caravaggio? Or written like Shakespeare?'

I pause. I've probably been rumbled here.

She pushes on. 'And, as a scientist, you couldn't possibly entertain the notion of intelligent design?'

'I don't see the connection. There's no such thing as God-given talent. If "intelligent design" existed, I wouldn't have to suffer mouth ulcers. And stuff that was bad for us wouldn't taste so bloody good.'

Again, the look. I've pricked her curiosity but she doesn't follow this up. Maybe she senses the conversation would spiral into even more uncomfortable territory if she did.

'What will you do with your fortnight away from work?' she asks.

'I've got a few things to sort out for my mother before the weekend.'

'Your parents were divorced, right?'

I nod. 'I've been thinking about the circumstances behind their separation a lot. I found this old diary when I was in Becksmouth...'

The waiter comes over yet again to ask us how we're finding the meal.

'It's disgusting,' Mariana jokes.

The waiter gets the message and goes to hide in the kitchen.

'So what's it like? The diary, not the food.'

'It's... weird. I mean, I'd forgotten most of the stuff that happened.' This is hardly surprising. That summer soon ran away with itself, revelations crashing against one another in rapid succession like dominoes, and years of early morning PowerPoint presentations and Mumbling Frank's conspiracy theories have distanced me from what now seems the petty, unimportant angst of children. 'I'm some way through it already. I've got to the part where I find out my father's shagging another woman.'

The fork stops in front of her mouth. 'At least the nasty bit's happened and is out the way,' she consoles.

I stare at a splat of madras on the tablecloth. That blood never did come out of the hall carpet. It fanned out fast, dried even faster. My father bought a rug to hide the evidence the morning after he left me standing, quite literally, by the side of the road.

'Oh it gets *nastier*,' I say, concentrating on stilling my other hand, as Mariana reaches towards it across the table.

The centre of the universe is, briefly, the point where our fingertips meet.

'Well, at least it's all in the *past*,' she says, her tone apologetic, dabbing her exquisite mouth with a napkin. 'It's a shame you can't come to New York with me. Maybe that's what you need, a few days away. Central Park's *gorgeous* this time of year.'

Merely talking about America, her upbringing, the burning summers and sub-zero winters, Macy's window at Christmas, seems to bring her colloquially closer to it. The 't' slips from the word 'water' and vowel sounds swap places in 'parents'.

After another long draught of champagne, she asks me, straight out, 'Lucas, are you remotely attracted to me?'

Her brown eyes give away a sparkle of expectation, armoured by drunkenness and her natural indifference.

'Very.'

She lowers her eyes, a knowing smile tempered by the sucking in of her bottom lip as unspoken confusions cut a cute pincer between her brows. 'The offer's there if you want it.'

I spear a piece of something with my fork. I'm still not hungry. 'Offer?'

'To come to New York. There'll be flights. Most mid-week departures are only half-full. What do you reckon?'

'I'd love to...'

'But?'

'But my mother would kill me.'

Outside the restaurant, we're kissing before I realise it.

Mariana's arms and shoulders are firm but not muscular,

evidencing cardiovascular workouts. She breaks back, says 'Dammit' with meaning, then presses her cheek to mine. We stay like that for some time.

'Lucas,' she says, still pressed against me. 'It wasn't alcohol you were addicted to, was it?'

'What do you mean?'

'You went... *strange* when I asked. You've quit drinking, I get that, but was there something else?'

Her cheek remains motionless against mine.

She's good. I track back over our conversation. I guess I did mention that alcohol became boring, which is seldom an objection of the binge drinker. I also said something ill-advised about bad things tasting good. Or is there something else she picked up on? Something in my very demeanour. My pallor. My self.

'I didn't mean to mislead you,' I say. 'Alcohol was a part of it, I guess. But, yeah, there was something else too.'

'What?'

'It doesn't matter anymore. I'm clean.'

A long time passes. Her body is curved perfectly into mine. Convex where I'm concave. Soft where I'm hard. We hold each other as though we're mourning.

'I better go,' she announces, finally peeling herself away. 'I've an early start and I need to pack up all the stuff I unpacked yesterday.'

I walk with her until she's able to hail a taxi, neither of us saying much. We kiss tenderly on the kerb. Longer than friends, far shorter than lovers.

'I'll see you when I see you, Mr Marr,' she says, dissolving into the cab's black leather.

When I get home, the budgie's baying his famine so I slot him some sunflower seeds. Within minutes, the ungrateful bugger's flinging them around his home with the fury of a sugar-dowsed eight-year-old. It's often said that owners come to resemble their pets, though the similitude is generally only applied to dogs, and I perceive a distinct parallel to my father: the thin face, proud beak and small unsatisfied eyes, a talent for messing up his own nest. At least my old man had company in his last few days; though for all I know this fictive Sophia fucked him to death.

I lie down and remove Laura's queen of hearts from my wallet, hold her spidery phone number under the bedside light. The card is stiff and calendered to a high quality, drawn from one of the casino's own professional decks. I won't see Mariana for a week. This seems to me, quite suddenly, like an injustice. And yet, I know, dialling this alternative would be a classic example of me playing my hand poorly.

It goes in the bin.

I pick up the slim diary, no longer the colossal ledger of childhood perceptions, from my bedside. My hands tremble.

But was the world I'm about to dip into really so different from this frankly bewildering adult one? Didn't the camps and clubs merely foretell the coteries and conspiracy theories of adulthood? Didn't the reading of superhero fictions prefigure a life of newsreader-divulged battles between 'good' and 'evil', the Godly and the Godless? The signs were all there for us, the templates prepared: the love triangles, instead played out amongst same-sex friends and rivals; the threats of 'bigger boys'; our ghosts next door.

As I remove the bookmark, the phone explodes beside my bed.

I fumble for the landline. 'Hello?'

'Lucas…? I've got some…'

I slam the phone down and yank at its cable, which unsockets and whiplashes a hair's breadth from my face. The diary flops onto the floor.

The voice was the same, fifteen years on. I try to compose myself, lying dizzy on the bed, the ceiling a fiercely undulating white sheet.

It can't have been. It simply *can't* have been.

I reconnect, stab 1471 into my phone then cross-reference

the number with the one I was called by on my mobile on Friday night. It's the same.

I unfold my laptop and open Google. Sinton Hospital doesn't have a website but, on an obscure South Eastern wellbeing portal, it's described as 'a Psychiatric Hospital with facilities for Crisis Stabilisation and long-term Secure Unit patients.'

In the UK, there exist a number of small secure units. These are modern buildings with up to date security features and are locally sited to help with patients' reintegration into society once medication has stabilised their condition (after, on average, two to three years). However not all forensic patients can meet this criteria and some patients, such as the criminally insane, end up spending a number of years on site. An example of a secure unit which caters for both medium-term and long-term patients is the Sinton Hospital, located to the north of Becksmouth on the south coast.

It's a prison, effectively, for the mentally ill.

Long after I've turned the computer off, I continue to hear that voice. In the wake of my father's death I should've expected a few ghosts from the past. But this is the last one I imagined hearing from.

I pick up my mobile again, scroll through my contacts and depress the green call button on a recently added name. A second later, before I even hear the first ring, I'm stabbing the red one to hang up.

After several minutes deep breathing, my eyes closed tight, I try again.

She answers immediately.

As steadily as I'm able, I ask, 'Mariana, does that offer to come with you to New York still stand?'

CHAPTER NINE

I lost my virginity because my mother met Clint.

She'd probably known him less than three weeks when we all set off for Majorca. Looking back, her motivation is clearer – it was a failed attempt to recreate a foursquare family unit, five years after she divorced my father. Not surprisingly, it was an uncomfortable holiday, though the sea was sauna-warm and a multitude of semi-nudes were baked beautiful by a tumour-bestowing sun. My mother and Clint talked about nothing but behavioural management strategies, having met recently on Becksmouth College's teacher training course, while I walked around Palma Nova draped in a teenager's black sulk, assuming looking cool would keep me cool. Ryan tagged along behind, too young to talk to anyone on their level, too old to covet everyone's attention.

Clint tried desperately hard to be the alpha, complete with Hawaiian shirts and the spouting of cod-Spanish in restaurants that only served British cuisine. Colonialism was alive and well, though looped episodes of *Only Fools and Horses* in the coastal bars looked daft juxtaposed with the lizards shinning up our hotel walls in their frenzied, zoetrope motions.

I had to share a twin room with Ryan, though we hardly spoke any more in those days than we do now. Most evenings, he played *Sonic the Hedgehog* on his Game Gear, or tried to convince me he could see dinosaurs or sailing boats within the autostereograms in his *Magic Eye* books.

On the fourth night, I climbed out the window and moseyed into Magaluf.

I don't remember much of the night after my fifth vodka, but certainly recall being dragged back to a beachside hotel by an English girl two years my senior.

Naturally, I equipped myself in a way customary to the first-timer and the magnitude of the occasion left me entirely sober. The physical, penile, aspect of the act wasn't Earth-shatteringly dissimilar to masturbation (still a recently-discovered delight at this stage, and one temporarily scuppered by having to share a room with Ryan), but the female body *was* new, its folds and sweeps and swells, its pliability and scents. I remained awake all night, relieved. A prisoner pardoned. A graduate.

I was probably hard to get rid of the next morning, only quitting her bed upon guarantee of a further tryst that evening. Once I'd made my way to the correct hotel, I found a mother too intimidated by the notion of my autonomy to be angry about me slipping out during the night, and a father-in-waiting waggling Terry Thomas eyebrows. For the rest of the afternoon, I sat alone by the hotel pool, feeling like the King of the Fucking Universe as I watched poor excuses for men – balding men, overweight men, sunburnt elders well past their prime – plunge in and out of the water.

I waited three hours for her outside the souvenir shop on the seafront, until long after the sun slid down behind the glass of the ocean.

The rejection must've shown in my face that night because when I returned my mother and Clint seasoned my nightly scrambled eggs with an empathy I'd hitherto been unaware was within their spectrum. For the first time in five years, I experienced a moment of genuine domesticity.

On our last night, I saw my *inamorata* with another guy, kissing on a bench by a pharmacy. He had his hand clamped to a breast, his tongue a driving piston between her teeth. 'Find a room,' my mother mumbled as we headed for the restaurant in which Clint trusted enough by now to order bangers and mash.

In many ways, that girl affirmed to me the benefits of remaining distant. I forced myself to believe that, like cortisone on my mosquito bites, the pain of that experience would be worth the long-term paybacks. I considered it a useful lesson.

Through my headache, in the back of a taxi on the way to Mariana's house, I have to admit to myself that I've enjoyed flirting with her – protean signals, double entendres, those suggestive smiles. I like the way she plays me, the way she casually extracts me from myself, how the thought of meeting her waters my palms. But, cards on the table, the reason I originally turned down the offer to accompany her to New York was out of a fear that, in doing so, she might be cut out of my life too soon. Flirting's very purpose, after all, presupposes another destiny.

She's better than a one-night-stand. But am I?

'Awright, mate?' the driver asks. He's about fifty and couldn't be more Cockney if he were dressed as a Pearly King. A miniature West Ham kit pogoes from his rear-view mirror. 'Want me to pull over or summink?'

I take my head from my hands, tell him it's a migraine. He nods, unconvinced, but turns off the radio anyway, avoiding my eyes in the mirror all the way to Southgate.

Mariana teases open the front door to her ground floor flat, then trudges off, leaving me to close it after myself.

'You ready?' I ask, following her through a lounge-cum-dining area into a tightly-furnished but uncluttered kitchen. Her tiny garden doesn't get much light at this time of morning but every flower's upright outside her window, awaiting what little sun they can acquire.

She yawns a reply, failing to cover her mouth, and offers me a coffee.

I accept, mumble something about how cosy her flat is.

Such lacklustre small talk is to be expected. We've both had a night to sleep off yesterday's kiss. She probably did the right thing by going home, so soon after the promise; she's not after the smash-and-grab. She seeks the long game. In her eyes, have I passed the test by agreeing to come with her, thus proving a capability for commitment?

'You haven't brought much stuff,' she says, nodding at my shoulder bag.

'I like to travel light.' I tap my jacket pocket.

'Ooh, let's have a look at your passport.'

Reluctantly, I hand it over to a nasal guffaw.

It's not hard to see her point: the lank hair and thick-rimmed spectacles at odds with the complete lack of erudition in the half-pout, the gormless quizzing of the eyes. It's impossible to believe this petulant try-hard put himself through seven years of chemistry exams, and harder still that any country on Earth permits me through customs.

'So your parents don't mind me coming with you?' I ask, taking back the passport.

'They won't object. Provided you're on your best behaviour. So, what changed your mind, in the end?'

'Oh, you know. I had a few days spare...'

When she disappears into her bedroom, to collect some nearly-forgotten accoutrement for her suitcase, I wander the lounge. CDs by Suzanne Vega and Joni Mitchell. A DVD collection comprised mainly of Spanish-language films. Books penned by proponents of Magic Realism.

'Who's this?' I ask, when she returns, pointing at a photo of a dark-haired man in his early thirties who peers into the camera in a tired, slightly Don-like way, as though auditioning for a role in a cheap TV rip-off of *Goodfellas*.

'That's Jorge.' She unzips her case and stuffs in a pair of jeans without folding them. 'The photo was taken a few years ago, about six months before he died.'

'I'm sorry. Who was he?'

'An uncle.' She answers quickly, keen to move on.

Human lives are recurrently influenced by the losses and rejections of other people: the house that was no longer suitable for the previous owner; the vacated position before you joined the company; the lover's lover who changed their mind. It would be an invidious man indeed who begrudged someone their past. However, an immediate and unjustifiable aversion to this 'uncle' develops within my gut.

She opens the door and strides into the sunlight.

'Did you think, maybe, he was my boyfriend?'

'Um... I wondered if...'

'Get a move on,' she chides. 'We'll miss the plane.'

My mother rings as we enter Heathrow's departure lounge, grey, bright and with the acoustics of a supermarket. I only answer because things got uncomfortable the last time I refused to acknowledge her calls in Mariana's presence and I disappear back towards the duty free, out of Mariana's earshot, upon hearing the serious tone of her voice.

'Are you sitting down?' she asks.

'I think we've already had this conversation, Mum.'

She doesn't think this is funny.

'Your father was poisoned,' she says.

'You fucking *what*?' The entire airport falls silent.

'Language, Lucas.'

In light of recent events, I vow never to pick up my phone again. 'But... Who would...? I mean... Surely there's been...'

Heathrow quickly regains its energy. A toddler knocks a rack of airport paperbacks across the terminal book shop. Mariana looks up from an issue of *Marie Claire* and grins at me without concern.

'Where are you?' my mother asks. 'Can I hear flight announcements? You're not vanishing off on *holiday* are you?'

'Are you sure he was poisoned? Doesn't that strike you as somewhat ridiculous?'

'Of course it does. I'm just telling you what the police are saying. Lucas, I absolutely forbid you to leave the country.'

'Mum, even if I were going somewhere, what would it matter?'

'What would it *matter*? Think about how it looks: you never made any secret of the fact that you disliked your father; you're a scientist with access to all sorts of chemicals; you're flying off to… where are you going?'

'Nowhere. I told you.'

'Lucas.' A hard edge finds purchase in her voice. 'Grow up and stop playing games. Your father's been *murdered*.'

THE SECOND PART
OF THE DIARY

Monday 4th September 1989

School sucks. Mrs O'Hanlon forces us to play lame games like 'school rules hangman' and I look spastic because my uniform is too big. In Mr Kemptons English class we had to write 2 paragraphs about something that happened over the summer so I wrote about Mrs Smithson dying. I didn't speak to anyone all day.

When I got home Mum asked if I was ill. She said 'You'll cheer up when you look in your room. Theres a surprise!'

On my bed was a telescope and the side of the box said 'Thrill to the Magic of the Night Sky!' She said Dad bought it for me to celebrate my first day at my new school and the telescope came with a star chart and I found Orion, Ursa Major and the bright star in the middle of Taurus. I spied on the Gemini constellation and The Pleiades, a cluster of 7 stars like this

I don't know what my star chart means when it says 'first magnitude' and 'variable star' but some are brighter than others. I will call my telescope Arcturus, which is a red giant and was the first thing I spotted with my new present.

I was in bed when Dad knocked. I pretended to be asleep but he stayed at my door for ages and eventually I went 'Thank you for my telescope' and he said that because I've started big school now I am becoming part of a world that is strange and mysterious and that sometimes things will happen that I might not fully understand and he said that if I need to talk to him about anything I can but 'maybe its best if you don't talk to your mother about what you think you saw yesterday.'

Tuesday 5th September 1989

I saw one of the bigger boys from Sinton Woods in the canteen, the one with the shaved head, so ate my sandwiches behind the Geography hut. The tomato made the bread go soggy. When I got home I found this note had come through the door for me in a sealed envelope

I've been doing some detecting. I asked my dad about The Old Mint House. He said it was used for photography classes about a year after the antique shop closed. This is why a red bulb was in the room and other things. I am sending this note because I didn't want to knock for you in case your dad answered and shouted rude words at me again.

Are your parents getting a divorce? Flossie Benedict's parents in 4C got divorced last year and she started throwing eggs at buses and telling people she smoked. How long has your dad been seeing that lady? Who is she? Did you get in trouble?

I haven't told anyone about it. It's our secret.
Julian.

Wednesday 6th September 1989

The screaming started after Mum got a call from Mr Kempton and before Ryan pooed on my floor.

Mum mentioned my English story about Mrs Smithson at dinner. She said she told Mr Kempton I'd always had a 'vivid imagination' and that Dad won't be buying me any more books on ghosts. She made an angry face at him across the table as she chopped up Ryans sausages and told me the noises in the night are just the water pipes.

After dinner I went upstairs and sat with Arcturus. It wasn't dark enough for proper starspying so I peeked in a few houses and watched lights come on as the sky went purple, so windows looked like floating squares which disappeared when people in their pants pulled their curtains together. When I spotted two flashing torch lights heading to the bottom of Julians garden the sides of my head tingled.

I ran downstairs and asked Mum if I could go outside too but she said I had to do my homework. Dad was in the dining room muttering to himself. He doesn't have a moustache anymore. I asked him 'Can I go outside and see Julian? Mum said I had to ask you.'

He thought about it then went 'I don't see why not.'

I was halfway down the drive when Mum shouted 'Going somewhere young man?' and the torches went off at the bottom of Julians garden.

Mum also said 'Your becoming rather sneaky' and I went 'ME???' and Mum asked 'What does that mean?' and Dad was quiet behind her. I could hear Julian and Daniel creeping in the garden, trying to listen to what was going on. They weren't very skill because I could hear twigs snapping.

Mum said that if I didn't go inside that minute and do my homework she would take away my telescope and I said she couldn't because it was Dad who bought it for me and Mum went something like 'Dad and I do things together and if I say I'll take away the telescope it means Dad will support me.'

Dad couldn't look me in the eye as I stormed past him back into the house. Mum was saying that she didn't know what happened to me in the last few days. She went, 'First he climbs out his window and the next minute a teachers calling about him hearing dead people!' and Dad said 'You know what boys are like.'

'What are boys like?' I shouted at Dad. 'WHAT ARE BOYS LIKE? I DID hear a ghost. And I saw one too. In The Old Mint. An UGLY *BITCH GHOST!*'

Dad shouted 'That's enough!' and I ran upstairs.

At some point after that Dad must have told Mum the truth because there was sobbing, slammed doors and yelling, all of it by Mum. While it was going on I stared at blue Venus through Arcturus, even when something smashed downstairs. Then I remembered that Dad bought me the telescope to pretend nothing happened in the Old Mint House, but now everybody knows EVERYTHING, so I lifted it way above my head and hurled it to the floor. It broke into a million pieces.

Someone said my name. Ryan was sitting on my bed all confused so I went over and gave him a hug and he said 'Mummy and Daddy fighting.' We played with Lego for a bit and then that's when I smelled the poo.

Thursday 7th September 1989

I bunked school today.

The camp was cold this morning and I had to ration my sandwiches like army men do. There were some blackberries left so I ate those and when I had to pee I did it into the bushes.

No matter how hard I thought I couldn't work out why Dad was doing what he was doing with that woman at The Old Mint. I wondered if Mum had done something wrong or whether Ryan or I had. I decided that even when school ended I still wouldn't leave the camp. When Mum and Dad realised I wasn't ever coming home they would tell the police I was missing and Julians policeman dad would go round and tell them off for being such crappy parents. Maybe they would stop screaming at each other.

At half past 3 it started to rain and the raindrops hitting the ceiling of the camp were machineguns and the thunder was bombs. The water dripped through and the camp started to smell of slugs and the colours got squelchy. It was cold in my wet clothes.

At quarter to 5 there was the sound of someone pushing through the brambleweeds and then Julian popped in. He was wearing his black mackintosh and the hood was tight and squeezed his face so it was round like the Moon. 'Your mums here' he said. 'She's looking for you.'

I told him Mum found out about Dad because I dobbed him in.

Julian whispered 'So its not a secret anymore is it, if your mum knows?'

Then there was crunching and rustling and Mum struggled into the camp. Her hair was running down her face and Julian went 'Hello Mrs Marr' and I thought she was going to be angry but she said I had to come home because I was really wet. Her lip wobbled.

Later Mum brought me some hot chocolate in bed and tried to talk to me about why I was 'in the hedge' in the rain but my head was all space and tunnels like at the beginning of *Doctor Who*. Theres no sign of Dad.

Friday 8th September 1989

Still no sign of Dad.

Arcturus didn't really break into a million pieces, but the lens inside is cracked. I had to mend it with selotape, so now when I look at the moon it has a black line down it and one half is the same as the other. I was trying to hunt for Betelgeuse when I realised I was crying.

Mum heard and came up with Ryan. Mum said things like 'for the best' and 'no ones blaming you' and 'that skeletons such a grim thing to have in your room Lucas.'

She patted my leg and said something weird like 'You've always been a brave boy. I thought so the moment I met you.' Then she went 'I mean the FIRST TIME I saw you as your OWN PERSON and not a helpless baby' and something about a mother having to wait before 'she truly sees her child'. She said something about how it was at a party at Julians house and when I went up to her I 'introduced myself' as a spaceman, all confident like a much older boy. Mums definitely cracking up.

I asked Mum if Dad was staying at Uncle Jeffreys house but this made her cry so I hugged her until she stopped. I think Dad has been fibbing about visiting Uncle Jeffrey.

Saturday 9th September 1989

There are only 6 ways to die in *Cluedo* and 3 of those are the same. Stabbed by a knife, thwacked with lead piping, strangled with rope, thwacked with a candlestick, shot with a revolver and thwacked with a spanner. No one is poisoned or pushed under a tractor.

Me and Ryan are staying at Granny and Granddads house for the weekend. We are to be on our best behaviour because Granddad has only just come back from hospital.

I like visiting Granny and Granddad. They are wiser than my parents because they don't shout at each other and Granddad killed Nazis. The only problem is they don't like much TV. Granny and Granddad have the television turned off for HOURS.

Mum collected Ryan in the evening and gave me a long hug before she left, like I wasn't going to see her for ages, which is silly because I'm only staying here for the weekend. Granny and Granddad were extra nice when Mum went and Granddad and me did drawings of each other but when I suggested we give the drawings to Mum, to cheer her up, he just looked out the window and said 'That's a nice idea'.

Professor Plum did it in the ballroom with the lead piping and Granny won.

Sunday 10th September 1989

I only went out with Julian and Daniel after dinner because Granddad was sleeping and Granny was knitting.

When Daniel went into Candy Corner Julian asked if I had found out who Dad was kissing and I told him I haven't seen Dad since Wednesday and that I think him and Mum are doing their shouting while I'm with Granny and Granddad. We 'dropped the subject' when Daniel walked out of Candy Corner with his pockets bulging. He showed us 7 packets of Jawbreakers, 3 Tic Tacs and a HubbaBubba. I noticed a big brown bruise on his hip when he pulled up his Tshirt to get the bubble gum.

'It was well easy to nick them' he boasted. 'Theres an old woman in there.'

He turned to Julian and said 'Your turn' and searched Julians pockets for money. I wondered if Daniel had bought the sweets he said he nicked, because we never got to frisk him, but I guess he did nick them because buying 7 packets of Jawbreakers is pretty dumb. When Julian came out he was shaking. He said the old woman was suspicious but pulled out a pocketful of cola bottles and strawberry laces.

'Those are well easy to get' Daniel said when he saw Julians sweets. 'The chocolate on the counter is the hardest stuff.'

'YOU didn't get any chocolate' I pointed out.

I don't think Daniel liked this because his top lip curled

like a Cheesy Quaver. 'Right Lucas, you have to get a Marathon. And a bottle of Panda Pop, the blue one.'

I walked into Candy Corner. Daniel had given me an impossible mission.

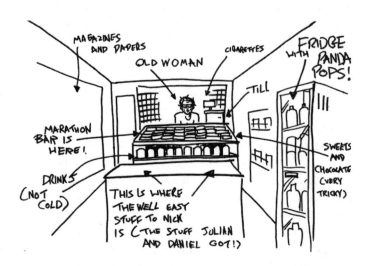

The woman behind the counter had thick glasses with black frames and her hair was grey and tied back and she was wearing a red jumper even though it wasn't cold. She always says hello to Mum because she has a magazine reserved and we used to have a paper delivered until Dad argued with the paperboy. Being last on this nicking mission was a problem. 2 of us had already been in the shop and not bought anything so she was super suspicious and her wrinkly eyes followed me everywhere.

I came up with a plan.

'I've come to collect a magazine for my mum' I said, walking bravely to the counter.

'Ah' she said. 'I think I know the one.' When she ducked down to flick through the pile of magazines they keep for customers I quickly grabbed a Marathon and took a Panda Pop from the fridge and stuffed them in my pockets.

She stood up again, her face well beetrooty. 'Sorry love I don't think its here' she said and I went 'Don't worry' and walked out all cool before running as fast as I could.

We sat on a grave outside Mums church and ate our sweets then walked down a path to the church. The door opened and Daniel ran to the pulpit and went 'Shall we turn Jesus upside down?' He tried to pull Jesus off but Jesus was well nailed.

'Give us a leg up' Daniel said. Julian put his hands into a cradle so Daniel could stand on them and he climbed up and put one foot on the edge of the big font and unzipped his trousers and started peeing in the holy water. As Julian was holding up Daniel his sleeve slipped down and I noticed Julian had 2 friendship bands on his wrist. Then I looked at Daniel's wrist. He was wearing a friendship bracelet EXACTLY the same as mine!

I didn't know what to do so I ran out the church and started pulling some bark off a big tree in the graveyard. I couldn't stop. Every time I snapped a piece off I imagined Daniel and Julian could feel it and I decided I would keep on going until the tree had no bark left. The wood underneath was pale and yellow and soon I'd made a big barkless patch. After a while I decided it would take too long to pull all the bark off and I got tired and anyway Julian and Daniel were chased out by the priest.

They were still laughing when we got back to the shops. Candy Corner had its big metal portcullis down.

We stopped outside Granny and Granddads house and I saw Granddad spying at the living room window. Daniel asked why I was staying here at the moment but I was ready for this and said that my bedrooms being painted.

Daniel looked at me with a sort of snakes smile. 'Julian said it was because your dad was doing it with some prostitute.'

Julian stopped laughing.

Then Granddad came out and asked if I had a nice time with my friends but I was so angry I didn't bother answering and I stormed inside. The door to the spare bedroom was closed and there was a large bag outside.

It was Mums.

In the lounge I was surprised to see Dad and not Mum sitting on an armchair. He looked older. I wondered if Dad watched lots of horrors this morning. He finished his tea and went 'Aaahh, very nice Granny' then said it was time for me to go home with him. Granny and Granddad were standing by the door looking at the carpet.

I asked where was Mum. Dad scratched behind his ear then went 'Don't worry, you'll be able to visit her.'

Monday 11th September 1989

I'm back home. Mums left with Ryan and they are staying with Granny and Granddad.

I know Dad drank a lot of beer last night because the bin was full of cans this morning. We ate fish and chips after school. When I told Dad he's fucked everything up he looked at me sort of angry then said it was an 'accurate postulation'. He didn't even tell me off for swearing, so I must have done a REALLY accurate postulation.

Now he's keeping me awake by singing 'Love, love will tear us apart again' downstairs and his singing is worse than Grannys and shes tone deaf.

Tuesday 12th September 1989

I spied on THE BACKSTABBER and Daniel as they played wargames with Daniels sister. Their having more fun without me, and with a girl. I saw Daniel run up his garden with this wiggly rope in his hand. 'It's a snake!' he yelled, dangling a slowworm in front of THE BACKSTABBER, who screamed like a fat spastic and ran to the other end.

Later, Daniel knocked on the wall and shouted 'homo'. I don't think he meant homo sapien and anyway when I'd been watching his sister being sat on by him and THE BACKSTABBER and water pistoled on the knickers I got a strange feeling and my willy went painful because all the skin got tight around the tip but later it went normal size again.

So I'm not a homo actually Daniel, you massive massive idiot.

Wednesday 13th September 1989

The bigger boy with the shaved head has spotted me. He told everyone he was going to kung fu me after school.

To avoid him I hid in the library after period 5 and read 22 pages of a book called *The Catcher in the Rye* which is a rubbish book I think because its got lots of 'goddam' and 'ya' and 'flunkin' in it and its just people talking. No one was waiting to get me when I left.

When I got home, Dad wasn't back from work so I took *The Omen* out of its fake book case. I still don't know why Dad took a video with him to see his girlfriend.

The devil chopped someones head off by taking the handbrake off a lorry and he did a terrible thing to a vicar.

When Dad got back I pretended I'd been watching *Art Attack*.

Now that Dad has to do all the things Mum did, like washing clothes and cooking dinner, I bet he wishes he didn't make her leave. He is rubbish at these things. Today he burned some chips and scraped them into the bin and called them 'bastard chips'. Before I could escape upstairs Dad went 'Wait. I've got something for you' and grabbed a parcel from underneath the telephone table. It was wrapped in blue paper.

'Open it' he said. He was speaking slowly and his eyes were all red and droopy.

It was a Tshirt with a shuttle on it. The fire coming from the rocket boosters was whooshing off the landing bay and underneath it said 'Apollo 11 1969.' I think the Tshirt is well cool, but I didn't say so. I said 'Why am I with you and not Mum? Why haven't YOU moved out?'

He was silent for a bit then sat at the bottom of the stairs. He has a circle on the top of his head which is like bits of dust and not hair. I hope I don't go bald when I'm older.

Dad said Mum still loves me but that its easier for her to live with Granny and Granddad at the moment because Ryans young and needs Mum more.

'Whats the name of that lady from The Old Mint?' I asked. 'Was she a prostitute?'

'No' he said firmly 'she most certainly was not.' He sighed and went on about how stupid them meeting in The Old Mint was and how when he saw me run out of that cabinet he'd never felt so awful in his whole life and how much he misses Mum and Ryan and feels sorry for me because I don't deserve to lose them either. He said everything was 'complicated.'

I told him it wasn't complicated. It was simple. He shouldn't have been a dickhead.

Dad shouted 'Oh what the hell do you know? Your 11!'

Thats when I started to eat the Tshirt. Dad was horrified and tried to pull the Tshirt out my mouth but I wouldn't let go and bit harder. I made sounds like a dog. Then I raced up to my bedroom and pushed the bed against the door so Dad couldn't get in and I haven't left all evening.

I had to wee in a cup.

Very late, Wednesday night

I woke up about 15 minutes ago and heard voices downstairs and dragged my bed away from the door and crept out of my room to listen from the bend halfway down the stairs. Dad was talking to a woman at the front door.

'You shouldn't have come here' he went and the woman said 'I don't have much to say. You'll never see me again. Sorry for fucking things up for you.' This was sarcasm, which is a tone of voice adults use when they aren't being honest.

The rest of there conversation went a bit like this.

'Jenny... we've been here before.'

'I mean it. You'll never see me again. I managed without you for 10 years. I'll manage again. Look at the state of you... Your wasted.'

'Shhh. Keep your voice down. You'll wake Lucas.'

'How is he?'

'Like YOU give a shit.'

She went 'Thats low, even for you.'

'Yeah? Tell me how many times over the last 10 years Lucas has even crossed your mind?'

'Don't start. You know my reasons. You know...'

Then I trod on the creaky corner stair and they stopped. Dad turned and stared at me with horror on his face and the Jenny woman had walked into the hall and was standing behind him and her blonde or blond hair was down around her shoulders and she was thin and pale and was looking at me in a mega weird way as if she was struggling not to cry.

I screamed at her but I don't remember what, even though it was only a few minutes ago. Dad told me to stop shouting and tried to come up the stairs but I started punching so he stepped back again to avoid my flying fists. 'Calm down' he was saying. 'Calm down.' There were black bags under his eyes. He turned to the Jenny woman and said 'Get out of our house.'

I thought she was going to say something, or burst into tears, but she just spinned round and left. Dad closed the front door and leaned against it. There was the sound of a car zooming away.

I ran back upstairs and barricaded myself and am now writing in this diary. 2 facts keep hitting against each other in my head.

The Jenny woman said she'd managed without Dad for 10 years.

Mum has taken Ryan but not me away from Dad.

I just got up, turned the light on and looked into the mirror on my wardrobe. My hair is mega blonde or blond under the light.

And

I remembered something Mum said last Friday that I thought was weird and read back through the evidence in this diary. She said about the first time she met me and then, well embarrassed, told me a story about how mums don't 'see' their children until a long time after their born. Apparently I introduced myself to her at Julians birthday party but why would I have introduced myself to my own mum? Unless

OH MY GOD

It WAS the first time she met me.

This is the most horrible thi

PART THREE

CHAPTER TEN

Stepping from the subway, the sheer height of Manhattan staggers me. Even the sky's bigger here, swollen, free, soaring down to meet four horizons at the crossroads.

Mariana's parents live in an apartment on the corner of Central Park West and Seventy-First but we've come up for air several blocks north of Times Square, having taken the AirTrain to the subway. The police weren't waiting for me at the airport, which was something of a surprise.

I'm initially struck with the unfamiliarity of the place. Walking through this end of Central Park, a place I've always been led to believe was something of a natural oasis in the middle of Manhattan, I'm shocked by the number of roads that intersect us, the volume of canary-coloured taxis powering through its arteries. But it's my first glimpse of Central Park West – all zigzagged fire escapes, smoking road grilles, cable-suspended traffic lights; the visual frilling on a thousand Hollywood rom-coms and gangster flicks – which convinces me that, though these steps on American soil are my first, I've lived here all my life. The dollars sleeping in my pocket have always been there.

I haven't told Mariana about my mother's latest revelation. I'm angry it's taken so long, that those who actually care about my father have to wait on the faxing of stats, for Death's paperwork. It's taken the coroner a preposterously long time to clarify that my father was poisoned. I could probably, given access to his body, have told them within minutes how he died.

'You're quiet,' Mariana informs me.

'Sorry.'

'It's pretty awe-inspiring, isn't it?'

We arrive at the apartment block and step into a spacious, mirrored elevator. Mariana depresses the button for the eighth floor and we emerge into a wide, white foyer. Six doors lead off from this open space and Mariana rings the bell of the fifth.

'Go easy on them,' she says.

A tall man in a light blue suit jerks open the door. He's older than I'd been expecting, but his eyebrows, set against the severe greying of his hair, are so black they seem absurdly false. He has a handsome, intelligent face and the smooth and sloping Venezuelan pedigree of the cheekbones is confirmed by the burst of urgent, unexpected Spanish with which he greets his daughter.

'Hi there,' he says to me, juicing my fingers of feeling with a handshake so unnecessarily painful I wonder whether I'm at all welcome. 'You must be… Um, sorry. What was it? Lucas. That's it. Well come through, both of you. Let me take your bags.'

Mariana's mother now hovers behind her husband. She's about his age but her auburn hair hasn't lost its hold yet, and the skin around green eyes seems weathered only minimally by life's anxieties. As Mariana claimed over dinner yesterday, the resemblance between mother and daughter is plain. Upon closer inspection, there's something not-quite North American about her too, in the full lips, the proud width of the face. Maybe Mariana's parents, as courting twentysomethings, didn't see money in Latin America. They certainly found it here.

'Sit down, sit down,' her mother requests. 'I'll make coffee.'

The apartment is large and opulently furnished. A wooden floor is covered in a number of thick rugs woven with complicated, arabesque designs. I refuse both Chesterfield sofas in favour of standing to inspect the bookcase. It contains the usual American heavyweights amongst the foreign-language texts. One large Rauschenberg print dominates the wall to the right of the long window.

No, wait, it's an original.

And outside, Central Park: their vast, perfectly quadrilateral garden, the towers of the East Side a picket fence forming a neat, trim border behind the fairylike joggers in its bowers. The view of lower Manhattan is awesome and the sky is a solid, flat blue.

I'm fascinated by the view until long after the family's congregated behind me on the sofas and are sipping coffee, bitching about aunts and cousins back in Caracas.

The conversation shifts to Syngestia. It's clear that Mariana, from her father's gushing praise, is expected to forge a career as a computer whiz kid, as he once did. I take my cue to sit down next to a beaming Mariana, who praises my handling of the lab cock-up, explaining that we're only here because the crisis is partially, potentially averted. Her father wants to hear all about it, even though he doesn't understand any of the lab-speak, and both parents suddenly act like they're casting for the role of son-in-law.

It transpires that three tickets have been booked for a show at The Lyceum this evening. Her father is adamant another ticket wouldn't be hard to obtain but, stressing I've no wish to disturb a family affair, I insist I'll be fine left to my own devices. In fact, I'd rather it that way. I've got the last part of my diary to finish.

Her father compromises by offering to lend me a map.

'Anywhere I shouldn't go?' I ask, mindful of what I perceive to be frightening crime statistics.

'Nah,' Mariana says. 'Perfectly safe. Everywhere.'

'But stay clear of anywhere north of One-Hundred-and-Ninth and avoid the Lower East Side,' her father gravely adds. 'And don't go into Chinatown or Midtown west of Broadway. The financial district will be full of gangs in a few hours, and don't even bother with Tribeca or SoHo. And stay off the subway after dark.'

Mariana turns towards me, crosses her eyes and purses her lips; the child challenging a surrogate sibling not to laugh at the absurd paranoia of a parent. Taken aback, it takes all my strength not to snigger.

'Does that leave anywhere?' I joke.

Mariana's father doesn't laugh. Instead he asks about my parents, keen to know the stock I come from. I tell him my mother has her own design company, which is a whopping lie. She *sometimes* makes greetings cards and sells them through eBay.

'And your father?' he asks.

A week ago, I would've replied that I didn't have one. 'He was a writer.'

'Was?'

Mariana steps in. 'Lucas's dad passed away recently.'

'Oh, I'm sorry,' he says.

I nod, shrug, try to pull the appropriate face.

'That must've been hard,' her mother muses. 'You're so young.'

Mariana's father looks at me with his mouth set to 'intrigue', his dark eyebrows at 'sympathetic'.

'The funeral's this weekend,' I tell them. 'At least it was meant to be. The police now think someone killed him.'

Her parents' faces freeze with their carefully cast expressions of deepest compassion. Mariana asks me if I'd like to see my room and then leads me out of the lounge to the sound of rattling coffee spoons and nervous coughing.

'Nice work, Lucas. It only took you five minutes to totally freak everyone the fuck out.'

Manhattan, according to my map, is a giant tooth, a girded and gridded fang. I walk down Seventh Avenue, through Times Square and its flashing, rippling neon, under the 3D M&M characters and Mr Peanut, and then head down

Broadway. I walk for hours, through the areas Mariana's father has told me not to, to the very tip of the fang, to Battery Park and the World Trade Center site, that part of the tooth now irretrievably chipped.

When I looked through the plane's window, diary in lap, a sleeping Mariana by my side, and saw our aircraft's shadow on the Atlantic, like a leviathan giving chase thirty-five-thousand feet below, it was plain to me: I was doing the right thing. Maybe, I thought, looking her over, nothing else matters.

But now... Swallowed by the size of New York, little more than a worm in the Big Apple, it occurs to me that I'm three-and-a-half-thousand miles from Becksmouth.

From home.

From the place of my father's murder.

On my way back up Broadway, I enter a bar called The Old Peculiar. It looks quiet.

The establishment is not unlike many British pubs, with several booths and tables clustered around a central bar. The place is air conditioned by two disconsolately spinning ceiling fans, performing, with slow munificence, the job of moving the smoke around so everyone can breathe it in. Sweat beads on the barman's forehead as he draws pints for chinless puffers, their ashtrays overflowing in the smoker's tricolour: lipstick red, filter orange, tar black. I was under the impression smoking was banned in New York; presumably this place is carrying on the fine tradition of the speakeasy.

Even ordering a single glass of Coke, I'm advised to set up a tab. A down-and-out eyes me with envy over the meniscus of his Super Cool.

I unfold a *New York Post* someone's left on a booth table. Amid the articles on prostitute-murdering Wall Street bankers and bellicose letters rubbishing the current administration's policies in Iraq, I find a piece on the closing down of a series of nightclubs, due to the sale of drugs. *What else?* West Twenty-Seventh, Twenty-Sixth, all just off Eighth Avenue. So Chelsea might be a part of town worth avoiding too, given I just felt my heart rate increase at the thought of it. I fold up the paper and sling it to one side when my drink's ferried over. Do I tip the barman? Do I stick the extra on the tab? Do I offer him fifty cents?

A voice from a neighbouring table interrupts my minor panic. 'Y' English?'

'Yes.'

'Thought so. Thought I heard the English accent. Thought I did.'

'You did.'

Pausing to scratch a bristled cheek, the hobo gestures to the empty chair opposite me. 'Mind if I...?'

I shrug to indicate that I'm not bothered and he scrapes himself over with his beer, gathering the bottom of his tatty greatcoat around his middle as if to stop it touching furniture. I hope this guy's got good stories. I hope he's lived well. A greased yellow-white blade of hair cuts across his craggy face, his teeth are mossy stumps and two patches of thick brown hair sprout below his eyes, old-man-growth too high on the cheeks to trouble the razor's well-practised trajectories.

'Don't like seein' young fellers like y'self drinkin' on their lonesomes,' he says. 'What y' thinkin' 'bout? Y' look glum, boy, like death warmed over.'

'Nothing. I'm fine.'

'Woman trouble, is it?'

He commences a bronchial coughing session. I wait for the performance to finish before saying, 'Not really, no.'

'Not a woman?' He flops back in his seat, cracks a crooked smile. 'Hot damn! Y' not from Greenwich Village, are y'?'

I wonder whether this is his way of accusing me of being homosexual. To get him off my back, I announce my father's recent demise. 'We never saw eye to eye, but I'm still, you know, shaken.'

'Ah, it's different when they're gone, ain't it?'

'Is it?' I honestly thought he'd have taken the hint by now.

'Hell yeah. Y' see 'em in a different light don'tcha? You're not s'posed to speak ill of the dead, but sometimes, if y' called a spade a spade durin' their life, why shouldn'tcha? But a dad's different, ain't he? He's flesh 'n' bone. The apple don't fall far from the tree 'n' all that. Suddenly, I bet, y' thinks to y'self, he can't have done nothin' *that* bad.'

This, it should be noted, is my *interpretation* of his wisdom, pieced together from the words I can actually discern through the stream of gruff incoherence. It would appear that shared DNA counts for something to non-scientists too, that 'flesh 'n' bone' elevates people to a height from which faults can be overlooked. To disprove his theory, I tell him about my father's affair, who it was with, where it occurred, everything.

'Shit, fire 'n' thunderation.' He shakes his head, casts his features into a mournful jowl, then drops an octave from his voice. 'The poor guy.'

'What "poor guy"?'

'He loved y' real mother, but couldn't be with her. Sad.' He shakes his head, coughs. 'What were the reasons for 'em not gettin' together? Y' real mom and dad?'

'They *were* together, for a while.' I sigh. 'They were both young – perhaps too young – and my real mother left us when I was too little to remember. Soon after, my father moved house and met... the woman who would become my brother's mother. The reasons for my real parents' split hardly mattered to an eleven-year-old. I couldn't understand why my actual mother came back for my father, but not for me. And I couldn't understand why my father, a man I once respected and trusted more than anyone, chose to ruin everything for the love of a woman who'd rejected me.'

The tramp takes out his cigarettes. 'Mind if I...?'

'Go ahead,' I say, shaking my head to decline his offer of one.

He strikes a match and lights the cigarette over-cautiously, as though outside in a fierce wind, and then furiously chews at the white cylinder until silver smoke plumes and twists from his mouth. He gulps the rest of his drink then fixes me a thirsty look. I feel duty-bound to order him another.

'Thanks, pal,' the hobo says as the barman adds it to my tab. 'Why was y' dad getting dirty with her in that antiques place? Sordid little detail, that is.'

'It was probably their idea of an exciting tryst. The house next to ours was unoccupied for a time and The Old Mint must've seemed like a safe place. My mother, my *real* mother, was in town only occasionally. My father could hardly invite her round the house, could he?'

'But...'

'Hey. That's the story. I don't know any more "sordid little details". And I never will now, will I?'

'And what about y' real mom? What happened to her?'

'She wanted nothing to do with me, so vice versa. She can rot for all I care.'

'Gee. Y're a right one, ain't y'? So y' know nothin' about her?'

I tell him about the time I caught her and my father arguing at the front door. Over the years, I've invented her afresh, based on that sighting. Her eyes – I remember, perhaps incorrectly – were as wild as her tousled, flower-child hair. Hardheartedness, pride, indulgence: the eyes of a woman who knew she was beautiful. Beyond that, I don't know who she was at all. A few ornaments remained in my father's possession, long after my mother took my brother and cleared out, that were certainly neither to his nor her taste. A statuette of a kissing couple. A blue tea towel soaked in star signs. Quartz crystal.

My impromptu drinking partner hacks out a phlegmy gurgle then announces, 'Mebbe she turned up at y' door to deliberately ruin things for y' father. Mebbe she was jealous of his marriage. Mebbe she was even jealous that he ended up with *you*.'

I stare into his haggard face. Perhaps he's wiser than I gave him credit for.

'Who knows?' My father certainly changed at that moment. He became colder. Much colder. 'You've no idea what it was like living with him after that.'

Smoke curls through his spindly fingers. 'Not many places let y' smoke in New York these days. This place has been fined somethin' like fifty times in the last year. Anyways, between you, me 'n' the fencepost, I still reckon y're bein' harsh on y' old man. If he's the worst thing that ever happened to y', you'll be lucky. He had a few affairs. So what? Don't let him rattle y' bones. Y' know what us men're like.'

I shudder at this ruined old man's assumption that the two of us are similar, beyond the Y chromosome and choice of dubious drinking establishment. I down the rest of my glass then tell him I have to meet someone.

'Watch y'self,' he mumbles. 'Stay off the cross streets and stick to the avenues, y'know what I'm sayin'?'

Like Mariana's father, he's lived through Manhattan's darker days. He sees outsiders like me at ease in his city, treading streets that used to be no-go zones. New York's pulled itself out of the mire but the memory lingers, keeps her citizens fearful.

I say my goodbyes and he discloses his name. 'Not Sam,' he says. 'Samuel.'

At the bar, I'm told there's a minimum with American Express, which I haven't reached, so I reluctantly pay for Samuel's next two beers. As they're poured, I watch the embracing amber bubbles sparkle and rush under the halogen bulbs.

The barkeeper slides them over. I'm still looking at them, mesmerised, when he asks, 'So what say I put a little rum in that Coke of yours? On the house.' He polishes a glass and racks it above his head.

It occurs to me that the glory days of last week, when the past remained in the past and I could simply resent my living, breathing father without guilt, are gone forever. This is what the future tastes like.

'What?' I ask.

'Another drink? For you. No charge.'

'Um… No thanks.'

Samuel gurns a toothless, confused jaw as I ferry his drinks over. 'I still don't get it. Y' hated y' dad but, unlike y' mom, he stuck around. Seems to me that…'

I don't want to get drawn into this again. I put Samuel at ease with an old story, one finally confirmed by yesterday's phone call.

'It wasn't that my real mother didn't want me. I think she did. She just wasn't able to raise me. She wasn't capable. There were rumours from within my family, you see, after the affair. Rumours that she was ill… mentally.'

'Yeah well,' he says, launching himself at his next beer. 'Ain't we all.'

CHAPTER ELEVEN

Mariana's father parks a can of Labatt Blue in my hand and slumps down opposite, cracks one open himself. I stare at the beer in horror. His wife and daughter are discussing the play in the kitchen and I fear I'm going to have to sit through some kind of 'man chat'.

'So where'd you end up then?' he asks.

'Just went wandering.'

He sips his beer.

'Like Johnny Cash, eh?'

'I guess. You don't happen to have a soft drink, do you? I don't actually drink alcohol.'

'No? Why's that?'

'Allergic.'

'Oh, you poor bastard. Grab yourself something from the icebox.'

He reaches for the television remote and begins chuckling at one of the late-night chat shows as I slouch to the kitchen, switch the beer for *yet another* soda.

'So where'd you go?' he asks upon my return. He doesn't unpeel his eyes from the screen.

'Um. I found the Flatiron. Went down to Lower Manhattan and saw a very misty Statue of Liberty. Had a Coke in a bar.'

'Which one?'

It turns out The Old Peculiar is quite a well-known dive. Mariana's father assures me I'm lucky 'nothing too shady' happened and that my drink was 'almost undoubtedly' spiked.

'My drink wasn't spiked.' *Chance would be a fine thing*, I hear a deep part of myself whisper.

He swigs again. 'I bet it was,' he says, serious.

We watch the TV for a while, laugh at the prescribed moments. On the shelf behind the television, Mariana's parents have the same framed photo of the peering, tired-eyed 'uncle' Mariana displays on her mantelpiece in Southgate. Next to it is a picture of Mariana's school-age self, hinting at the woman this child would go on to become. Most notably in the large, acerbic eyes and wide, toothy grin.

I announce my intention to take a shower and go to bed.

'Be my guest,' Mariana's father says.

On my way past a low shelving unit, I catch something with my hip and a sickening crash speeds Mariana and her mother from the kitchen, screaming their worry like opera singers. I apologise profusely and attempt to gather together the splinters of orange and blue pottery while Mariana's mother tries hard to assure me the vase wasn't 'too expensive'. Her father remains in his armchair, smug and chuckling, as though proved right about the inevitable, dizzying dangers of visiting local hobo hangouts.

I've removed my diary from my bag and settled down into the bed, when there's a knock on the door.

Mariana sticks her head round. 'Decent?'

I stretch and casually push back the sheet to expose my torso, though I haven't done so many press-ups lately. She might as well take a look. As she enters the room, she remarks how skinny I appear. I hide myself again and place the diary on the bedside.

Mariana perches on the edge of the bed and looks straight at me, something that might be mirth flinching behind her irises. She wears a darker version of the dress her mother wore, but the exposed skin is lighter, the neck smoother. She's left the door ajar.

'Your hair's wet,' she informs me. 'You'll get pneumonia.'

She takes the towel I've left on the chair by the door and starts drying my hair in short, tender tousles. She has to lean across me slightly to accomplish this and I detect her perfume, now mixed with her own scent. Sweet, strong and feminine: a nuclear core fermented in rose petals.

'I never liked that heirloom anyway,' she says.

'Was it expensive? I'll pay for it.'

She slings the towel back on the chair and pulls a small, travel hairdryer from the bottom bedside drawer. The faint smirk is still just beyond detection, hidden behind deadpan features. 'It was about twenty-thousand dollars, last estimate.'

I consider saying that the vase shouldn't have been put in such a foolish place in the first place but she turns the hairdryer on. Her soothing hands work their way through my hair gently as the warm air blows across my scalp and I feel myself stir beneath the sheets. All worries about the price of the 'heirloom' evaporate.

I never want her to stop doing this.

'There, all finished.' She turns the dryer off and retakes her position at the end of the bed. 'Anything else I can do for you, Mr Marr? Hot chocolate? Bedtime story?'

'I wouldn't say no to a goodnight kiss.' It doesn't come out right. It's hard to do jovial with this much desire between your legs.

She looks over her shoulder at the half-closed door, then leans forward and pecks me a platonic kiss, betraying the fact that her parents, in their home at least, still have considerable authority. Then, as if acknowledging my unspoken psychology, she places a hand to my freshly-shaved face and kisses me on the lips. 'If you need anything, my room's the other side of the lounge,' she whispers.

I understand the inference. The ball's in my court.

The light from midtown skyscrapers bleeds through the window, a faint blur, edgy, cinematic. The traffic on Central Park West purrs.

I've waited about as long as it's humanly possible. The lights have gone off in the rest of the apartment and I'm pretty sure everybody has gone to bed. Wearing boxers and T-shirt, I gently open the bedroom door and steal my way into the hallway like some diarrhoeic secret agent.

This is ridiculous.

Hoping my eyes will soon adjust to the darkness, I creep through the lounge until the sole of my right foot is pricked by something. Fighting the urge to shriek in pain, I reach down and, with difficulty, extract a tiny thorn of pottery. After what seems like an age, in which I've no idea how I don't break anything else, I eventually make it to the other side of the room and knock, very faintly, on Mariana's door.

I wait.

She opens the door, her face knowing and suggestive. 'What can I do for you?' she breathes, wearing nothing but a blue T-shirt which she tugs down for modesty at the front with both hands, tightening the fabric across her chest. It's all wonderfully calculated.

'I was wondering if I could have that story?'

She retreats back into her low-lit room. I can almost feel my memory sharpen; I know I'll have perfect recall of this moment in ten years. I see her in silhouette as her long legs stride her back to bed, the T-shirt forming a shelf at her hips, where it gathers above her backside. She swiftly hides herself back in bed.

Maybe invited, maybe not, I walk forward and crouch at the end of her bed. Her room is decorated with a *Breakfast at Tiffany's* poster, while her shelves contain computing tomes and a modest collection of bears. I wonder how many of the grinning friends tacked onto corkboard she still speaks to. In one corner about fifteen canvasses of varying sizes are leaning against one another, all turned towards the wall.

I nod towards them. 'Are those yours?'

'Yep.'

'Can I see them?'

'Are you kidding?'

'What's the harm?'

'The harm?' Her eyebrows clench. 'You'll dislike them but will feel obliged to tell me they're good. In which case, one of two things will happen. One, I'll be able to tell you're lying and we'll both feel awkward. Two, I'll believe you and a little bit of me will want to start painting all over again, even though I suck.'

She leans back in her bed. It no longer sounds like it's worth looking at the paintings to me.

In the mirror on the back of the door I notice what appears to be bruising around my mouth. It's lipstick, from when she kissed me goodnight.

'What's the matter?' she asks.

'I've got your polyethylene on my face.'

'Gee, I love it when scientists talk dirty.'

She crawls towards me across the bed, slowly. Our bodies are perhaps a foot apart when she asks, 'What's that?'

She's looking – not horrified, just interested – at the marking on my left arm.

The scars might heal eventually. Oddly, I stopped feeling much shame over them a while back. If anything, pride became the prevalent emotion. Pride that they're just that: scars, no longer fresh wounds. But now I find them taking on a new symbolism. They're a warning that temptation is still there, that the body doesn't heal itself overnight.

'Needle tracks.'

'Oh.'

'You were right. I mean, I didn't lie to you. I did quit drinking, but it wasn't the drinking that was a problem. I quit *everything*. I had to. I have an obsessive personality.'

She sits down in front of me, cross-legged. Again, the hands knead and pull at the hem of her T-shirt to cover herself.

I hold my arm up. 'I've been clean from this for a year. The drinking… There was a lapse recently. When I heard about my father's death my first reaction was to have a pint. I fear I made quite a fool of myself at the funeral parlour.'

'Good. It shows you're human. I was beginning to wonder.'

We look into each other's faces, not saying anything, our eyes wandering over the other's features. I've never sat so close to anyone for so long without saying a word; it's an uncannily erotic experience. After a while, she picks up my left forearm and looks closely at it.

'I've always felt *normal* after a few drinks,' she confesses. 'You know, like I was born two pints short or something.'

'I know exactly what you mean. I always needed a drink to start conversations, to feel at ease. But with... diamorphine...' A carefully chosen, safely medical term. '...it was about living for the moment. Feeling *more* than myself.'

'Living for the moment?'

'Posterity counts for little when you're high. That eternal moment is all that matters. I might not be explaining myself very well. I still crave it, as I do alcohol. But I know addiction itself is the bigger picture. The diamorphine habit came from the same place, the same part of me – that part of me that was missing – that alcohol dependence did.'

'Are we talking about the drug I think we're talking about? You mean heroin, yeah?'

The word's been uttered.

I nod.

'How did you stop?'

'With difficulty. And a lot of Suboxone from the lab.'

'Who knew about all this?'

'No one. Except Aaron.'

'He was the only one?'

'Others may have suspected. But I was good at hiding it. I had to be.'

She wriggles a little on the bed, then rotates her shoulders. 'I can't imagine you... You know.'

'Burgling old women for a fix? Shooting up behind the town hall with my trousers full of piss? It's perfectly possible to lead a healthy, normal life with a clean, regular supply. At least for a while.'

'So… What *is* it?'

'It's a member of a class of narcotic analgesics called opioids. It is a diacetyl ester of morphine and is processed from extracts of the *papaver somniferum* seedpod.'

'You what?'

'It's The Devil.'

'But it's… nice, yeah? I mean, it must be.'

My laugh is unavoidable. 'You have no idea.'

I get the impression she's been fishing for a description of its effects with her last few questions and I haven't been giving her the answer she's wanted.

'People have used it for centuries,' I explain. 'The poppy was cultivated in Mesopotamia about… I don't actually know. Three thousand years ago? But it was first processed in London at the end of the nineteenth century by a chemist working at St. Mary's Hospital, though the drug wasn't named heroin until a German pharmaceutical company, twenty-something years later, deemed it *heroisch*. People in field studies claimed, understandably, to feel "heroic". For over ten years, in one of the medical world's most infamous cock-ups, heroin was sold as a cough medicine for children.'

'You've done your research.'

'As have you, with your wines. It pays to know what you're getting into bed with.' This comment, intended innocently, suddenly feels utterly inappropriate. I doubt anything's going to happen now. This conversation has turned me off, so I dread to think what it's done to her.

'So what's it like?' Here we go.

'What do you mean?'

'When you inject. What does it feel like?'

'It wipes you clean. It's a reset button.' I've never tried to describe it before, and I'm not sure I can, accurately. 'Time

141

stops. The ache in your muscles and bones, your pain, your grief, goes. The mind gives up the fight. Your body too. You're whole.'

She's looking at me sideways as she pushes herself back towards the headboard.

'Go on,' she says, as though playing the part of the counsellor. But her body language has changed. She curls to one side, her body closed to me.

'For me, it was always as much to do with the preparation as it was the *penetration*. The anticipation as you set up the cotton wool, the cooking can, a shiny new needle, the clear bag of white powder. It's medicine, that's what it is. Liquefying it, dropping in the cotton and watching it puff up like a sponge, pushing the needle into the cotton, drawing it up through the syringe and, finally, laying the needle flat across the length of the major vein at the inner elbow and injecting in small, hesitant strokes to prolong the initial rush…'

I stop, almost breathless.

'Lucas? You okay?'

She's looking at me sideways. Her breathing has quickened too and I can see the sheet rise and fall across her stomach. There's a vulnerability to her, a renewed innocence – a concern – which shames me.

Hastily, I peel myself from the bed. 'I'm sorry. I didn't realise it was quite so late. I'm… I'm pretty tired.' I make my way to the door.

'Lucas…' I hear her call after me, but I'm already creeping, once again, across the black obstacle course of her parents' living room.

I don't sleep a wink.

CHAPTER TWELVE

'*New York*?'

'Relax,' I tell my mother. 'It's only for a couple of days. I'll be back in plenty of time for the funeral. Whenever it is.' I'm standing in Mariana's parents' lounge, scrutinising this millionaire's view, this verdant parallelogram carved into the serrated steel of the East Side. 'I'm ringing because I want to know if you've given my number – mobile or landline – to anyone lately.'

'Who?'

'To *anyone*. I've been getting... calls.'

'I don't know what you're talking about. *I've* been trying to call you. What are you up to, Lucas?'

'Look, I only came to New York because I didn't think I'd be of use to anyone back home. And, at the time, perhaps I doubted the validity of this whole "murder" thing. You know, I read not too long ago about a woman from Wimbledon who'd been declared missing for three weeks before her body was discovered behind her sofa. The local police assumed her home had already been searched by the CID, so practically drained the river looking for a corpse...'

'So what?' my mother interjects. 'Is that your argument for running to New York? That you don't believe the coroner?'

'The coroner's made his report already? That's quick. What happened?'

'We don't have the report yet.'

'Then how do you *know* he was murdered?'

'The police spoke to me. There was a trace of something in his blood, and not something, you know, normal. I explained to them that I don't know the man anymore. I mean, any clues about his life, his friends, his *enemies*, weren't going to come from me. The last time I spoke to him was probably three years ago.'

I sigh so hard it hurts. 'So was he *murdered*?'

'That's the angle the police are investigating. But all I know, and all you need to know, is that the funeral's going ahead Saturday, as planned.'

Her voice is less urgent than yesterday, her tone defensive. She was never able to lie as convincingly as my father. 'Why do I feel like you're not telling me the truth? If they've released the body, that suggests the inquest is over, or abandoned. What's going on?'

'Oh, I'm sorry. I'm not telling *you* the truth? You're the other side of the world, Lucas.' How are mothers able to say your name and make it sound like an insult? Is it because they chose it, a reminder of a gestalt authority from before your own birth? 'Listen to me for a minute. As far as I know there hasn't been an inquest. Okay, got that? No inquest. The post-mortem report hasn't been received from the pathologist yet. Apparently, it can take somewhere between three to eight weeks before the report's made available. Especially in situations where a toxi-something-or-other report is required.'

'Toxicology.'

'Yes, that's it.'

This tit-for-tat method of communication is nothing new, though I can't blame her entirely in this instance. I'm sure the police aren't informing her about every development. After all, as she's just pointed out, she divorced my father a long time back; she's just reading between the lines.

'What about this Sophia character?' I ask.

'Still no news,' she tells me, in the cold sulk to which I've become accustomed.

'And what does Ryan make of all this?'

'He doesn't know. Ryan still believes, as we all did, that his father died of a heart attack. And that's how it's going to stay. It's been very hard for Ryan, you know, but he's been a tremendous help with the arrangements. He's going to say something at the service. We've managed to get in touch with some of your father's friends, old colleagues from the bank, and I think there'll be a half-decent number. Barely any family though, obviously. You *are* going to turn up, aren't you? I know he had his faults but...'

'I'll be there.' I'm worn out now and can't hide it in my voice. 'I've got to go, Mum.'

'Before you do, there's *one* thing I need from you...'

I read her my credit card number. I want to argue this, I really do, but I can see her predicament. Why should she pay? Why should Clint? Ryan certainly can't. At least the sale of my father's flat will reimburse me these funeral costs.

I ask something that's been on my mind for a while. 'Mum? Why do you think he left me his flat?'

'You're his son.'

'Yes, but why not split it with Ryan? It seems kind of unfair. From what I can tell, Dad was hardly prepared for his death; he stipulated a song for the service and that's it. Yet he had the forethought, for some reason, to leave the flat to me. Why?'

'It wasn't *left* to you; it was always yours. We found that he used your identity when buying it in the first place. He was just about able to scrape the deposit together, but your details made the purchase look less of a risk. I guess he faked your signature on a consent form at some stage, sent off copies of your birth certificate. You know what he was like. He probably knew you were still using your trust fund account and was able to show them the money was there.'

145

And here I was thinking maybe he felt he owed me something.

'Put it on the market immediately,' I tell her.

Gazing up at the ceiling of the New York Public Library's reading room, the gold-leafed roses enclosing a dawn-singed Renaissance sky, I wonder who commissioned this artwork, and why. Did the architect insist Heaven was painted on the underside of the roof to emphasise the infinity, the liberty, of knowledge, or was it purely to distract visitors such as myself from their studies?

My diary has taught me much so far – that Daniel's sister was capable of giving me a hard-on, that my father was useless in the kitchen, that I couldn't tell the difference between they're, there and their – but it's handed me no clues, so far, about who might've poisoned him. After all, how could it? I've been sitting here for an hour and haven't looked further than its off-centre Letraset title. Instilled within me – from where, I don't know – is a sense that the diary will decipher a host of mysteries, including my father's murder. I'm aware this theory is hardly scientific but, after all, my early hunch that he died under suspicious circumstances was proved correct. I believe clues *are* inside this diary, if I dare myself to look deep enough.

There's one thing the diary can't do, though.

A voice from my past. *Hi, Lucas...? I've got some...* Reading the diary won't complete the phrase.

I've got some*thing important to say*

I've got some *bad news for you*

I've got some *time out for the funeral*

Whatever she was going to add, I got the message. My father's dead and my real mother's alive.

A lot's changed in a week.

I slide the diary in my shoulder bag and skulk back through the library, postponing the task still further. Reading it has been more painful than I realised it would be.

146

The sun is a blowtorch on my face and arms as I saunter down the main steps between the library's two guardian lions. Four guys breakdance for money on the street, a large crowd around them. I veer left, back towards the apartment.

Mariana's meeting an old school friend of hers in Brooklyn. She did say I could accompany her but the date was knowingly undersold with the line, 'She's just had a baby, so it'll be really boring, but you can come if you like.' I told her I'd meet her a little later, in the afternoon, and there flashed a tangible suggestion of disappointment in her face, as if I'd failed some secret test.

Last night wasn't mentioned, almost as though we'd slept together and were both slightly embarrassed about it. To all intents and purposes, because I opened myself up to her, we did.

'Did you enjoy it?' a voice asks.

'Sorry?' I turn on the last step to see a slim redhead. Long-sleeved grey top, white mini, long brown boots. She's pretty, though her eyes appear ringed with severe tiredness.

'I saw you in there. Good book?'

'Um… It's okay.'

'My name's Leah.' She flashes a white smear of teeth, looks me up and down. Her voice is nasal, as though she's suffering with the aftermath of influenza.

'Lucas. Nice to meet you.' I consider moving on, but she still watches me, as though expecting more. She's not flirting – her crossed-armed posture is positively distant – but this anticipation in her eyes makes it hard to leave. She wants something. 'Hot today, isn't it?' I say.

'English?'

'Since I left my bowler hat at home, I assume your guess was based solely on my appraisal of the weather?'

Her eyes lose their fatigue for the duration of an honest, croaky laugh. 'Where you heading?'

I wave downtown, uptown, shrug. 'Nowhere really.'

'I know a nice place that sells coffee?'

Stepping closer to me, she appears whiter, gaunter, her skin waxier. Her clothes have seen better days. Her eyes show trauma. She's an addict.

Perhaps this is why I accompany her to her suggested 'nice place'.

Disappointingly, it turns out to be Starbucks, just round the corner. We sit by the window and I watch life speed past over her shoulder: the floating skirts swinging shopping bags, the briefcases hailing cabs. Leah tells me she's studying law at one of the universities but won't divulge her age, and when I announce I'm in pharmacology she nods without emotion, as though this was obvious, starts fingering the salt shaker. When she lifts her head from the contents of her coffee cup there's a faint smile struggling to break free, one which I attempt to reciprocate.

'What brings you to New York?' she asks.

'I'm on the run.'

Leah chuckles, but her previous humour has drained away. She no longer makes much of an effort to entertain me, to pretend to be entertained, and can't even summon the energy to scoop more than a postage stamp-sized morsel of chocolate brownie into her mouth. I'm eventually asked how much it rains in London.

'Not as much as your movies reckon.' I'm now irretrievably bored. I turned down a morning in Mariana's company for this.

Leah reaches for her handbag and gropes around inside. 'Oh. My. Gaaad. My purse's been stolen,' she says, the words a pantomime synonym for 'I can't believe I'm trying this on *again*.'

I look around, embarrassed, but no one's looking our way or remotely cares about her desperate performance. She rifles through her bag a bit more, churning up lipsticks, sore throat palliatives and balls of tissue, until I make the inevitable offer to pay. 'You sure? Gee, thanks.' Po-faced, she replaces her handbag on the seat next to her, happy enough that her routine's procured a chain-store coffee and three crumbs of cake. This is not the most professional of tricksters.

I sling ten dollars to the table and tell her I have to fly.

'Wait!' She thrusts out an arm and grabs my wrist. Our fellow customers still ignore us.

Leah gazes through me, her pupils the graphite points of sharpened pencils, the mouth mumbling silent entreaties.

Does she see, somehow, through those hopeless, suffering eyes, a fellow addict? Or is she just reaching out to the first person not rushing around Manhattan like they've got a motor jammed up them? Last night, Mariana observed I was thin but I certainly don't look ill, not like this. But maybe it takes one to know one. It's bad of me, I know, but a pride wells up in me, a pride that I lived through the days of constant cold-like symptoms, memory fatigue, listlessness, and didn't become what I now see in front of me.

Sitting back down, I prise her trembling fingers from my arm.

I can help this girl.

'Listen,' I say. 'I've been there. I can…'

'Fuck you, shit-for-brains,' she yells, then snatches my ten dollars and bolts from the café.

It's not long before I catch sight of her again, coughing and hacking the short distance to Grand Central, weaving a mercury route amongst pedestrians. I assume she's late for a train until she slips into a phone booth and begins shouting down the line.

I find myself watching her from the shade, curious. I don't know whether it's being in this city, but I almost feel like I'm in a film. Following her all the way from the coffee shop was odd behaviour, I accept that. I certainly don't want my ten dollars back.

But what is it I *do* want?

She jabs the phone down then paces back and forth, every exhalation is desperate, every knuckle bitten. It's not long

149

before some lowlife sneaks up and hands her a white bag before ambling off with an urban limp. And then Leah's strolling away in the opposite direction, back towards me, checking her bounty with fraught expression. She darts north up Park Avenue then jaywalks the road and crouches in the tree-lined island between traffic lanes. She wastes no time in publicly strapping her arm and searching for a vein.

Unbeknown to her, about twenty feet from where Leah squats, are two blue-vested cops in octagonal caps. To my dismay, they're ambling in her direction.

I jog to the other side of the road and snatch the white bag from the dry ground in front of Leah, who immediately yells and gives chase through the jolting traffic on the other side. The cops don't appear to have noticed over the horn blasts, even though Leah's shouting blue murder.

After allowing her to chase me for a block, I hail a taxi and wait for her inside it. She trots up, breathless and snarls through the door. I cradle her bag on my lap.

'Are you getting in or what?' I ask.

'How long have you lived here?'

The décor is clearly that of an aging couple – not to mention the photos of an adult daughter, the *hiking boots* – but Leah doesn't appear to notice. She just sees a big apartment with a big view. She just wants the skag.

'Not long.'

She sits on the floor, refusing the Chesterfields, and delves into her bag. Her body language becomes noticeably sharper upon seeing the aluminium foil wrap, the sharp bevel of a hypodermic, and she gazes at it all with Christmas-morning amazement. I'll let her have her fix then kick her the hell out of here. The responsibility I felt for her has long gone and Mariana's parents will be back from work in a few hours.

She carefully, devoutly, removes the heroin from its wrap and I find myself leaning forward to get a better look. I never tried this black tar stuff, so I've no idea whether its gumminess, its far-from-faint smell of vinegar, is normal. It looks to be cut with large quantities of either coffee or treacle.

She rummages in her pockets, then fires the wick of a tealight and bends a spoon, twice; once at its narrowest point and once halfway down the handle, so it forms three sides of a square. She positions it on the floor, the concave bowl of the spoon facing the ceiling, and slides the candle into the mouth of the spoon's three planes, forming a makeshift burner. She could be in any bedsit, squat or alleyway in the world.

I watch, fascinated. My eyes won't tear themselves away. An ache returns.

The heroin takes ages to liquefy in the heated steel, but once it's done she places some cotton on it to soak up any germs or other particles. She's not labouring under the misapprehension that this stuff's pure. She draws up the heroin with the syringe then holds it upright, depressing the plunger until a tiny bead appears at the needle's tip. She flicks the hypodermic twice then applies it to her vein.

It slams her backwards, but she doesn't appear to lose consciousness. Sickness and pleasure meet in her eyes.

Time passes.

I ask her how she's doing and am greeted by a vacant, gurning rictus.

And then she asks the question I've been waiting for.

'You want some?' She nods towards the needle on the floor.

'No.'

'No?'

'No.'

'So why am I here?' she has the sense to ask.

Power. Release. Self-righteousness. Maybe all those things.

'I was saving you from the police. You should quit this stuff. You're better than this, you know that?' But I sense that my tone is no longer as convincing as I'd like it to sound. There's plenty of heroin left.

151

'Let me guess,' she slurs. 'You're clean? And you're on a mission from God to clean me up too? It'll happen, what-ever-your-name-is, but on my terms. I don't need no Born Again preaching to me 'bout how great life is on the other side. I'm in *control*, man. I've got my studies. I've got my shit together. I'll quit, one day. Don't worry 'bout little old me.'

The cruel, beautiful irony of diamorphine is that the only time you don't think about it, don't crave it, is when you're on it, when you're reminded how warm and relaxing and *bloody wonderful* it is. It's easy to think you're seeing clearly, easy to make these bold promises. She genuinely believes she'll quit.

I attempt a paternal smile, which is obviously read very differently to how it was intended because, in one fearsome bound, she smashes forward and kisses me with a grinding, arrhythmic tongue. I push her off, hold her at arm's length. This doesn't disconcert her; she takes my hand and plants it on a small, aroused breast.

'This isn't why you're here,' I protest.

But why *is* she here? We could have gone anywhere. I feel cheap and ugly, a crude ghost of Mariana's hospitality. Did I feel so flattered, in my unworthiness, to be shown that welcome that I went and passed it on, to an old self?

And yet I could easily lose myself in the curious sensation of Leah's doped gratefulness. She's peeling off her clothing, crawling towards me, her eyes full of numb desire. I close my own and try to think of Mariana, but can't bring her face to mind. Instead, I see a carousel of female faces upon Leah's: Anna-or-Tanya from the funeral directors; Laura from the casino; the Queen of Hearts, a rather severe-looking line drawing with thin lips and masculine eyebrows.

The light from the window is intense, the taxis swearing foghorns out at sea, as Leah attempts to tug my trousers off. Then, once I've successfully prevented this, pulls at my T-shirt instead. I push her away. She gets the hint. Right now, she's the last person in the world I'd want to infect with my DNA.

Mariana's uncle Jorge looks reproachfully at me from the mantelpiece.

Leah grabs her chunk of black tar and makes for the door. Then she stops and, in what seems a moment of clarity, turns and says, 'Thank you,' though I'm not sure what for. She takes a pen from a desk and scrawls her number on a notepad and hands it to me.

And then she leaves, stopping short of calling me a shit-for-brains again.

I close the door, slam my head against it, then tear the paper in half as many times as possible before taking the pieces to the window and casting them outside. The white squares twist and spiral like ticker tape towards the ground. The external door to the block opens and Leah exits through the falling scraps and crosses the road towards Central Park, wherein she shuffles down to Strawberry Fields and disappears under the rustling canopy of hackberry and tupelo.

I jump into the bathroom and splash her scent from my body, her perspiration from my lips, but I feel no cleaner upon draining the sink. I strike myself hard across the face, once, twice, then return to the living room and hastily collect together the apparatus she left in the white bag and conceal it all inside my travel kit; I don't need Mariana's mother finding it in the kitchen pedal bin. I straighten the rug on the floor.

The house phone rings. After some hesitation, I answer it.

'Hi.' It's Mariana. Her voice is both calm and calming. 'What you doing inside on a nice day like this? Never mind. I'm on my way back now and just got a call from my friends Mark and Charli. They're at a bar on Twenty Third. Fancy it?'

I tell her I've seen the inside of enough bars to last me a lifetime.

'Oh, okay.' Before the pause becomes too uncomfortable, she adds, 'What do you want to do instead then, Mr Marr?'

I gaze at the yawning metropolis through the window, suddenly hungry. 'What are visitors to The City That Never Sleeps *supposed* to do? Shouldn't I be trying a pastrami sandwich? A white truffle burger? Maybe a fried Twinkie?'

'Get real, Lucas.' She adopts a saucy tone of voice. 'If you like, I can take you to Heaven and back.'

'Does that mean what I hope it means?'

'Sure does. Meet me at the Empire State Building.'

CHAPTER THIRTEEN

After queuing for over an hour we finally emerge, dizzy from the elevator's swift ascent, to a windy observation deck atop the Empire State. I'm anxious all of a sudden, restless. Tourists of every conceivable nationality jostle me as they rush to peer through the criss-crossed grille at a city composed entirely of straight lines, an undulant heat surfing across its metal body. Times Square flashes and jigs somewhere inside our enormous, Midtown-straddling shadow.

'This is so cheesy,' I complain.

'What's so cheesy about this? We're both tourists.'

That's not strictly true, considering it's only a work visa that binds Mariana to Britain, but I sense nervousness as she looks towards the fierce point of the Chrysler. She steadfastly refuses to look down.

'Odd choice of date for someone with vertigo.'

'I don't have vertigo.'

She let the 'date' mention go though.

It occurs to me that she's not nervous of the height; September the eleventh is still fresh in her – in everyone's – mind. Understandably, she scans the skyline for sharking planes.

I'm fidgety and uneasy myself as we pace the platform, Mariana always several footsteps from the edge, gingerly pointing out landmarks, New Jersey, her favourite deli. Nothing happened between Leah and me, yet there's guilt there. The notion that I *cheated* on Mariana would, surely, only be a valid one if we were now in some kind of relationship, but nothing of the sort has been intimated beyond the odd kiss, a fleeting touch of fingers.

She asks me, shyly, to take a photo of her. On the digital camera's screen, she looks beautiful, big teeth, big eyes; I've always found her attractive, but never *beautiful* before. It's as though she suddenly conforms to my type. And yet the image of her against Manhattan's undulating steel hills is coy, coquettish, posing. All the things she's not.

'The last time I was here,' she says, 'was on an elementary school trip. While we were up here our teacher passed on the news that Reagan had just been shot.'

'How old...?'

'Elementary school is kind of like your junior school,' she explains.

We spend another few minutes wandering before settling on the view of the financial district. The foamy wakes of ships in the Hudson and East Rivers speed in comparison with the slow-moving traffic of Broadway. I'm gazing towards the puny-looking islands, Liberty and Ellis, when the mathematics creeps up on me.

'When was Reagan shot? It was just after his first election win, wasn't it? That can't be right. If you were eleven then...'

'No, no. I'd only just started school.'

'Even so. Say you were seven in – what was it? – 1981, 1982, that makes you...'

'A little older than you. Is that... a problem?'

Maybe surprise floods my face, just briefly, and maybe disappointment bleaches hers in return. It's hard to tell up here amongst the winds. She was unnecessarily defensive there. A good sign. I kiss her to prove nothing's changed, and in doing so everything probably changes.

Someone coughs, over-loud, then brushes past us on the crowded gantry. We part. I get a mouthful of her hair.

'My toyboy,' she coos.

I find the confidence to press another aspect of her life.

'Remember our dinner in Mayfair, and when I asked you what you did before you came to work for Syngestia? You got sort of coy…'

'Did I?'

'You did.'

She sighs, embarrassed. 'You're so successful… It makes my career path look sort of pathetic.'

'It's fine. If you don't want to tell me what you used to do, you don't have to.'

She stares out at the city. 'Okay, but please remember I was kind of rebelling against my parents' expectations…'

I hope my smile is appropriate, that she's about to tell me she did something legal but mildly contemptible.

'After college, I worked for the New York sewer department. Every Sunday, I would go underground to where the sewer lines converged, and hose down the grinders. After that, I became a quality controller of cat food. Then there was a stint in a pie shop. I can't remember if my time as a fence painter was before or after… Anyway, I spent five years doing that sort of baloney, convinced I was going to be an artist. My jobs just subsidised what I did in my spare time. I didn't care that there was no future in them. In fact, that was the point. Anyway, I grew out of the ambition eventually.'

She *grew out of it*? This reaction to her failure to achieve a goal strikes me as more than sad, that those times taste like wasted years. Instantly, I gain an appreciation of her *laissez-passer* mannerisms, that sarcastic and slightly bitter sense of humour. She didn't 'grow out' of her ambition. The ambition proved unsustainable.

'The worst job I ever had,' she continues, 'was as a monkey handler at a safari zoo. You know the kind of place. You drive around from one reserve to another and, when you arrive at the monkey enclosure, the capuchins enjoy a free ride. At the exit of this particular reserve a zoo worker was equipped with a stick, to prevent monkeys from leaving on a car. That zoo worker was me. Eight hours a day chasing monkeys and trying not to get run over. In the blazing sun.'

As much as I feel I'm supposed to laugh about this, I'm now utterly depressed. I really wish I'd looked at her paintings last night, told her they were beautiful.

I swing a telescope round and pop a dollar inside, unsure what to angle it on. It doesn't matter, to be honest. It's the whole view or nothing, and cross-hairing in on a heat-hazed block three-quarters of a mile away is admittedly pointless. I sweep the telescope down the perpendicular lengths of the city, scan the neglected railway track, smoking road grilles, fuzzy apartment windows. A man glares back at me, his naked and unworked-out back visible under candlelight. He sports seventies sideburns and a look of enmity. I snatch my face away from Arcturus.

'What's the matter?'

Looking again, the man's gone. I see a rusty water tank, a vested old Jew sitting on a rooftop deckchair. I hand the viewer over to Mariana but she's not impressed by the scrawling sights and I didn't think she would be.

'Everything's so *nothing* from up here,' she says.

The money ticks out and the coin's ingested. As soon as we're done, another couple take over viewing duties.

Marina walks me on.

'So what now?' she asks. 'There are a few really cool rooftop bars near here. Bad wine, generally. Seven out of tens, if you're lucky.'

'Never ask for the house wine. Most offer a generic tannin taste which, quite often, is not the fault of the wine but of oxidation, a result of heat overexposure.'

'Is that so? Look, I know you're teetotal but... I just don't know where else to go. I really don't. That's why I suggested here. Cinema maybe? Think there's that new Tom Cruise one on.'

I may be imagining it, but a physical distance seems to have again squeezed its way between us. Knowing more about each other, we're perhaps somehow less familiar; we've redefined ourselves. The cinema would be proper, old-school romancing, I guess – a stealthy arm around the shoulder on Regal Theater backrests in the popcorny dark – but I genuinely don't know that I can sit, twitching and jittery, throughout the entirety of *War of the Worlds* without her picking up on my latest unwelcome bout of cold turkey. 'I'm not the biggest fan of Tom Cruise,' I flounder.

'What's wrong with him?'

Uh oh. I detect a fan. 'Nothing. He's a brilliant, brilliant actor. I, er... I just don't know that he's made the right film choices lately.'

She's winding me up. 'God, you're so serious.'

'I am not.'

'You are so. All this "your lipstick's polyethylene" and "a crap wine is over-oxidised" stuff. Man, you scientists. Lighten up.'

I look at the others around us, posing for photos. Making a single moment last an eternity. It strikes me how Manhattan's skyscrapers resemble vast fields of hypodermic syringes.

'I'm sorry,' she says. 'I forgot. Fuck. I'm such an idiot. Jesus. Sometimes I just shouldn't say anything. You know, my nickname at school was Mouth. Sometimes, I think, I just get kind of nervous around people. You know, certain people. I tend to talk too much.'

'What are you going on about?'

'I shouldn't criticise you for being so serious. I mean... You're mourning.'

'I am?'

'Of course you are. And *obviously* you don't want to see a film about death and destruction right now. Man, am I a doofus.'

'Mariana, I don't think your nickname had anything to do with your talkative personality.'

'No?'

'No. I mean you kind of have a rather... *big* mouth.'

'It's not that big.'

I say nothing.

'Oh my god. Is that why they…?'

'It's no bad thing. You have a lovely mouth.'

She's pinching her lips together with finger and thumb, as though trying to measure it. I can't stop laughing. She hits me on the arm.

'Stop it, Lucas!'

She's actually covering it now, even as she curses me.

'There are worse nicknames.' My chest hurts.

'I can't believe this…' She's gurning into every passing reflection. A welcome cloud blots out the sun and vanishes the shadows from her face.

I head to the elevator. 'Come along, Mouth.'

Afterwards, in the taxi, during a slow, forgiving kiss, the city hurries past like a thousand fireflies, a congregation of tail lights.

I wonder if other men fear sex. As a user, I certainly had a few non-events, and those poor performances were hard to bounce back from. Drugs do absolutely nothing for your libido.

Back at the apartment, I'm led through like a secret. Her mother and father smile at their daughter's happiness but scowl at me; Mariana's an adult, but it must be horrible, knowing that a man's got their dirty eye on her. She unlocks her fingers from mine, heads to the bathroom to freshen up, shooting me a 'give me five minutes' look. I flee to my room to avoid her parents.

As I rummage through my wash bag for a condom, Leah's white paper bag of drug paraphernalia flumps out onto the carpet. Without really thinking, I peer inside. There's a small foil wrapper in there, empty.

The acetylation reaction used to convert morphine to heroin creates acetic acid as a by-product, hence the drug's often vinegary odour. The smell's divine. I remember the days when, out of a desire to put off the kicks and the sweats and the shivering, out of a desire to postpone an existence

160

where I'm taking heroin to disguise the side effects of heroin, I was utterly addicted to this scent. Tentatively, and without really knowing what I'm doing, I place a lighter under the foil and breathe in the vapour.

A tiny hit. A momentary chill of astral pleasure.

I stuff it all back again when I hear her leave the bathroom, then begin the embarrassingly public walk across the apartment to her bedroom.

The exuberance created by my minor relapse lasts all of the ten or so seconds it takes to reach her door. It wasn't enough. *I want more*.

It's ajar, I suppose to spare me the embarrassment of knocking, so I slip, unchallenged, inside. She's already in bed, which means I have to disrobe with her watching. I take off my shoes and socks and place them together at the foot of her bed, then my trousers. She laughs.

'What's the matter? What's funny?' I ask, unable to conceal the paranoia.

'Are you going to say anything?'

'I was concentrating.'

This sets her off even more.

I elect to keep my boxers on and sneak into the warm bed beside her. I can't help but notice she's already naked, so go through the rigmarole of removing my undergarments.

'Ready?' she teases.

'Not quite. Probably we should instigate some kind of... you know. Foreplay?'

'Is this not it?'

I'm mildly horrified. Is every step of the way going to be gently mocked like this? I'm abnormally nervous as it is, and don't think I'd be able to cope if I'm halfway through making love to her when she asks whether or not I've started yet. These sarcastic comments have all been in response to my dumb ones, so the best thing to do, I reckon, is just to start kissing her, to shut us both up.

'That's more like it', she says, reaching down between my legs. 'My my, what have we here?'

'That'll, er... be my penis.'

A lustful complexion overcomes her. 'How do you want me?' she asks, all big eyes and flushing skin.

'How do I...?'

'I'm yours. How do you want me?'

During the time it takes me to formulate a half-sensible reply to this magnificent question, she disappears under the sheets.

'While you're making up your mind, how about I show you why I'm *really* called Mouth,' she murmurs.

So I needn't have worried. It turns out that sex with Mariana is much like Mariana herself: funny, erotic, beautiful, ineffable.

While she sleeps, illuminated by the City's eternal lights, I risk a peek at her paintings.

While it's true I'm no expert in the visual arts, I know enough to understand that I don't need to be. 'Good' art is something you like, not something you have to understand. So, cutting through what these pictures might *mean*, I can state with confidence that Mariana's painstakingly-rendered photorealistic cityscapes – primarily of New York – and portraits – mainly of family members – are superb.

One picture that really stands out is already familiar to me. Jorge, Mariana's uncle, has been lovingly, expertly rendered from the photo I've seen a couple of times now. It could almost be a high-resolution digital image; the brushwork is tight, precise, the portrait astonishingly lifelike, even down to the pores of his skin, the specular reflections on his corneas. It appears to have been created with acrylics and a faint pencil grid is still visible through the paint in one corner.

Mariana stirs on the bed; her head raises itself. Faintly puffy eyes focus upon me and she smiles, pleased to have caught me out.

'Thought I told you not to look at those.'

'They're amazing, really.' I hold up the painting I've been looking over. 'Who's this?'

She yawns. 'I told you, that's Uncle Jorge. He died. Four years ago.'

'How come?'

'Pulmonary embolism. Very sudden.'

I examine the work closely. It's not possible to see the septum but the nasal cartilage has certainly melted away on one side, as a result of narrowed blood vessels, causing a small cavity. 'Cocaine, was it?'

'Yes,' she replies, half impressed, half horrified that I can tell. 'I painted it shortly after he passed away. It was the last one I ever completed.'

'I don't understand why you didn't stick with it. How do you know your stuff wouldn't be in MoMA by now if you'd kept going?'

'I don't.' She sits up, rubs her eyes with the heels of her palms. 'But this way it's my choice that they're *not* there. It was liberating, you know, just *giving up* the ambitions. A relief. It felt good.'

'You mean it felt better than the rejection did?' I don't mean this to sound harsh, but I fear it does.

She slumps back down and stares at the ceiling, chews her gums. I doubt she's going to go back to sleep now. Then she looks at me and smiles, badly.

'Yes. Let me put it like this: I quit painting because, even though I enjoyed it, it ultimately made me feel bad. Sound familiar?'

'Not really.' I think I know where this is heading. Has she brought this up to punish me for questioning her motives for putting aside an ambition?

'You quit drugs and drink for the same reasons, didn't you?'

'No. I wasn't "talented" at heroin. I didn't win prizes for it. The way I shoved a needle into my vein didn't elevate it to an art form. I stopped because I have addictive tendencies. Like my father, in many ways.' I don't know why I add this afterthought.

'What do you mean?'

'He couldn't let go. He just couldn't.'

'So you quit to avoid becoming like him?'

'I didn't say that.'

'Well, whatever the reason, you found the strength to move on. That's...' Her voice seems to falter. 'That's what I love about you.'

A detonating silence.

'Pardon?'

'Figure of speech, Lucas. Figure of speech.' She turns to face away from me, and I start talking about something else, anything.

CHAPTER FOURTEEN

It's another hot afternoon, the horizon shimmering with a mirage of such heat that The Bronx seems to samba. Mariana lies back in her new sunglasses, says, 'What a fantastic day.' She's lost that hard, almost sarcastic voice I've known since she first wandered into my life six months ago to fix the laboratory printer I kicked in a moment of impatience.

Mariana obviously has an affinity for this green rectangle the New Yorkers refer to as their backyard, and she points out her parents' apartment from Sheep Meadow as we slump amongst an untidy scattering of other couples. She tells me about the summer days of her childhood, but I fail to imagine growing up in a city such as this one, probably because we've barely seen any children over the last forty-eight hours. All I can do is compare these glimpses into her past to my own tree-climbing, bike-riding, star-gazing and ghost-hunting antics. Maybe she presumes my provincial childhood to have been boring in comparison to her own but, looking back, deconstructing our experiences in that tragic, adult way, staring down the wrong end of the telescope, all of us perceive a life more important than anyone else's; see a childhood rosy with undoubted promise. Like the reddish light that filters through the Earth's atmosphere during a lunar eclipse, making the moon appear briefly like Mars, the past only becomes vividly beautiful and transcendent because of the comparative darkness, the shadow, you're standing in.

She senses my mind has wandered. 'Are you worried about Saturday?' she asks, buried in my neck.

'Saturday?'

'The funeral.'

'Not really. What day is it today?'

She tells me it's Thursday. 'The flight lands early Saturday morning, so if you want me to come with you, if that would help... It's up to you.'

'Come to the funeral?'

'If you want.'

The sound of teenagers chasing each other with water-pistols carries from the shores of The Ramble. Involuntarily, I scratch at the insides of my left forearm.

'Lucas... I don't mean to pry but... Why do – *did* – you hate your father so much?'

'I told you.'

'You didn't. You told me you were reading your old diary and that you'd got to the part where you found out he was having an affair but... like... where would the two of you stand if he was alive today? Would there be any chance of re-acquaintance?' My silence forces a disclaimer of sorts. 'I mean, I'm sure a rivalry, naturally, exists between a father and son. Animals locked together in cages will always fight. It's just... I'm close to my family. I find it hard to...'

'There'd be no chance of re-acquaintance,' I tell her. 'Well... I don't know. If I'd known he was going to die, things might've been different. Then again, he wasn't *supposed* to.'

'How do you mean?'

'The police think he was murdered. Poisoned. My mother's being annoyingly vague about it all, actually.'

She freezes. 'Lucas... Shit. When you said that to my parents, I thought... I thought you were *joking*.'

'I hadn't spoken to him for years,' I continue. 'And I had no desire to, whatsoever, not after a nightmare five years living alone with that lying, gutless, selfish excuse for a man.

Everyone goes through an Oedipal period at some point in their lives but mine lasted a lot longer. I have *two* mothers after all.'

'You have… two mothers?'

'Well, not really. One's dead to me, obviously. Or I thought so. Believe it or not, I received a call from my real one just before I came out here with you. Scared the shit out of me.'

My tongue's running away from me; it's not the most romantic of days anymore. My biological parents, even now, are capable of souring the mood.

'So… your real mom… she's…?'

'In a mental hospital.'

I can't distinguish Mariana's eyes behind her tinted lenses but, her mouth ajar, she affects a nodded, unconvinced understanding. 'Lucas… Are you for real? Your father was *killed*…?' She's trying to deal with one discovery at a time, skips back to the first. I know what she's really asking. She's asking *Do I know this man at all?* Mariana was keeping a few things back herself – her age, her paintings – but nothing on this scale.

I can see the relief break out in her face when her phone rings.

'Shall I answer it?' She shows me her mobile. Aaron's name flashes on the tiny screen.

I shrug and bury myself into her lap. 'If you want.'

Aaron wants to know where she is, and if she's alright. He's a bit worried, what with 'today's events'.

'What's that madman on about?' I ask. 'What "events"?'

She holds her hand up to silence me. 'Of course I'm alright,' she says to him. 'Why wouldn't I be?'

Her phone's volume is loud and I hear every word Aaron says. Three bombs exploded on the London Underground and another went off on a bus at Tavistock Place. It's reckoned over fifty people are dead and maybe up to a thousand injured. 'Where you been all day?' he asks. 'Outer space? You must've seen the news on the telly. The city's empty.

Totally deserted. A ghost town. I've never seen anything like it. Al-Qaeda, everyone's saying.'

Mariana sits upright and sways slightly, as though inebriated, swears a couple of times. She tells Aaron she's in New York.

'Right, that's okay then. How are things over there?'

'A bit *weird* actually.' She smiles at me.

'You haven't heard from Lucas, have you? I can't get in touch with him.'

The liar. He hasn't even tried.

She errs on the side of caution. 'Um... I think he might've gone home. You know, for the funeral.'

'Ah, yes. Are you going to that? I used to know his dad, back in the day, so I'll be there... In fact, when you get back, do you fancy...?'

A Frisbee lands at my feet. A topless jock eyes Mariana with obvious hunger as he jogs over to collect it, and I feel a stab of superiority raise my own jaw as I toss it back to him. I get up to stretch my legs and from ten feet away, out of aural range, I watch Mariana sitting on the grass with her knees raised against her chin, phone pressed to an ear.

I've been here before, of course, at the starting line of relationships – petitioned by hormonal first years in dingy university dorms, or in the beds of married women who casually remark upon the differences between their husband's sexual technique and mine – but I've always been able to ignore the more voluble pleas for reciprocation and maintained an affectionless distance. This feels different: I don't want to leave her.

Laughter interrupts my thinking.

Mariana's giggling now into the phone, rocking back slightly with the effort of it. I try to imagine what Aaron's said that's amused her so much, on the day London's been attacked by terrorists, but can't fathom a worthy subject. I keep on walking. When I'm thirty feet from her, I look back. She's still laughing, wiping her eyes of mirth.

At the edge of the Meadow, I reach out and touch the rough, dry bark of a plane tree. Before I can even acknowledge my irritation, I dig my fingernails underneath a nook of bark and peel away a small, palm-sized section. I find another loose piece and pull that away to reveal yellow-white periderm. I experience an emotion I haven't felt for years. I feel jealousy. I see Aaron as a rival. Another layer of hard, brown, dead tissue is torn away. The action calms me, almost mechanically, and I keep peeling at the bark until I've decorticated an area about the same size as a tabloid newspaper. Tranquilised, I walk back to Mariana.

She glumly turns off her phone and places it in her lap.

'You should've told him I was here,' I say. 'You should've been honest with him.'

Ignoring me, Mariana points towards lower Manhattan. 'The towers stuck up over there,' she says, indicating the right of the skyscrapered horizon. 'You used to be able to see them from here. I was a graduate at the time and slept right through the attack. I saw them collapse though, saw the dust in their place, hovering for miles. Ash was all over here.' She indicates the grass we sit on. 'Burned paper documents from the offices, falling everywhere. Horrible. People were shit-scared. No one had known anything like it before. Strangers talking to you about it in the street would start crying. It was such an intrusion, like your house had been burglarised, you know?' She gazes at the ghost of the World Trade Center, plays with her hair. 'It was so... indiscriminate. Who would do such a thing?'

'Cowards.' I wonder if flights to the UK have been affected. My mother might *just* accept the detonation of explosive backpacks on rush-hour transport as a valid excuse for missing the funeral.

'Just think if we'd been there...'

'It's only been, what, three explosions did he say? Four? We'd have been fine.'

'What's making you so blasé about it?' she asks.

Good question. Had I seen it coming: a subtle escalation of fear and violence, sensationalist journalists peddling a dislike for the unlike? Am I too involved with, distanced by, my childhood? Or did apathy, even then, meet the shriek of cornering ambulances and the blood which splattered a concrete driveway on the evening I was left by the wayside?

'Aaron's sweet, isn't he?' she says. 'I mean, he suffers from a rather anxious temperament but he's well-meaning. To be honest, I wasn't sure about him to start with. I thought he was a bit pretentious and incompetent, but he seems fun. How did you meet him? I never asked.'

'It was a long time ago. What was he telling you that was so amusing?'

'He does a fantastic impression of you. Have you heard it?'

I watch a plane soar above Manhattan's rooftops, moving at what seems a leisurely, touristic pace through the Wedgwood sky. I watch a lone cirrus cloud. I watch the grass bow under a gentle breeze.

Mariana twists my right earlobe, breaks me from my jealousy. 'Come on, let's go.' She reaches out a hand to help me up, attempts a stately dance spin and folds herself into my side.

As we walk out of the park and onto Central Park West, I spot a familiar figure waltzing towards us through the taxis, wearing a blue mini and long-sleeved white top to hide the track marks on supermodel-thin arms.

Fuck. What are the odds?

Seeing no other escape route available, I grab Mariana and embrace her.

I kiss her for at least a minute. Mariana makes strange cooing sounds throughout. Once enough time has elapsed for Leah, surely, to have passed by, I break off.

The junkie's three feet away, staring at me.

'I left some,' Leah says, tears in her eyes.

Mariana jumps and detaches herself from my arms. 'What the...?'

'Do I know you?' I ask.

She looks from me to Mariana, a dawning comprehension of the awkward situation I'm in misting bloodshot eyes. 'It's me,' she beseeches, but in a way that tells me she doubts the validity of her own words. She's as high as I've ever seen anyone in my life. 'Don't you remember? Yesterday?'

'Who are you?' Mariana asks.

'Please,' Leah says, shaking, feverish, kneading her upper arm. 'There was some left in the bag. I know there was. I just want the last of it.'

'You've mistaken me for someone else,' I say. I start to lead Mariana away.

'Wait!' Leah shouts, her face convulsing with effort. 'I can't remember your name. But… we went to your apartment. You live over there…' She waves in the wrong direction, piling a merciful credibility onto my story.

'I don't live in this city,' I tell her. 'I don't even live in this country. Good afternoon.'

She yells out again as we attempt to walk on.

'You can't do this to me!' Her face shows real, raw fear. 'I'm desperate. Please. Have some compassion. Please!'

Mariana spins and jabs her finger in Leah's face. 'Leave us alone. Or, God help me, I'll do something I'll regret.' This eruption silences Leah, who, sensibly, backs off. I can't help but feel sorry for her; this hint of what lies growling deeper inside Mariana shocks me too. 'Come on,' she orders me. 'Let's get out of here.'

Leah spins round and storms across the street.

'I'm sorry about that,' Mariana says, taking responsibility. 'One of our resident loonies.'

We head to the apartment.

In the moaning elevator, all chrome and mirrors and lights and dials, I catch a glimpse of myself, cornered, culpable, an inverted blonde question mark of hair hanging too long over a rutted brow. The doors open. 'I think I should be packing,' I tell her. 'My father's funeral is in two days.' I can hear the hysteria in my voice.

In my room, I start slinging things into my bag. The diary, my clothes, my washing kit. I look inside Leah's crumpled paper carrier and, lurking under her broken spoon, the tatty strip of aluminium glinting in the low sun coursing through the window, I see the remnants of the black tar she was on about in Central Park. It's about the size of a jelly bean, but undoubtedly worth a hit to a junkie. I shove it all in my bag.

Mariana's sitting on the sofa. Her mother's at the desk on the far side of the room.

'Want me to come with you to the airport?' Mariana asks, standing.

'It's fine. I'll go tomorrow. I was just…'

Even though her mother's in the same room, I drop my bag on the sofa and take a step towards her. Mariana was looking a little freaked out by my behaviour in the elevator and I feel the need to hug those suspicions out of her.

From under my right foot, comes a soft but terrible crack. I know at once what it is.

We both look down to the rug.

'What was that?' She crouches. 'Step off it.'

Powerless, I do as I'm told. There's nothing there.

She peels back the edge of the rug to reveal Leah's broken syringe.

There's an all-too brief moment when she just stares at it, confused, before turning an accusatory eye on me.

'Lucas?'

'What's the matter?' her mother asks, sensing a scene and scudding over. She probably thinks I've broken yet another heirloom.

She eyes the hypodermic and her face begins to change. 'I don't want junkies in my house,' she snarls quietly. 'My God, we had enough shit in this family with Jorge.'

'Mom, it's alright. Let me deal with this.' There's buried fury in her voice.

'Out!' her mother hisses, gesturing to the door. 'You must think we were born yesterday.'

Mariana calmly picks my bag off the sofa, hands it to me. 'You need help.' Her voice is composed. The indifference leaves me cold.

At the front door, I turn round to speak.

'Don't say anything.' Her voice is losing its strength now, is nowhere near as hard as her features. I can see her fighting to reign in the temper she directed at Leah.

'I just want to say…'

'*Don't.*'

'It's all been a terrible misunderstanding. Me and Leah didn't…'

With tears in her eyes, she punches me in the face.

I stumble out into the wide foyer, massaging my left eye. Only then do I realise my mistake: Leah never mentioned her name.

'Please. Mariana. Let me explain…'

The door slams and, through it, her mother calmly informs me they own a gun.

Outside, I hail a cab. The Afro-Caribbean driver smiles as he tells me a drive to JFK will cost sixty dollars, plus tolls, an audacious swindle even for this city. I slide in and watch Mariana's parents' apartment recede all the way down Central Park West.

'You headin' any place nice?'

I tell him I'm off to London, but he doesn't mention the bombings. News from my island hasn't reached him yet. It's small change, as they say. I declare I'm due to attend my father's funeral, solve a murder. My driver locks his eyes on the road then turns the radio up.

Back through the steel and glass we travel, under bridges, road signs and pleas to drive safely. We motor through Queens with the Manhattan skyline behind us and the tidy, carbon-copied suburban estates to our left and right. I watch the bruising of my eye in the rear-view mirror and, in no time at all, the socket's a purplish dime of shadow.

THE FINAL PART OF
THE DIARY

Friday 15th September 1989

Shit fucking shit bastard bumholes.

Monday 18th September 1989

I don't know what the point of this diary is anymore. I thought I might want to write in it but I don't. This will probably be my last entry so goodbye forever.

Wednesday 20th September 1989

Nothings been washed, not even my pants. Some boys at school said I had turdy trousers so last night I washed them in the bathroom sink then hanged them on my door skeleton to dry. In the morning they were still wet but I had to wear them to school anyway.

Thursday 21st September 1989

I didn't want to speak to Daniel but Dad had already let him in. He had a red mark on his neck and when I asked him about it he said 'Thats nothing' and pulled up his sleeve to show me all these black bruises on his arm and shoulder. I asked how he got them and he curled his lip and went 'I got beats' then told me he's heard things creaking in the night. I showed him a book about ghosts and had to explain what 'apparition' and 'parapsychology' meant because he's not a super skill reader like me and has to use his finger to follow sentences. He told me he's going to exorcise Mrs Smithson this evening by reading the Bible and holding up a cross (my book says this counts as a 'symbol, icon or amulet, etc'). He said he would throw holy water at her.

I asked him where he got holy water from and he said he took it from the drain outside that church we broke into and I went 'Your going to throw rainwater round your room?' and he said 'Holy rainwater.'

Daniel then showed me the flick knife he won in some bet at school. He said if the holy water and exorcism fails he'll stab the ghost up 'good n proper'.

I was pleased when he left.

Dad and I ate beans on toast and afterwards he asked me if I wanted to go and look at the stars. I didn't. Instead I went upstairs to listen to Daniel shouting next door. He went something like 'In the beginning God created heaven and Earth and there was darkness all over everywhere and God said "Let there be light" and there was light and out demons, *out*!' Then there was a crash and Daniel screamed.

WHAT. A. RETARD.

Friday 22nd September 1989

Mum and Ryan picked me up after school. Mums eyes had dark rings and her nostrils had flakes of peeling skin on them. We went to Bowling City where the balls are heavy but I got eight pins down in one go.

When Mum dropped me off at the front gate I asked 'Why can't you be my mum anymore? Why does that Jenny woman have to be my mum?' Her lip wobbled and she hugged me tighter and said that she's still my mum and always will be and 'Please don't mention that womans name around me. She doesn't love you like I do.' She couldn't believe that Dad told me any of this stuff about her. I told her he hadn't, and that I detected it from all the evidence available. Mum ruffled my hair. I asked when I could move in with them but Mum said she is going to move to a flat to look after Ryan but that, if coppers got involved, Dad would get me because he's earning more and is the 'biological' parent.

Then Dad pulled open the front door and staggered outside and Mum grabbed Ryan and ran off down the road before he could breathe beery breath on them.

Saturday 23rd September 1989

Dad tried to outdo Mum today by taking me to the cinema to watch *Batman*. Afterwards he asked if I liked the film. Its the best film I've ever seen in my life but I said 'No' to annoy him.

Later, Dad set the curtains on fire.

Sunday 24th September 1989

I am hiding from Dad in my room and it is raining. I wrote more than this today but just tore the pages out. Everything is utterly horrible and ruined and

Monday 25th September 1989

Fight day.

Someone pushed me in the playground and suddenly all these people came running over from different parts of the playground chanting 'fight fight' and the bigger boy with the shaved head started boxing near my face. I said 'Why don't you pick on someone in your own year?' and then all the anger exploded out of me and I duffed him on the chin and he fell on the floor. The crowd went 'Oooh.' I thought he was going to spring up and hit me so I kicked him in the stomach fifty times. Then Mr Johns stood between us and we both had to go with him to see the big eared headmaster.

I lied and said that it was self-defence and never wanted to fight in the first place but Mr Johns said there's 'never any excuse for violence' and that he saw me kick Aaron when he was on the floor.

I had to sit in the headmasters office, which smells of coffee and old paper, while the office women tried for ages to ring home. Eventually I told the headmaster Mum left us to live with Granny and Granddad and he called Dad at the bank to say I'm going to be excluded from school for 4 days.

Dad came to collect me at the end of the day and spoke to the headmaster while I waited outside the office. On the wall were long photos of old school groups, all sitting in rows with teachers at the front. The photos go back to 1962 and the teachers get older and unhappier as each year goes by.

I was working on my revenging plan when Dad came out of the office. I caught the headmaster saying, in a voice all sympathetic, 'Don't blame yourself, Mr Marr.'

Tuesday 26th September 1989

Day 1 of my exclusion.

There are black rings in the bath, plants are dead, toilet paper has run out and plates are dirty. Plus the living room smells of fire and beer. I ate some frozen chips and watched 9 minutes 52 seconds of a video called *The Shining*.

When Dad came home I asked him why there was no food in the house and he said, trying to be all smiley, 'When did you become so obstreperous, Lucas?'

'Why didn't my real mum want me?' I asked. 'And why did she come back?'

Dad said he didn't want to talk about it and that 'It doesn't matter' but it bloody does matter. I asked him why he hurt Mum and he looked lost then quietly went 'I don't know. I really love her, champ.'

I asked who he meant and he said 'Mum, of course.'

'Which one?'

'Mum. Proper Mum. *Mum* Mum.'

I told him I hated him and that I wished I had never been born and Dad looked at me with his eyes wide. 'Don't *EVER* say that' he said. He said he wanted Mum back too but Granny and Granddad won't let her talk to him. He was talking like he was tired, but he couldn't have been because it was only 6 o'clock. Then I asked 'Why did my real mum leave me?' I thought if I asked enough times he would have to answer. 'Was it because of you?'

He didn't answer so I asked again and again.

And then Dad exploded and went 'She was insane, forget about the bitch!' He said my real mum had something called paranoid schizophrenia and that they split up because Dad came home one day and caught her trying to do something terrible to me because she couldn't hack my crying or something and Dad said he didn't know if it was the first time she'd tried to hurt me but 'I made sure it was the last.'

I shouted something like 'So you DID make her leave, like you did Mum! I knew it. Nobody wants you!'

I know how much it hurts when your told nobody wants you so I wasn't surprised when Dad got angry, but I was surprised when he tried to grab my neck and I fell and cracked my head on the radiator.

He was shouting he was sorry as I ran up the stairs and when I got to my room I dragged the bed back against the door. Dad was banging on the door. My cheek hurt and I could feel a swelling. Suddenly the door made a crack and a hinge smashed and the skeleton flew across the room as the door crashed onto the bed and Dad was standing outside my room. I picked up my telescope and swung it like a sword. I told him I was going to hit him round the head if he came near me.

'Are you alright, champ?' he asked.

I screamed until he went away.

Wednesday 27th September 1989

I have to stay with Granny and Granddad during the day now to do my exclusion catch up work. Today I learned that Hastings was invaded in 1066 and Harold was hacked up by Frenchmen after they pretended to retreat. This was a clever tactic because it means we now have places like Herstmonceux and Cul-de-Sac. Everyone thinks my bruise is because of the fight with Aaron.

I thought it would be fun to see Mum but she acts sad all the time.

When Granddad came out of his bedroom after his afternoon nap I told him I was developing a revenging plan, to take Julian and Daniel down a 'peg or two'. He whispered 'I understand your confused and that you have a lot of new emotions, but you can't take it out on your friends.' His hair is greyer after his heart attack and he asked me why I was so angry and I told him no one wants me and everyones lying to me and he didn't have a reply to that.

Thursday 28th September 1989

Julian and Daniel are on the cover of this weeks *Becksmouth Observer* under a small headline saying 'Ghostbusters Too'. I told Mum *Ghostbusters II* had just come out and she said the title was a pun. The photo shows the morons standing outside Daniel's house and Daniel is holding Keegan's cross (which he STOLE from my garden) and Julian is holding what looks like a thermometer, with his fat hands on his fat hips. Underneath the photo it says 'Look out spirits, the Ghostbusters are in town! Halloween may still be over a month away but ghosts are busy all year long, which is why Becksmouth residents Julian Pendle and Daniel King, both 11, have turned their talents to freelance exorcism, starting with a pesky poltergeist haunting Daniel's bedroom. "It was ten feet tall," says Daniel, "but we exorcised it and it's finally at rest." The pair used holy water, bible recitations and a "secret trick" to banish the ghoul and now want to hear about any other unwanted phantasms in the neighbourhood. Who you gonna call?'

Mum said the article was 'tongue and cheek' and I should be pleased for my friends.

Now I'm back at home in my barricaded room. The house stinks of those weird cigarettes Dad was smoking with my real mum in The Old Mint and, just now, Dad went into the garden and started burning things on a bonfire while talking to himself.

Friday 29ᵗʰ September 1989

A chemistry book told me everything in the solar system is made of the same elements from the periodic table. Iron (Fe) atoms found on Earth are identical to iron atoms on meteorites and these same iron atoms make Mars red. Also, the electrons that orbit the nucleus of an atom do exactly what satellites do to planets. I want to learn more about the periodic table because Arcturus isn't working well at the moment because its casing is made of weak Aluminium (Al). Also I stamped on it on Wednesday because I was cross.

Dad knocked on my barricaded door while I was perfecting my revenging plan to ask if I was ever going to 'cease this silliness' so I strengthened my barricade with books.

Saturday 30th September 1989

I wrote a note out on Mums old typewriter and put it through Daniels door. It said

Dear Daniel King, Ghostbuster,

I recognised your house from the recent Observer *article. I am writing concerning a matter of grave importance and have information regarding an ectoplasmic entity in The Old Mint House. Many local children have complained of hauntings there, as I'm sure your aware, and my own children have seen the ghostly antiques ghost on several occasions, but always on the third day of the month, at dusk, maybe because this was when an evil deed was committed, perhaps with an axe or something.*

I read about your skills and know you and your friend are the right boys for this job. I can sense things. When I was a little girl my mother told me I had second sight.

I am also rich beyond belief and can pay you 500 pounds each if you can exorcise the malignant spirit with ionization detectors or EMF sensors or whatever. Please, please rid us of the depraved phantasm, before even more innocent children get scared.

Yours in fear for my children's safety,

Mrs Omen Shining

I made up the history of the ghost and nicked 'ectoplasmic entity', 'malignant spirit' and 'depraved phantasm' from a library book. The 2 morons won't know about EMF sensors and ionization detectors but it definitely helped the letter look proper.

'Operation Ghost' will take place on the third of October because there is never anything good on TV on Wednesdays.

Sunday 31st September 1989

I found Dad asleep in the bath this morning with his clothes on. We went to Spar. I put everything Mum used to buy into the basket, plus loads of Angel Delight, and he put in beer, which he called 'hair of the dogs'.

When we got back, Julians dad was in the driveway washing his car. Julians dad is tall, because he's a policeman, and has green eyes and short black hair. He looks more modern than Dad. The dads shook hands and Julians asked 'How are you? How is Susan?' with his hand on Dads shoulder.

Dad told me to go inside but I went into the garden instead to throw stones at a pyramid of old fizzy drink cans (Al or Sn and steel, which is an alloy of Fe, Ni and Cr). When the dads went, I detected lots of burnt paper and black photos in a small ashy pyramid at the bottom of the garden. In the ashes I could see happy faces.

A girls voice asked me what I was doing and I turned and saw Daniels sister standing at the chicken wire wearing a white Tshirt and jeans. It seemed she was a bit taller than me so I didn't go over to her, in case she was.

Lucy's quite pretty, because her hair is long and she doesn't look like Daniel. I wondered if they are real brothers and sisters, like me and Ryan aren't.

'I know all about you' she said. 'Daniel told me what you 3 get up to, all the nicking and breaking into churches. Bor-ing. Did you see him and Julian in the paper? What a pair of divs!' She had her hands on the fence and was on tiptoe. She wanted to know what happened to Mum and if shes left forever. She said she heard Dad was having an affair and then she told me shes had 2 affairs with Robert Oastler and one with Tim Witton. The affair with Tim lasted 3 weeks and they used to kiss in his greenhouse. Then she looked at me and said 'Have you ever kissed anyone?' and 'Will you show me your secret camp?'

We walked behind the sheds into Julians garden and I showed her the hidden entrance. I crawled inside the camp then she followed me and we sat together. She smelt of bubblegum. After a few seconds she put her head to one side then pressed her hot mouth against mine. It was wet and our tongues did somersaults for ages and I got funny feelings in my stomach and between my legs. She let me put my arms round her while we kissed. It was nice for a while but I was relieved when someone shouted 'Lucy!' because my neck was hurting.

Daniel was in the camp entrance with his weird snake grin on his face.

'Bog off! Get lost!' Lucy shouted, crawling to the entrance.

Daniel went 'Beat it or I'll tell Dad what I just saw. I need to talk to Lucas.'

She ran off and left me and Daniel together. His neck still had horrid red marks on it and he pulled his flick knife out of his pocket. 'I got beats because of you last week.'

'I'm sorry' I said. And I was. I remember how it felt when Dad duffed me against the radiator.

'You told me the best way to exorcise Mrs Smithson was by throwing water around my room.' He crawled forwards and waved the knife in front of my face, making slashes. 'Your full of shit. She's still in the walls. But me and Julian have information about a ghost that will make us well famous so tell me how to exorcise a ghost properly or I'll hack your tongue out.'

I screamed as loud as I could for Dad and shut my eyes. When I opened them Daniel had gone.

I found Dad in front of the TV. The whole house smelt of grassy cigarettes and the white bits of Dads eyes were bloodshot. 'Were you calling me?' he asked, without moving his head. I went upstairs.

Monday 1st October 1989

I thought Aaron was probably after a rematch so I pretended not to see him when he came over to me at lunchtime but he jumped in front of me with his hand out.

He said 'No hard feelings?' then 'Aaron, at your service,' in a well fancy way. He bought me a canteen chocolate doughnut and told me he likes Nintendo. He said he only started fighting me because everyone had made a circle round us and was chanting. He's well impressed I've got a girlfriend.

Later, when I got home I found lots of stuff missing like chairs and books and plates and I thought we'd been burgled until I detected all the photo albums with Ryan in them had gone too. Mum had been sneaky and come round when Dad was at work.

I went upstairs to see what else was missing and looked in Mum and Dads wardrobe and during my detecting I found one of the fake leather video boxes. I thought it might be a horror that was too scary to have downstairs but when I opened it up I was disappointed to find a bag with green grass inside. I leaned forward and gave it a good sniff and it stunk of Dads cigarettes. None of Mums clothes were left. She's never going to move back in.

I think this annoyed Dad because when he got home he kicked the television to death.

2 days until 'Operation Ghost'.

Tuesday 2nd October 1989

A man came round today to bang a sign up in our front garden that had a galloping green horse on it and said 'For Sale'. Dad says we have no choice about moving now Mum is filing for divorce. He wants to leave our area of Becksmouth and move to the other side of town, closer to his work. He says there are 'too many good memories' here.

After chips, I watched Dad sprinkle some of his grassy stuff into a small bit of paper. He put some tobacco on top and then rolled it up with his thumbs into a big cigarette and smoked it and sat in front of the broken TV and burnt curtains until he got sleepy.

'Why do you hate me?' I asked. 'Is it because I remind you of her?'

He looked at me for ages like he couldn't see me properly, but didn't say anything. He didn't need to say Yes so he just cried instead and I went upstairs.

Wednesday 3rd October 1989

My hands are shaking and there might be some blood and I've only got a few pages left so I'm writing this small because I want to fit in everything.

Aaron came round this evening. I wasn't too pleased to see him at first because I thought my revenging would be ruined. But I worried for no reason because once I told him about my plan he wanted to be part of it. I didn't want him to meet Lucy though because someone told me Aarons already had loads of girlfriends and I thought she might fancy him because he's older than me.

We went into my garden and climbed over the fence into the back of The Old Mint. I had already tied my skeleton to the beam of the Victorian building before school and stored it in a bit of the roof that hangs over the main door. I tied it with a loose butterfly knot and put ketchup on the skull so it looked scarier and so Julian wouldn't recognise it as the one I bought from Gamleys.

My trap was in 2 parts. Part 1 involved the skeleton falling down when I yanked a string. This was to scare Julian and Daniel and activate Part 2, which was me making them properly shit themselves when they tried to run away by jumping out dressed in an old bedsheet with eyeholes cut out. Aaron said it would work better if he put on the ghost costume while I hid on one of the metal crates at the back to pull the string. Aaron picked up a massive stick in case of a combat situation.

Here is a drawing of the important parts of the revenging plan

At precisely 7.51 we saw them approach and went to our positions. I watched Julian and Daniel walk up to the Victorian building, looking suspiciously through windows. I wasn't expecting such careful detecting and was worried they would spot the skeleton. As they went to look around the back I heard Julian blabbing about how this was where he'd seen Dad with a naked prostitute. It was beginning to get dark already.

Then something unexpected happened. Dad walked down the drive carrying a black plastic bin liner. He was staggering a bit. He dropped his keys and when he picked them up he got distracted by the stars which were coming out and he looked up at them for a while before letting himself into the Victorian building. I crawled on my elbows towards the edge of the crate so I could get a better look through a window. Dad had turned the red light on and was throwing things into the bin liner, like the chipped blue mug and the candles and the glass ashtray with the cigarette butts that didn't smell of cigarettes and the out of date newspaper.

Julian and Daniel came out from behind the building. Daniel opened his bag and pulled out Keegans cross, 2 water pistols and a Bible we were all given in junior school. They walked around the building firing muddy water at the windows.

As they got nearer and nearer to the skeleton I prepared to give the string a good tug. Daniel had the cross in one hand and Julian started reading from the bible. They were almost at the door.

I pulled the string and nothing happened.

Julian was shouting now, all that stuff about Gods face and water and light. Then there was a scraping noise and the door shot open and Dad marched out.

And that's when Daniel, all scared or surprised or both, turned round and stabbed him.

I couldn't speak, like everything I was watching was just happening in one of Dad's horrors. I saw Daniel drop his flick knife and run up the drive as Julian screamed. Aaron heard the scream and assumed the skeleton trick had worked and jumped out with his stick and went 'Woooo'. Daniel ran past him but Julian fell down and smacked his face on the concrete. Aaron took his costume off to see if Julian was alright and I saw how confused Julian was, wondering why one of the bigger boys who threatened us in Sinton Woods had set up a trap with Dad. Then he got up and ran after Daniel. The skeleton flopped down and bounced on its string but no one saw it.

When I got to Dad there was blood all over his shirt. I was scared he was going to be angry again like when I hit my head but he looked all calm and just said 'Do us a favour champ. Call 999 will you?'

I ran home and called 999. A woman asked what department I wanted and I said 'Ambulance' and they asked me what the problem was and I said 'stabbing.'

Aaron helped Dad up the drive and into the house and Dad took a blue tea towel with star signs on it from the kitchen drawer and pressed it to his side and tried to hide the wound from me but when he lifted his shirt I saw a little hole, like a dark red eye. There were bloody handprints on everything, like the drawer handle and the wall. There were spots of blood on the hall carpet.

'That Daniel is flipping mental,' Aaron said as he was trying to clean the blood away from the floor with a dishcloth. The dishcloth just smeared the blood around.

The ambulance arrived, all blue lights and sirens and black windows and 2 paramedics came into the house. Their snot-coloured jackets were crackling like foil.

'Are we going to hospital?' I asked one of them.

'I think we better,' she said, looking at Dads wound.

Dad asked her name and said something dumb about falling on a knife which she thought was a joke but I knew was just another lie. She was pretty and had brown eyes and Dad grabbed her hand and smiled at her like he was Timothy Dalton.

Dad was put on a stretcher and we went outside. The lights in The Old Mint were angry red eyes and I saw Julian duck behind his bedroom curtain when I looked up. He never was very skill. Then the police came and listened to Aaron grass up Daniel and went with him to ring his doorbell to start their detecting.

The paramedics lifted Dad into the back of the ambulance and I started to climb in too but Dad boomed 'No! I don't want HIM coming with me. Does he look like a flipping medical genius to you?' He actually pushed me away into the road, like *I* was the one who stabbed him. The female paramedic turned to me and said 'Um, maybe its best if you stay here, young man.' I know I should have been pleased when she added, all jokey, 'Your lucky. Your dad's lost a lot of blood but he's going to live, this time,' but I didn't feel anything.

Dad would rather be in an ambulance with a pretty lady than with me.

A policeman agreed to take me to Granny and Granddad and then doors were slammed and Dad vanished behind the black windows and the siren started again and cars stopped as the driver smashed his foot on the accelerator and I was left standing as unwanted as ever on the pavement and that was when I realised I didn't care, even if Dad wasn't going to be alright. The thought of him being dead doesn't make me sad me at all.

Thursday 19th April 1990

Just found this again. I've only got a few lines left so might as well fill them. Keeping a diary started off a fun experiment I guess but I definitely picked the wrong time to keep it. Perhaps one day I'll write another one. I doubt it though.

Hello, older me, if you're reading this. I hope you got away in the end.

PART FOUR

CHAPTER FIFTEEN

Something's wrong. Unfamiliarity fills the air. Not a scent, a feeling. My heart thumps with nauseous anticipation. I've been burgled.

I kick the front door shut behind me and let it slam. Only silence is returned. I sling my bag into the hallway and cuff the light switch. Radiance sweats from the sixty-watt.

It seems to me, as I quickly reconnoitre the flat to see what's left, that more than a few belongings have been overturned. Though the computer, DVD player and stereo are present and correct, a swathe of breadcrumbs decorate the kitchen counter with all the inelegance of an irregular galaxy, and an array of strange garments have buried the sofa. A newspaper I've never bought before sits atop a television staring its standby redeye and a half-eaten chicken korma spoils the dining table. Next to this is a yellow Post-It bearing the bizarre proclamation that 'Lamigstrm: the petentsofe agaw.' An equally indecipherable 020 telephone number is scribbled underneath.

None of this matters. I have better things to see to right now.

I follow the smell of musty sheets and budgerigar into my bedroom, where I'm surprised to find that I left the window open. The bird tweets and trips around on his pedestal, squawking hunger. I'll feed him later; first I need to see to my own nourishment.

From the bottom of my wardrobe, hidden beneath the dry-cleaned suits and poorly-ironed shirts, I carefully pull out a shoebox and place it upon the bed. My breath thrashes in my chest as I remove the lid to reveal the paraphernalia of my past addiction: cotton wool, an aluminium cooking can, shiny new hypodermic syringes, courtesy of Syngestia. The only thing missing is the white powder heroin, which, as a recovering-addict, I would've been a fool to have kept in my treasure chest. I don't quite know why I kept all this. I guess I thought that, without the heroin, it was harmless. How was I to know, one day, I'd be flying over a tar-black Atlantic with a tiny amount of New York's supply? It's all I've been thinking about for the last few hours.

There were a number of things I could've done to smuggle it through airport security. Cayenne pepper in my shoes to put the dogs off me. A paraffin wax coating inside a supplement bottle. Within a condom, up the backdoor. In the end, I employed none of these methods. I didn't care. I kept it in my pocket the whole time and simply walked through. They were far more concerned about explosives and weapons than a linty piece of poor-quality junk.

I break the small amount of Leah's tar in half and cook it up.

As I'm drawing it up the syringe, I stop myself. It's a tiny hit, I justify. One tiny, tiny hit. An ex-smoker's cigarette after a few pints. An advent calendar chocolate a day early. I can validate this to myself in the grand context of things. It's been a hard few days.

In it goes.

The heroin's warm and comforting, a miracle cure for the symptoms its absence has spawned. The need of the needle is out of my control, and that brings a kind of peace: I know what I want. I want heroin. Such things give one's life a steadying meaning.

The increased salivation that precedes vomiting begins and, before I know it, I'm hovering over the toilet. Afterwards, I turn on the shower and remain under for nearly an hour, lost in a fog of self-loathing.

My actions in New York were despicable but, strange as it may seem, I had little time to consider my betrayal during the flight. It was difficult enough getting my diary finished. And I almost wish I hadn't.

Under the water's dizzying heat, I often have to grasp the shower head to prevent myself falling over, while the crackling bathroom radio spews out some earnest boyband's croonings about love lost and wisdom earned, as though no one's ever put the two things together before. Personally, the human condition has long struck me as allotropic. After all, if charcoal and diamond can both be forms of carbon, why shouldn't affection and absence be borne from the same element, from a beautiful American woman who accidently admitted her love for me?

Eventually, I exit the cubicle a wrinkled, prune-like chewing of a human being, and plod to my spinning bed. I'm too tired to sleep, and haunted by actions I don't remember performing: a cool breeze fluttering net curtains, courtesy of the window I never opened; the mess of food and clothes in the other rooms. I'm haunted too by the converging of my past and my present, the gap where they don't quite collide. I was wrong about the diary: there *doesn't* appear to be a link between then and now, no clues whatsoever as to my father's murder.

But it turned another, long-held assumption on its head.

My father wasn't simply throwing me into the road that night. That's how I saw it – perhaps understandably – as an eleven-year-old, but there was so much more to it...

The budgie squawks.

Victimised by thought, I leave the bed, close the window and open the birdcage to throw some seeds in. I stare at the remains of Leah's junk for a long time.

Almost from outside my own body, I watch as I crouch down and cook up the last of it.

The heroin kicks into me.

I was lucky the first time to get away with a mere moment

of dizziness in the shower, but this sends me straight to the carpet. I feel my tendons tightening, curling me foetal. My respiratory and cardiac systems are slowing; my heart's a failing metronome and the room drops several degrees in a matter of seconds.

It all happens so fast.

I take a last look around me. A shelf of healthcare textbooks. A few works of fiction, not as highbrow as I'd like to think. No photos of loved ones.

This is it.

My final heartbeat isn't a heartbeat at all. It's a window slamming.

A man stands in my bedroom. Upon his face, shock and concern have coalesced to form something that resembles my brother.

Ryan says, 'What the *fuck*…?'

I pull the needle from my arm. The consequent arc of blood confirms my heart to still be operational.

'Ryan,' I croak, 'pass me that box.' I nod towards my addict's trove. 'Quick!'

He hands the shoebox over, eyes wide with repulsion, and I clutch within for a bag of powder and a syringe then demand the glass of water by my bed. I pour all but a hundred grams onto the floor then empty half the bag into the glass.

'Naloxone,' I explain, not that he asked. 'It counters the effects of the over… *Christ!*' The contents of my chest punch against my ribs and Ryan ducks forward to snatch the glass from my hand before I drop it. 'Stir,' I gasp, slumped at the foot of my bed as catatonia infects my muscles.

Unquestionably, I'm dying.

Ryan uses a pen to help dissolve the powder and, somehow, I summon enough strength to direct him to draw the mixture up through the syringe. I persuade him to stab it into my arm, guiding him feebly, and hold my breath as the opioid antagonist races into my blood. Ryan's breath smells faintly of the chicken korma from my dining table.

Something flickers and ripples underneath my skin, consciousness trying to breach the surface. For a while I don't think the naloxone's working but then, slowly, the cravings return. It's as though I never injected H in the first place.

'You saved my life,' I inform my brother.

He's slumped against the wall at the other end of my room, facing me across a floor of drug apparatus. He looks as confused and out of his depth as the three-year-old version of himself I've been reading about.

'You were lucky I came back when I did,' he mutters.

I stare at my alarm clock. The numerals don't make any sense.

'What you doing here?' I ask, as if it isn't obvious our mother's sent him to collect me in time for tomorrow's service.

He waits an eon before he answers. 'I needed somewhere to go. I tried Dad's first. You've got the only key to his flat so I had to break in through one of his windows.' Ryan's head falls back against the wall with a thud. He's panting more than I am, a sheen of sweat across his cheeks and forehead. If pressed, a stranger would find it hard to label the addict. 'He must've been in agony when he died. All the stuff from his briefcase on the floor... Whiskey all over the coffee table... I couldn't stay, so came here instead.' My bedroom window's wide open. Quite the cat burglar, my brother.

I'm not surprised by the revelation that he ran from his hometown. I too deferred my worries by flying to New York. The appeal of absconding, stopping the turn of the world for a moment, is quite an opiate. I have a feeling it gets stronger the older you become.

'Does Mum know where you are?'

'She thinks I'm at my girlfriend's,' he says. 'I had to vanish for a while, you know? Mum's being weird. I think there's something going on. There was a detective at the house yesterday.'

His eyes have been on the needles at my feet all this time.

'It was the impurity of the… stuff,' I explain. 'I'd been used to far better.'

'Fuck you. What are you doing this to yourself for?'

'I don't know.'

'It's disgusting.'

We lapse into another silence. I nod at the bedside phone. 'Has anyone called while I've been away?'

'I answered once. It was your work.'

Paranoia filters through me, leaving just one insoluble thought: Mariana has betrayed me in return by informing Syngestia of my habit.

'They left you a number to call,' Ryan says. 'A helpline.'

'A helpline?'

'I assumed because of, you know, the death. I wrote the number down for you on a Post-It in the front room. It was a guy called Lavingstrom or something. He asked me to send you his best wishes. He also said I was to tell you "the patent's safe again". Apparently you'd know what he meant.'

I'd forgotten all about work these last few days. Thoughts of a humdrum subsistence – eleven o'clock cups of coffee, flirtations with members of the IT department, solving minor analgesic patent crises – almost cheer me until I remember the shitheap of misery I've created out of Mariana's affection, and a tiredness which had been slowly tightening its noose now tugs at the knot. I climb onto my bed, coil into a ball. 'I need to sleep. We'll talk in the morning.' My legs start to buck as my fingers worm among the sheets.

'I should get you to a hospital.'

'No point. I'm not in danger anymore. Besides, the funeral's tomorrow.'

'Seriously, you look…'

'I'm fine. I'm fine! Leave me alone!' My anger is the agony of withdrawal.

He backs towards the door.

'Was he murdered, do you know? Dad. Was he murdered?'

'Close the door,' I say. I don't want Ryan seeing me like this.

After a few minutes, I hear the muted sound of the television. Now that I'm lying down, I'm no longer as tired as I thought I was; the naloxone has generated a heat that scalds my eyeballs. My teeth clash. My head drips. I'm starving.

I dial what I think might be Mariana's number. It goes to voicemail, but the words aren't delivered in her singsong timbre so, disappointed, I kill the call.

As I recover, a sort of dusty clarity settles upon me. I shouldn't have shouted at Ryan like that; the kid just saved my life.

And then the parallel fully dawns, an echo of the past that ought to be deafening but, thanks to the miracle drug in my system, is merely melancholic, obvious. I attempt to suppress it again, stuff it back into my subconscious, but this time, I can't shoot up to escape the truth.

Yes, my father shoved me, quite roughly, out of the ambulance. Yes, he barked at me to stay back. But he didn't want me to see him in a moment of weakness and pain. He was desperately trying, on the third of October, 1989, to hang on to his final strands of the paterfamilias mystique.

Everything I thought I remembered about that moment was wrong.

The silence circles, preys on me. Even that damn bird's quiet.

I raise my head to discover a vacant cage, the tiny steel door wide open. My window too is a curtain-flapping empty space, outside of which the sun's splashed red against Alexandra Palace and a hundred free birds sing to protect their nests.

CHAPTER SIXTEEN

Ryan and I leave early, at the first tube-rumblings of dawn. It's evident from his darkly haloed eyes he's barely slept.

Which makes two of us.

I can feel the city's shock even here, in the backwaters. Each pair we sidestep in Crouch End talk about the bombed bus ten minutes ahead of them, the twisted, smoking train to Liverpool Street they missed by a whisker, affirming their lives by glorying in a proximity to death. Londoners seem full of both indignant relief and angry trepidation, but I wonder how long it will be before the ambivalent veil drops back down, the mask my fellow citizens would wear all the time if they weren't duty bound to heave their guts every night at The Bricklayers Arms or The Pillars of Hercules.

Ryan and I don't talk much on the tube. At Victoria we board the 8.15 for Becksmouth. The carriage is almost empty and every time we change tracks I feel afresh the eviscerating hell of a heroin hangover.

Deep breaths. Relax. Think of running water.

I know how it's going to sound, but I have to share the information with *someone*. And this silence is driving me crazy.

'I've been getting calls from my real mother. From Sinton Secure Unit.'

My half-sibling looks doubtful. Twelve hours ago, he found me with a belt round my arm and a needle in my vein. 'You what?'

'I was surprised too. We didn't speak, but it was definitely her.'

His clear brow knots, somehow unnaturally; the elasticity of his skin soon leaves little trace of his scepticism. 'How can you be so sure it was her if you didn't actually *speak*?'

'Who else would call me in the wake of Dad's death? It had to have been her. She said, "I've got some...," and then I hung up.'

I've got some*thing to say that can't wait any longer*

I've got some *information about your father's killer*

I've got some *time out of the Unit, for his funeral*

He still looks unconvinced. 'Where did you say she called from?'

'Sinton Hospital.'

'You mean... she's a *mentalist*?'

'Didn't you know?' There's never been much communication within our family but I thought Ryan would've been informed of an elementary fact like this.

My brother seeks a distraction out the window. End of conversation.

I ask to borrow his mobile, announce that I want to call Syngestia to see how my colleagues are, following the bombing. Grudgingly, he hands it to me and I head down the shivering carriage to the toilet. My master plan is thus: if I call Mariana from a number she doesn't recognise as mine, she might answer.

She doesn't.

I re-join Ryan, hand him back his phone. We don't say anything else until well past Gatwick. It's obviously not the best time to talk about our father's poisoning, the subject of which, despite Mum's appeal to the contrary, I was going to raise – it's time members of this family were honest with one another. Fearing the same withering, teenage disregard that met my previous revelation, I instead say, 'I'm afraid I've got some bad news about Dad's budgie.'

'Oh no. Although that can happen, can't it? When a pet's owner dies? The grief and that.'

Another station flashes past.

'I remember a large garden,' he says, his voice nervous, thin, 'and a long landing.' I'm surprised by his choice of conversation, but he seems genuinely curious about the house we grew up in. He has only vague memories of its layout and décor, and even these are probably pilfered from photographs he's seen. 'You, um, babysat me, didn't you, when Mum and Dad were out? We played with Lego.' He smiles at the thought of it, our momentary family, and talks about the time he shared a roof with his father as though it were some kind of perpetual Christmas.

I remain silent, lost in thought. Is the Lego incident he's remembering the same one I documented? Is he, without realising, referring to the fateful day I announced our father's infidelity to his mother? Has he fashioned *fond* memories from that September evening?

Ryan takes my silence as a rebuttal and springs into defence mode.

'Look, what memories I have of Dad are special to me. I know I wasn't the one growing up with him, so I don't know what it was like and all that, but he was still Dad. I'm sure it was dreadful after Mum and I left – you've told me enough times that it was – and I know you think he never forgave you for exposing his affair, that you felt constantly shoved behind women and drink and weed, and I'm sure it must annoy you, listening to my rosy little recollections, when all you got from him was five years of silence, but memories are all I have of Dad now.'

Ryan snaps his head back to the window. My brother, I know, has always resented my loathing of his father, and it's not the first time he's revealed this resentment, but a newfound maturity lends his frustration a powerful fury. And his discovery of my heroin dependence has hardly made me a more respectable figure.

He hasn't finished. 'You felt betrayed... Fine. Mum wasn't your mum... Fair enough. Dad embarrassed you by turning up wasted to parents' evenings, friends' houses... I've heard all the stories. I know that he shagged your real mother in that old antiques place. I've heard how those meetings disrespected Mum. And disrespected you. But, Lucas, he's dead. *He's dead.*' Water wells in Ryan's eyes.

I want to reply to this rage, appease it, but my tongue merely dries and clucks in my mouth. He's challenging me to defend my hatred and I can't.

'You weren't there,' I eventually croak. The old argument. 'You weren't there. No one was.'

Those are the last words of our journey. We spend the rest of it looking out the same window, shifting our gaze when the eyes of our reflections cross.

I hold back my trump card. I don't ask Ryan, 'If our father was so innocent, why would anybody want to murder him?'

Donning a rarely-worn black dress, and having announced a sarcastic, 'You cut it fine,' our mother runs through the day's agenda mere moments after we walk through the door.

I'm to go round to my grandparents' house at about midday before driving them to the same church Mum's visited every Sunday of her life, for the service. My grandfather's legs aren't so reliable these days.

As soon as he can, my brother bolts to his bedroom. The glimpse I afford of Freddie Flintoff posters corroborates his mere teenagehood.

I wonder how long Ryan will remain in the nest. By the time I was his age I'd been living by myself for a year, having left our father in unspectacular fashion. There was no fight, no argument. That wasn't our way; ours was a relationship of simmering conflict-avoidance. We were like people living in the aftermath of a massive earthquake, always expecting fresh tremors that never came. I probably said goodbye but don't remember doing so; I think we both assumed I'd be back after a couple of days of kipping on mates' floors, at least to collect more of my stuff. I never did return.

Before I set off for my grandparents', and after trying Mariana again from my mother's landline to no avail, I scrutinise myself in the bathroom mirror. To someone not in the know, seeing me in my blacks, the lines of tiredness and eye-haze of a likely new fight with addiction could almost pass for grief. I no longer feel as sick as I did a few hours ago, but this headache is *killing me*.

'That's quite a shiner you've got there,' my mother says from the doorway. 'Dare I ask how you got it?'

'I upset somebody.'

She moves forward and opens a mirrored cabinet above the sink. 'And what does the other feller look like?'

'It wasn't…'

'Stay still, will you?' She's swabbing my black eye with concealer. 'Don't tell me you were punched by a girl, Lucas? She must've really *liked* you.' She dabs my eye one more time then stands back, appraises the finished effect in the same proud manner she did the day I tried on my new school uniform.

'Any news on the inquest?'

She looks over her shoulder, to check Ryan's out of earshot. 'There was no inquest. I told you. The post-mortem report will be ready in about a month, they say. Because of that toxi-thing you mentioned.'

'So there's no criminal investigation at all now?'

'I didn't say that was the case, Lucas. There's been no *inquest*.'

'Do they know how he died?'

'I *don't know*.'

'And in the meantime we just sit back and wait for the results, do we? Where did these suspicions that he was poisoned come from? Was it heart failure or not?'

My mother replaces the make-up in the cabinet then casts another cautious eye in Ryan's direction. 'Look, I'll be honest with you. And I'm telling you this because I know it's hardly going to wound you. I don't actually *care* what killed him, alright?'

I leave the house forty-five minutes before I'm due to appear at my grandparents'.

Candy Corner, or rather the newly expanded 'superstore' that now stands in its place, is dense with people. All the CDs are in the wrong place and half the displays are barren. In no way does it resemble the shop I remember; its considerable extensions have swelled its aisles and plasticized its shelf edges in corporate-looking reds and greys. I hunt around the Pick 'n' Mix for a while but the figure I glimpsed last weekend is nowhere to be found. It's probably for the best. I don't know what I'd say to him anyway. In fact, I don't even know why I've come.

As I'm leaving the store I spot him.

He emerges from a stockroom and begins talking with a female colleague behind a till, explaining how to override a price via an intricate combination of chubby grey pushbuttons. She looks confused. He looks bored.

I'm shocked by his height, though he's not tall. I'm shocked by his age, though he's not old. I'm shocked by his frame, how scrawny he's become, how unpredictably his face has morphed. His nose is more retroussé than I remember and his hair is already thinning at the temples. Having fought off a childhood obesity, Julian Pendle was unfortunate never to accomplish good looks in maturity.

I'll leave him to it. This was a bad idea.

'Lucas! Lucas Marr!' Suddenly Julian's strolling past the two-for-one hoarding towards me. The voice is different. The walk is different. And yet it's clearly him. The eyes are the same. The skin flushes in giveaway discomfort. He's wearing a heavy and ill-fitting suit, the nametag bearing the Becksmouth Superstore legend.

'What on Earth are you doing here?' He wrings my hand. And then: 'Ah, yes. I heard about your dad. I'm very sorry.'

We walk out into the street. Listless pedestrians inch past, expending the energy of wasps left to die in jars. Julian pats his pockets for cigarettes. 'I'm a supervisor.' He gets in a self-deprecating shrug and his face refashions itself into steely ennui. 'It pays the bills. Plus I get thirty percent off stationery.'

I force a smile on his behalf. 'Great.'

'And you?'

'Oh, you know. Medicine.'

'Wow. Doctor?'

'Pharmacist.' I downsize my vocation; a pissing contest just doesn't seem right.

I'm waiting for the excuse, the 'Well, I better go and check on the troops. Can't be seen to be slacking,' but he just stands there, patting his pockets, a kind of vacancy tugging at the bags under his eyes. He finally finds his fags and sparks one up.

'So, how long's it been?' he asks. He needs to moisturise; dryness lines crinkle their way to the corners of his eyes as he sucks at his cigarette and there's a tiny, maggot-shaped scar on his chin, through which stubble refuses to grow. I wonder if this was formed when he fell face-first on the driveway, running from violence at The Old Mint House one Wednesday in 1989.

'Sixteen years,' I tell him.

'Wow.' A few seconds pass. 'You're looking well. You're living…?'

'London.'

He nods. Our conversation runs aground.

'It's a bit late,' I say, 'but I'm sorry about the letter and the plastic skeleton and the ghost and everything. I was jealous. Backfired badly, didn't it?' I fake a laugh.

'What are you talking about? What plastic skeleton?'

Julian clearly can't remember much about that night. And why should he? He probably didn't cement it through the action of writing it down. I'm not surprised he's confused

208

by my mention of a skeleton he never saw, but the jealousy should've been patent. I had one good friend, a fellow child in a world of betraying adults, and he couldn't even safeguard one secret. Not that I was able to keep my father's affair confidential, either.

'Nothing. It was a long time ago.'

'Are you talking about the time when…? You know, when Daniel stabbed…? That wasn't *your* fault. I think you're remembering it wrong. It was that Aaron kid who sent a letter and waited for us there, dressed as a ghost, in revenge for us all throwing bricks through his window. Remember?'

'Right. Of course. So how *is* Daniel these days?'

'Don't you know?' Julian's eyes widen a fraction and, for a second, I see him as he used to look, all the delights and expectations of storytelling smoothing out his features. He becomes that excited little boy who stood in The Old Mint and wrought facts from sketchy evidence. 'He's in prison.'

'*Prison*?'

Julian smirks. 'Yeah. You wouldn't believe what for.'

'Stabbing a man?'

My childhood best friend adopts a look of sympathy. Daniel received a nominal amount of community service for his spontaneous attack on my father and the pair of them attained a certain level of neighbourhood interest afterwards. Though it was my father's only moment of genuine fame, it seems Daniel went onto bigger things.

'Close. He tried to rob the bank three doors up, with a fake gun.' Julian waves up the street. 'He botched it, was wrestled to the floor by college kids. Got four years. I went to visit him about a week ago. Told him about your dad. He seemed very upset actually.' He flicks away his cigarette. 'You know, all that time, when we were kids… Well, his dad was quite handy, if you get what I mean. Daniel would often show me the results of his 'Beats'. I used to think he was showing off, but now I wonder whether it wasn't a cry for help. Sad really, that it was always going to end like this.'

I think of the time I saw Daniel scudding up the drive away from the scene of his first violent crime, full of fear and exhilaration, wearing his abuse in bruises all over his body. Is Julian right? Did Daniel's life *have* to end up like this?

Julian describes his call on Daniel's jail, the regime of meals and visiting hours, the grey walls and barred windows and clunky steel gates. 'A couple of pretty fit members of staff too,' he says, pursing his lips with intentionally comical irreverence. '*Women,*' he adds, too quickly, as though concerned I'd be offended if he'd turned out gay after all our secret missions and wargames. His adult personality is truly revealed to me, somewhat disappointingly, and he emerges petty and hidebound, the kind of provincial bore I left Becksmouth to avoid.

'"Fit members of staff"? Do they have female guards in male prisons?'

'Ah, well, it's a "Secure Adult Unit", if we must be specific. He's being held there due to prison crowding. They often keep prisoners there, apparently, round these parts. Ironic really, that he's at a mental hospital. He was never quite "all there" was he?'

I feel bile rising in my throat. 'Where's this Unit?' I ask, desperation returning my voice to its 1989 register.

He looks worriedly at me. 'Sinton, of course. The only one.'

I mutter something about running late and hear Julian call, 'Sorry again about your dad,' when I'm already ten feet down the street, pushing through hunched old ladies dressed as though it's ten degrees below freezing, tired young mums in Sainsbury's jeans.

At least one minor mystery has been solved.

Before she was due to hand over the phone to Daniel, one of those female members of staff Julian was so physically impressed by tried to confirm my identity with the words 'Hi Lucas…? I've got some*one here who'd like to speak to you.*'

CHAPTER SEVENTEEN

A shadow twitches a curtain and the waves of time roll back. My grandfather isn't explicitly harking back to a moment I captured in my diary – I'm sure he spies through the window most afternoons – but I can't help, on this of all days, but feel hounded.

The shock still hasn't thawed.

I was seconds away from speaking to *Daniel*. Not my real mother. Daniel. He requested permission to call me, to commiserate, to commit an act of kindness after all this time. And what did I do? I hung up, assuming that the past, after years of having left me alone, was now in pursuit. Even before one parent was cold in the clay, I exhumed the other.

How could I have thought it was my mother? *Why*?

The panel door is pulled open without my having knocked and the magnetism of my grandparents' embraces causes the hairs on my arms to stand like iron filings.

I can't resist a snoop around the old place, though I'm shamed it's been so long since I last stepped inside their red-bricked semi. Can it really be as long as a decade? My grandfather points out new wallpaper, the lino in the kitchen, an additional tea-service, but the home's sameness somehow transcends these new features. My mother's old bedroom is used as a storage room now but it still, though her belongings have long gone, retains the feeling of her. I slept here myself at weekends sometimes, just to escape Dad, and I was aware of that strong trace of her even then.

The little girl destined to become a woman who would pretend to be my mother.

There are still pencil notches on the inside of the bedroom door, where my grandfather measured my height in bi-monthly increments. My grandmother, somewhat over-keenly, produces the scribblings I created when I stayed here, including the – hilariously disproportioned – drawing I made of my grandfather after our documented game of *Cluedo*.

The tea brewed, the milk jugged, I'm gestured towards the sofa. My grandfather loses his years once ensconced in the matching, baize-green, tall-backed chair by the window and talks with the energy of a man half his age, his arms flailing propellers as his rigid, thin legs remain folded before him. My grandmother, whose cheeks are as downy as the skin of a ripened peach, does less of the talking, but when she chooses to embellish one of her husband's tangents with a date or name she radiates a wisdom it would be imprudent to argue with. They cite the past a great deal, as befitting a couple fast approaching their eighties, but it's remarkable how little they mention family. Perhaps this is for my benefit. The past is deemed a sore point, especially today.

'Are you alright, Lucas? You're sweating.'

I sluice off my forehead with the back of a hand, the nausea from my encounter with Julian still lingering. 'A bit hot, that's all, Granny.'

Replacing my teacup on the sideboard, I notice the black and white image of my grandparents' wedding. They look remarkably similar to how they appear fifty years on – my grandfather even wears the same pair of thick-rimmed spectacles, or ones very much like them – though the smiles were broader then. There's also a photo of Ryan and my mother, quite a recent one, in a golden frame next to a pot of African Violets.

'I don't know why that's there really,' my grandmother offers, shifting uneasily in her chair. 'We just liked the photo, I think.'

My eyes prick with tears when I spot a photo of my eleven-year-old self nestled there too. I'm sitting in practically the same place I'm sitting now, slightly dwarfed by the floral patterns on a throw covering the settee, and lost in a chemistry book. I don't even remember the photo being taken.

'You were always very independent.' My grandmother looks at the photo too. 'A bit like... Your father did some silly things in the past but he was a good man, Lucas. He didn't deserve to be taken at such a young age.'

My grandfather looks worried by his spouse's unscripted remark.

'He tried very hard with Ryan, he really did,' she adds. 'He was a good father to Ryan.'

Perhaps this is true. As time went on, my mother certainly relaxed her grip on her only child and let my father see more of him. Conceding *my* relationship with him to be a write-off, she thought he ought to make good the bond with his remaining son.

'I feel so sorry for Ryan. He adored his father. Such a sensitive boy. Do you remember how mortified he was when he found out you weren't his brother? He thought you were going to be taken away. He cried for a week.'

'My my, look at the time,' my grandfather says. 'We'd better get going.'

He accompanies me to the garage, muttering apologies, while my grandmother locks up the house. Once I've backed out their old Ford he climbs inelegantly in beside me to explain about the 'tricky' release button on the handbrake. My grandmother clambers into the back.

There's a pointless one-way system round these parts now and, despite having been given long-forgotten landmarks to watch out for and it only being a mile or so drive, I take a wrong turn a couple of times. This is treated humorously, but no one makes the joke, more appropriate for weddings, that I'm trying to avoid the church. By design or accident, we arrive in Windermere Road.

I slow down, then grind to a standstill outside Forty-One.

My old house sports new windows and a sizable extension now, its ground floor swelling smugly, but the place is still tiny compared to the fabrications of a child's memory. The walls are clad in white pebbledash, as they always were, and the front door is wooden and unpainted. I think the door used to be blue, or green. Perhaps it was different colours at different times.

'Are you alright Lucas?' my grandfather asks as a Volvo honks impatience behind us.

I slide their car into a parking space. 'Do you mind if I have a quick look around?'

The two of them stare back, quizzical, horrified at my willingness to break with an arranged schedule. I'm already out the car. 'You've got five minutes,' my grandfather yells after me, stabbing a finger towards his retirement timepiece.

It's a real summer's day. Heat swims up off the tarmac. The small recreation ground opposite my old house is constructed of completely alien dimensions from those of my recollection and features a wooden play-castle with rope bridges and curling slides and a soft, spongy black floor. A mother watches her two daughters haring about with the blithe panic borne by all mothers since time immemorial. There's a doctor's surgery where two bungalows used to stand. The Old Mint House has disappeared without a trace.

Its driveway now leads to a small red-bricked warehouse, seemingly recently built. The 'spooky' Victorian building has been pulled down and the prefabs and haulage crates have gone, though there's a faint reminder of their dynasty in the form of darker, unbleached squares on the concrete. A To Let sign hovers outside two empty office cubicles and, looking through the window of the third, I spy a small workshop, presumably rented by local tradesmen or artisans.

The same low, stone wall to my old garden remains. Without much thought, I scale it.

In the old days, I would've been out of sight of the house down here, in the 'allotment' area, as my mother used to label it, home of oddly-sprouting potatoes, Keegan's bones and broken flowers, but the garden is open plan now, scattered with gardening tools, flowerbeds and birdfeeders. A new shed stands on the old concrete base. Ghosts stir in an upstairs bedroom and I duck out of sight of the house, behind the shed, then climb the creosote-smelling fence that's been erected between Forty-One and Thirty-Nine.

The water butt, lawnmower, gazebo and barbeque could belong to any British garden but I doubt Julian's parents still live here; the newness of these artefacts somehow hints otherwise. Another fence has sprouted in wire criss-crosses at the rear, separating the garden from the overgrown chaos of weeds behind it. It's amazing the elderly lady's garden hasn't been tended in all this time, though I guess it's not impossible the old bird still clings to life. But this new fence means that, even if our old camp, or the vague form of it, were to have survived, access is denied.

This ancient world is a small place indeed. With the advantage of extra height, I can see above a succession of fences: the steel pyramidal spire of a child's swing; the smashed panes of abandoned greenhouses. The soft thrum of lawns being mowed competes with the gentle, distant whine of cars, and the sun blazes as it slips a cloud's moorings, intensifying the greens before me, the red berries.

I prise the wire fence up and it pings from its ground brackets without resistance.

Instinctively, I find the trail of old roof tiles, ones Julian and I pinched from several gardens in the wake of the Great Storm of '87, and crawl under, parting weeds and branches. The camp *has* retained a cramped memory of the space we used to occupy, though nature has vehemently repossessed it. I inch myself in, creating room as I press through the brambles. The scratching canopy of blackberry and ivy still filters the light through in thin lasers.

It's the smell that takes me back. Earth, sap and grass: the promise of a future; the peace after thunderstorms. A pleasant scent of rot, a fresh mould, makes me thirsty for earlier times, for the soaked bottoms of too-small trousers, for arms sore with nettle stings and lightsabers torn from English Oaks. I smell naivety, purity, and the fickleness of youth. Bike-riding friends one minute, foes the second.

The last time I sat here I snogged Daniel's sister. I wasn't allowed near her again after that. For the weeks up until my father and I departed Windermere Road, she was steered sharply into her house and the curtains snapped tight if I happened to be in my garden.

I take out my mobile to ring Mariana. There's no phone signal in 1989.

The retching begins, but there's nothing in my stomach, nothing to trouble the pharynx, so I just sit in the old camp with tears in my eyes and a pain in my core. I take in a lungful of moist air. And another.

If I don't get some diamorphine in me, I feel certain I'll die here.

After what feels like a few minutes recomposing myself, I check my watch. Somehow, almost quarter of an hour has passed. I begin to crawl from the camp.

As I do so, I'm aware of a noise coming from the garden, the sound of plastic bouncing off a body part, a clonking, hollow echo. Silence precedes a soft shuffle of feet.

I remain as still as possible, but the evidence of the torn fence hardly hides my unlawful conduct. The feet step closer.

Now, the lifting of the fence, the worming of an investigative body. The camp is about to be infiltrated. Indeed, my very childhood.

A child, no more than seven or eight, appears through the bracken. His eyes are huge and dark, the mouth a small pink bud, pressed open with curiosity.

'Hello,' I say.

The boy's expression changes to one of unfathomable

horror and the head shoots away. 'Daaaad!' he hollers, charging on his diminutive legs towards Thirty-Nine's open French windows, yellow toy sword springing at his hip.

I flail as fast as I can back under the fence, my knees caking themselves in mud, my elbows too. Something prevents me escaping fully into the daylight, a tugging of the camp on my belt, its reluctance to let me go, as a large, broad-shouldered figure appears on the patio, bends to comfort the boy, then swings his head sharply in my direction. 'Oi!' A deep, male voice. I summon an extra effort to tear myself out and there's the sound of ripping. Free, I clamber back over the taller fence leading to my old garden, run across its lawn, up the shared drive, then through the gate between the two houses.

My grandparents are still waiting for me in the car, faces carved into the pregnant, ever-watchful gazes of abandoned children. I bound into the driver's seat.

'Time to go,' I say, jovial, out of breath, twisting the ignition key. I wrench at the handbrake. The car stalls.

'I told you it was tricky,' my grandfather says.

The front door of number Thirty-Nine flies open and a furious blur bounds across his stubby front garden. I fire the engine again and, punching into first, arc the car into the road and whipcrack us away from the livid father, the sudden acceleration throwing my startled grandparents back in their seats like astronauts at launch time. Receding, the figure shakes his fist at us in the rear-view mirror, before flapping at the pluming black exhaust fumes now enveloping him.

'I suppose you have a good explanation for that, Lucas?' my grandmother asks.

The scarred patch still exists on the tree in the churchyard, child height, smoother and yellower than the rest of the trunk but darker than when I first ripped off the bark. In the years since, couples have crunched across acorns and cupules to carve their initials into the exposed wood, inscribing them within clumsy love hearts: BJP 4 NLM; STEFAN LUVS

LESHIA 24/7; J♥P. Someone has tagged SKAR or SHAK with a knife. The effect of it all is an ugly, cryptic nonsense. My rage, years ago, seemed to last longer than indicated by a bare patch no more than the size of a computer screen. Ironic, too, that it begat all these pronouncements of love.

I turn and walk back to the church.

The cortège is fifteen minutes late, a fact which pierces a grimace into the rusted face of Father Anthony. Bodily, the priest remains stoic, with only his charcoal vestments fluttering the breeze, but his occasional glances at the clock on the church tower expose consternation.

There are a number of people gathered outside the church, taking advantage of the sun. Yews, now in fruit for the hundredth time, wave gently by the far wall. The headstones stretch in tidy rows across the small graveyard, perched atop mounds of subsidence. As an adolescent I used to drink with school friends at the end of this cemetery, tossing empty cider bottles into the hawthorn, laughing at the archaic-sounding names on the stones – these Ingrids and Ermintrudes, Wilfreds and Gertrudes – in the knowledge that my own end was eternities away.

And here I stand, not even a decade later, lucky not to have died yesterday.

I set about brushing the mud from my suit. My grandfather's expression is unreadable, but no doubt the tear to my jacket is of concern. Ditto, the black eye.

I search amongst the alien faces for Mariana. Some hope.

There's the sound of crunching gravel and the crowd turns as one to see the flat nose of the hearse pass through church gates, fresh streak of seagull shit on its ebony bonnet. Father Anthony's face cracks into relief and he immediately starts directing the remainder of the murmuring congregation inside with those big flapping raven's wings of his.

My grandparents and I hang back to await the coffin.

The driver and his passenger, both funeral director staff, walk the length of the hearse and click open the boot. My mother and Clint, then Ryan and his girlfriend, slide out of the second car. The two paid undertakers pull my father's sleek, light-brown coffin with practiced grace towards Ryan and Clint, who receive a corner each. These four pallbearers gently haul my father onto their shoulders and turn him one-hundred-and-eighty degrees before beginning a slow march to the church door. Any guests remaining outside hold back to let the coffin float pass.

I should be helping to carry the body. I know this. But the time has long passed for any grandiose or sentimental gestures on my part, and I can only watch the four of them transport my father stiffly, steadily, into the church. They've evidently rehearsed this without me, just as they all, no doubt, visited my embalmed progenitor, once released by the coroner, during the time I buggered about in the US of A. I haven't gazed upon my father's face, dead or alive, since I was sixteen.

That fact has never shamed me before. It does now.

Before I can step inside the church, I'm stopped by the palm of a tall middle-aged man who's melted out from the brickwork. His hair has grown too long to flatter his recession and he suffers from mild rosacea on his puffy cheeks and high forehead. He quickly pulls a flash of silver from his black jacket.

'Can I speak to you later?' the detective asks. His voice is fraudulently kind.

I nod, then follow the body and my hobbling grandparents through the transept and into the nave.

Behind me, the detective stuffs his ID back in his pocket then finds himself a seat near the back. His eyes, I feel sure, never leave me.

CHAPTER EIGHTEEN

A slow piano piece overlaid with sliding guitars, sounding suspiciously like Pink Floyd, fades to a climax as my father is laid gingerly down upon the two fragile-looking trestles under a kind of proscenium arch at the front of the church.

I sit in the front row, on the right-hand side, between my grandmother and mother. Ryan has pride of place on the aisle seat and a few of his unidentified aunts and uncles fill in our pew, wiping restless hands down the thighs of newly-laundered skirts and trousers. My mother fumbles in her pocket for a handkerchief then passes it across me, to my grandmother, as the priest takes his place in front of the coffin.

My dad's in there. Dad. The man who punted footballs to me across the garden, who taught me chess and bought me books on ghosts, who provided me with green eyes and faithlessness, telescopes and T-shirts.

We stand for a hymn he liked, apparently.

About halfway through *How Great Thou Art*, I look over my shoulder, through the warbled wrong notes and trembling hymn sheets. There are far more people here than I expected. Maybe the death was mentioned in *The Becksmouth Observer*. Maybe he was *liked*.

I'm surprised to see Aaron sitting three pews behind me, in his rainbow leathers. He's worn his pulling jacket to a funeral.

He appears to be wiping his eyes, and nods to me

without shame when he spots me looking over. I stick up my thumb in response. This doesn't go down too well with the scowling row behind me, or indeed with the detective watching circumspectly from the back row. There's still no sign of Mariana, but I'm pleased Aaron made it. He's always believed his alacritous conduct and presence of mind helped save my father's life – I never had the heart to tell him Daniel's knife was far from precisely directed – so this must, in a way, feel like coming full circle to him.

A few seats to the left of Aaron, a fair-haired woman in late-middle age, skin sticky with sunscreen, flicks her eyes from mine, then returns them a few seconds later.

My blood runs cold.

Though I can barely remember her face, I'd recognise her if I saw her again. And this woman is too wide, too regally postured. But more people got wind of my father's death than I assumed would, so there's a chance, conceivably, that news got to her. Maybe my father continued to keep in touch with her throughout the last decade, despite what I've always been told.

Suddenly, after years of indifference, I'm terrified at the thought of what I'd do if we met. Panting, full of hate, remembering to breathe again, I scan the congregation for vestiges of my biology.

What about that woman over there? She's about the right age, has fairish hair, is looking at me with undisguised concern. And there's another contender. A middle-aged woman with too much blusher – a disguise? And four rows behind me, half-obscured by a shoulder, one more. Is *she* the woman who gave me up all those years ago?

I feel a sharp jab in my ribs. It's my mother. Susan, that is. She glares at me, screws her lips together and insists I face the front. The hymn ends.

For another ten minutes I listen to what kind of a man my father was from the mouths of strangers. Some beak-faced child of the sixties called Jerome, hair wisping from the few

221

places it still grows (the nostrils and ears), focuses on my father's writing and weed consumption. I'm not convinced these pursuits are totally appropriate, considering their respective futility and illegality, but Jerome's interminable anecdotes garner a few laughs, and even the priest, after a tale concerning how my father bought three grams of oregano off a Swedish prostitute, raises eyes to heaven.

Jerome resumes his seat and, after we've listened to the Simon and Garfunkel track my father specifically requested, Ryan stands for his turn. The church falls silent.

My brother looks ten years older in his suit, acquits himself without obvious nerves. He recounts a few childhood memories from the time just before I left Becksmouth, when the man we're saying goodbye to was allowed greater access to Ryan's life. My brother's voice cracks when he talks about the rounds of golf they played, the Champions League football matches watched, but regains his composure to the wholesale adoration and pride of the gathering. Although a steel glove pulls and wrenches at my insides, at the proof that so much attention was lavished on Ryan, that he was *fathered*, I'm proud of him too. It can't be easy up there.

At the creak of a door, I find myself spinning round.

A woman hovers at the back of the church, thin, anxious, her black twinset revealing bare arms. She peers around the room with guilty, brazen eyes, then half-hides behind a marble pillar.

I stand. Our eyes meet across the heads of the congregation.

When the detective rises and advances towards her, she hurries from the church into the sunlight, stilettos clicking on the flagstones.

Ryan's stopped speaking and every face turns to mine. I hear someone ask their partner who I am. They murmur that they haven't a clue.

My mother hisses, 'What the hell are you doing, Lucas? Get down!'

I sit, javelined by the fury in my brother's eyes and force myself to pay attention to the scenery throughout the rest of his eulogy: a golden Jesus, eye-rolling his patented pain; a stained-glass window depicting Jonah being retched from the mouth of a whale. If I close my eyes, I can see a small boy on another boy's shoulders, pissing in the font. And over there, where Ryan now stands, just before the chancel, my mother kneels to pray for her father's swift recovery after the heart attack that turned his hair white.

There are those all over the world who, when cursed with awareness of their impending death, once the doctor utters the dreaded words, will become a believer, will sink to their knees. Just under the surface of most of us lurks veneration for the invisible, the improbable. But not me. Religion, the wholesale worship of the accidental, of nature, of beautiful but random patterns, has always struck me as a terrible bore, not to mention a chore. Attending church to sing praise for our ability to breathe always felt like writing a thank you note for the present you never asked to be given.

There are other ways of coping. I think of my eleven-year-old self, blessed with the extraterrestrial logic of youth, and my ludicrous, macabre theory on cheating the reaper by jumping from my bed at the last minute. Much like my father, my more recent attempts to hide from mortality involved consuming to excess, living purely for a nihilistic moment. And my colleagues and I are no better: playing God as we dial for eternal life with the tungsten wheels of our microscopes.

The sudden but ironclad belief that it's my fault assaults me, that my father fell into the abyss and I, as a scientist, as a son, wasn't there to save him.

Ryan finishes his tribute and leaves the front. There's a breach of etiquette as the church erupts with applause and he blushes as he retakes his pew, looking yet another decade older. Or it could be the blood-red summer sun streaming through the stained glass. I wipe at something wet on my cheek and find the remainder of my mother's concealer on my fingers.

This time, I accompany my father on his short, final, journey.

At the journey's end, my mother, Clint, Ryan, his girlfriend and I squeeze our way out of the silent hearse. I go straight to the rear end, nominate myself as a pallbearer.

We convey the surprisingly heavy wooden box into the crematorium, a squat, pale stone building, and then through to a predominantly mahogany room not unlike Kirkby Funeral Consultants' Chapel of Rest. The coffin is placed onto a carpetless oblong, before sprays of fresh flowers and an amethyst curtain. Ryan joins his girlfriend on a pew at the very front of the room. Clint does the same, next to my mother. I sit between these two couples.

A middle-aged man from the crematorium, who bears a startling resemblance to Peter Sellers, enters and expresses his deep sympathy to us. Or, I should say, to Clint. He obviously assumes him, reposed and unruffled, his arm never leaving my mother's shoulders, to be the leader of the gang. Father Anthony, who's appeared out of nowhere, stands to one side of the casket and recites several more Thees, Thous and Thys from the Bible, a prayer seemingly asking for the deceased's absolution. Not long after, Peter Sellers depresses a button on a discreet panel of switches set into a lectern. There's a sharp hydraulic squeal and the coffin shudders.

In the middle of our row, gripping tight the hands of my mother and brother, I watch the box containing my father lowered towards the cremator.

No fire. No fanfare.

And then, he's gone.

CHAPTER NINETEEN

The colours cast onto Aaron's face flush from green to red as he nervously steps backwards, forwards within the stained glass of the vestibule.

I returned to the church with the now coffin-less hearse to find most people had already headed to the pub. My grandparents will need a lift home but are nowhere to be seen, are probably enjoying their yearly brandy with the others.

'You coming to The White Lion for the reception?' I ask.

'Nah. I signed the Book of Remembrance already. I arrived a bit early so I went over there first.' He steps forwards into green.

'You should've called round.'

'I didn't want to intrude, you know.' Backwards into red. I've never seen him so ill at ease.

Now's not the time to discuss the blood on the driveway, the red fingerprints on the kitchen drawer, but the memory of that evening is certainly stronger today, for both of us. The stabbing was hardly serious, but we didn't know that at the time and the drama of the moment helped forge a comradeship, just as, no doubt, seeing Mrs Smithson's corpse once did with me and Julian. Boys are morbid creatures.

'Got your pulling jacket on?' I nod towards his hideous blue and red leather.

'What? This old thing? No. No. Definitely not. No.'

'Heard from Mariana lately?' I ask, giving away the motivation for my earlier question. He obviously thought she'd be here.

'No...' I wonder why he fails to mention their transatlantic conversation on Thursday. Possibly my question sounded a tad rhetorical, challenging. 'I mean, why would I have?'

'She's not answering my calls,' I say. 'I screwed up there. I screwed up *big time*.' Eye contact is impossible. 'I do really care for her you know...'

'Look, mate, funerals are difficult times. You're emotional. Worry about Mariana another time, eh? I mean, today's about your family.'

'I guess you're right.'

His phone pings a text alert and he yanks it from his trousers. After scrutinising the device, he announces he has to leave and promises to give me a call soon.

We walk out into the sunshine, hug a nervy goodbye.

'Thanks for coming, man,' I tell him. Either he's bulked up lately or I'm losing weight; his embrace dwarfs mine.

My mother's standing with the priest on the driveway, presumably thanking him for the service, when she spots me.

'What *the hell* was that?' Her yell pierces the serenity of the cemetery. Father Anthony stiffens, looks appalled, and Aaron takes his opportunity to slip away.

'What was what?'

'What do you *think*?' She marches up to me. 'Standing up during your brother's talk.'

'I thought I recognised someone. My mistake.'

She's been bottling her anger up in preparation for this, but I've clearly thrown her. She peers at me through the sun, pulls back her head. Her eyes regard me with unbridled disappointment. 'Who?'

'Nobody. Just...' I release the information like a guilty schoolboy, staring at my shoes. 'My mother.'

'Jesus Christ!' she shouts. The priest winces again as he floats past. 'Lucas, your mother's long gone. Are you coming to the pub? Today's about *your father*, remember?'

'In a bit. I might.'

Me, in a pub? Today?

226

I'll give that a miss.

Over her shoulder, I spot the detective, rigid and stony-faced, in an arbour of the graveyard. He sits on a bench, holding a mobile phone which receives only superficial interest. I assume he's waiting for me.

My mother's fury cools during a long silence.

'Why did you think *she* would be here, darling?' Her fingers are warm upon my cheek. 'You really think she gives a damn about your father these days?'

'I don't know. I just… got a bit confused.'

'You wanted nothing to do with your real mother, remember? What's changed now?'

I don't answer. I'd have thought it was pretty obvious what's changed.

'Your mother's not here because she just doesn't care about you. I'm sorry Lucas. She didn't care about anyone.'

'But she must've cared about Dad, *once*. It wasn't her fault she was schizophrenic.'

My mother raises a tidy, thin eyebrow. 'Is that what he told you? That the hippy was insane? Good Lord! Messed up on wacky baccy more like.' She squints across the graves. 'Male pride,' she sighs.

'He said she tried to hurt me when I was a baby.'

'Well maybe that's true, I don't know. But she's a whole other story, Lucas. Forget about her. She's not a part of your life. She doesn't exist. You know, I remember taking you bowling once, shortly after the split – you probably don't remember – and you asked me, "Why can't *you* be my mum anymore?"'

'And you told me you still were. Of course I remember. You said something like, "I'm still your mum, Lucas. I always will be. Please don't mention that woman's name around me. She doesn't love you like I do."'

'My God. How can you *possibly* remember that?'

Tears well in her eyes, something my father's death failed to inspire, and she reaches for me as though to prevent herself falling. She stifles her emotion on my shoulder.

Above her head, I watch the detective stand and walk unhurriedly from his hiding place, up the gravel drive towards the road. No doubt he felt awkward watching us, and will wait for me at the lych-gate, but this action seems to vindicate me; I've proved my familial credentials, my innocence.

'I'm sorry,' my mother says, pulling herself back, wiping her eyes. 'It was so long ago. I shouldn't care anymore.' My mother spent a couple of years getting over my father, it's no secret. His infidelity changed her, toughened her; I can only assume it's the sense of occasion, and the fact we've never talked about those times before, that's responsible for this tearful blip. 'Your father was a gullible fool, I know that better than anyone, but he was… romantic in his own way. His problem was he could never let old dogs lie. One old dog in particular… Anyway, now he's gone. She's gone. But I'm here. Ryan's here.'

'I know…'

'So forget about her. Ryan told me you said she tried to call you…'

'I was wrong.'

'*Of course* you were wrong. Look, I'm no psychologist, but you want to know what I think? Well, I'm going to tell you anyway. Why do you think you're acting like this? Seeing your real mother everywhere after all this time? You're finally steering that anger at another in order to mourn your father. Ask yourself: did you really hate him, the man who loved you no matter what you thought of him over the years, who *wanted* you to stay with him when we split up, or were you merely directing your hate *at* him?' She jabs me in the chest with a long finger. 'You know something? You learned to hate at an immature age. It stuck. And you've been clinging to it out of habit ever since. You hate your real mother. You don't hate your father. You never have.'

I meander down to the bottom of the churchyard, wipe Estelle Catt (loving wife of Phillip Catt, born 1889, died 1968) of bottle-tops and sit on her.

I'm underwater. I'm thousands of miles above sea level. I'm listening to the leaves on the Great Oak whishing like the priest's vestments, trying to come up with an excuse not to join the funeral party at The White Lion. New mourners are gathering at the church door and Death's protocol is repeated under waving cemetery trees: the unsure body language of near-strangers; the priest glancing at the steeple clock.

The crowd by the church shuffles and swells under the merciless sun, on a day we're obligated to wear black, and from this modest gathering a woman walks out towards me. I watch her slink through the graves, bare arms swinging. She's the woman who gatecrashed my father's funeral earlier, this time more decisive in her manner, steeled. Though she's nowhere near my biological mother's age, I can see why I thought she might've been her. She definitely doesn't appear to want to hang around long.

She stops three feet from me.

'You must be Lucas.' She delivers this as though it breaks her heart. 'Has that policeman gone?'

'Who are you?'

'My name's Sophia. We need to talk.' Panic strains her voice.

A young, slender body. An apprehensive, unhappy beauty shadowed beneath unkempt dark hair. It's not too hard to imagine this woman on my father's arm twenty years ago, but I can't fathom how a destitute almost-fiftysomething could've snared her.

'I wondered about you,' I say.

'Likewise.' She perches on a neighbouring grave, pushes a weave of hair from her sallow features. I'm sure Ryan said she was twenty but she looks much older, though this is perhaps due to exhaustion, mourning. She keeps tense eyes on the church. 'Your father told me a lot about you.'

I assume 'a lot' to be something of an exaggeration. 'Did you know my father well?' A stupid question.

She inhales as though it hurts her lungs to do so, then turns to inspect me. 'You look like him. You really do.'

'Why didn't you come to the funeral? Properly, I mean.'

'It would've been awkward.' We sit in silence for a while, pretending this *isn't* awkward. 'Several times over the last year,' she says, 'your father almost called you up, but... You have your own life.' Her voice is so soft, pitched at such a monotone, it defies any kind of accent. Her eyes seem too green for her rich tresses, betraying a possible Eastern European ancestry. Something about her dispossessed, hunted air reminds me of Leah. 'It was hard for him, I think, knowing his firstborn had left his life forever. He treated you all – his family – terribly, he knew that.'

'What happened? There's talk he was murdered.'

She looks away, waits for the church bells to finish pealing three o'clock. 'It was a heart attack, the paramedic said.' She talks without feeling, a bad actress reciting practised lines.

'I don't believe you. Where have you been all week? Apparently you found him.'

A fingertip taps the stone beneath her, a heel the grave-rail.

'Sophia, you *have* to help me. You were probably closer to my father than anybody. Tell me what's happened.'

When she turns back I see beyond her grief and fear for the first time. I see what my father saw: those green eyes reveal an intelligence few people convey without words. 'I *wasn't* particularly close to him,' she admits. 'He was a difficult man to get close to. You think you're close, but then... well, he made it very clear I was just a fling.'

'Sophia, you've got to tell me what you know about how he died. First there's talk of murder, then the inquest isn't necessary, now there's a policeman sniffing about...'

My words haven't registered. She stares beyond me, past the sky. 'I didn't mind. The truth is, he never got over her. His "big love". I caught him looking at her photo a few times, or stuffing it back in the desk if I entered his study unannounced, but I never said anything. How could I have? He was nearly thirty years older. He came with baggage.

230

Some days it seemed as though he lived almost entirely within his memories…'

My impatience spills over. 'Look, I'm very sorry he treated you badly. *Quelle surprise*. But they think my father was *killed*.'

She winces. 'I know.'

'*Was* he?'

Her voice catches. 'I'm sorry.' She stands, pulls at the hem of her skirt for a few more inches of modesty. 'I thought I could help you… I'm sorry. I'm really, really sorry.'

'But… why did you come to find me?'

She's already walking away from me when she says, 'To do your father a last favour. To do something he didn't have the strength to. To tell you he loved you.' She twists back round.

I laugh without humour. Everyone's telling me this today.

When she breaks into a run I give chase through the graves. 'Wait! It was you who tidied his flat, wasn't it? What were you trying to cover over? What happened? Why are you so desperate to avoid the police?'

Though she's in heels, she makes fast progress and is soon amongst the black suits of nonplussed, grieving strangers, struggling against them, and heading towards the tall wooden lych-gate. I too fight through the crowd, the brutal searchlight of today's sun, only to find my way blocked by Father Anthony. He stands, erect and solemn, watching the approach of another hearse. In this one, the word 'Sister' is spelt out with white flowers on one side. The vehicle turns right, then stops, preparing to enter the church grounds. 'Daughter' decorates the other window.

I stand back to let the vehicle pass. Once it's done so, Sophia's vanished.

The scent of mould once again greets me in my father's hallway, the odour of a house unaired, hermetically sealed. With the door closed, Becksmouth is all but silent, the whine of cars on the coast road barely audible. A gull pads softly about the roof.

I head straight to the study. My briefcase is still on floor, its contents a disembowelled concertina of papers beside it: the first few pages of a magazine Aaron and I started to design, full of star charts and espionage stats; exercise books filled with sci-fi stories from bored Sundays. In the third drawer down on the right-hand side of his desk, sporting a brighter, well-worn handle, I find the photo Sophia mentioned.

It's half-hidden under a stack of correspondence in a legion of handwritings. The photo's slightly singed, as though pulled, last minute, from a fire.

The image is of my father, younger than I am now, beside a blonde woman wearing a tie-dyed T-shirt. They might be in a beer garden, cold but in high spirits. My father sports an ostentatious, and very seventies, handlebar moustache – one which, I realise, he was briefly persuaded, in 1989, to re-grow. His hair is the same length it generally tended to be, curling to just short of his collar, but is much darker than I remember. Typically, he's not *quite* looking at the camera.

I find myself scanning the other face for signs of insanity, as though such things would be obvious via an anonymous photographer's viewfinder. She looks completely different to the way I remember her on our doorstep. Yes, she's blonde and pale and thin and good-looking but there's nothing but delight and optimism in those blue eyes. Her mouth is wide open in mid-laughter, the top of her nose wrinkled with the authenticity of the emotion. It's probably my imagination, but there is a passing resemblance to Sophia after all, in the lean shape of the face, the elfin nature of the chin.

Perhaps this moment in time is misleading, perhaps as soon as the shutter snapped the smiles were wiped away and this shared, unquantifiably happy look is nothing but an accident. But I don't think so. Whatever went wrong after this will never be explained to me now. It's no wonder my father kept this old photo, its edges curled by flame, the colours tanning. Here – 1978, it states on the back – is where his love jammed, remained stuck in a groove for the rest of his life.

I take the photo and walk into my father's lounge. I try to experience the world he inhabited when gazing out the window at the backs of Edwardian houses, what he might've felt, in this hot and unventilated place, when he looked upon my smiling school photo on the mantelpiece or listened to the lonely sonata of high tide.

I inspect the window Ryan climbed in through. The lock's been forced and torn from the wood, rendering it unusable. This flat's on the second floor so he must've shinned up a drainpipe to get here, clearly leaving through the front door and relying on the deadlock for matters of security.

My attention is drawn to the DVDs under the television – all horror films, naturally, and nothing from the last twenty years – and that old video box in the fake leather I spotted last time I was here. I open it up, expecting to see the 'green tobacco' I found in my father's Windermere Road wardrobe, or at least an old VHS copy of *Night of the Demon*. But it's empty. Out of curiosity, to check whether this was indeed the case he still kept his weed in, I duck forwards to smell inside. It's slightly redolent of skunk, true, but beyond that, overpoweringly, is another scent: the unmistakable, vinegary smell of acetic acid.

Everything falls into place.

There's the click of a door lock and I bolt upright.

I'm frozen, powerless to move as the swish of a bag follows the ticking of shoes. The door slams. Feet slip across the hallway. Another door, probably the study, groans open.

I actually contemplate hiding behind the sofa. Times have changed since Julian and I holed out in The Old Mint, young spies with worldly secrets to uncover. Why am I so reluctant to show my face? Worried I'll look soft, hunting round my father's memories?

'Hello?' a woman shouts.

Footsteps in the hall precede the opening of the lounge door.

I turn around to face the intruder, who stares at me with the look of an animal aware of its impending journey to the slaughterhouse.

'I killed your father,' Sophia says, the five syllables echoing like gunfire round the room.

'No, you didn't. It was an accident.'

Sophia slumps to the sofa, casting a set of keys beside her. All her poise and dignity has vanished, her chartreuse eyes now look cold, even her mourning clothes seem cheap.

'Why did you run away from me?' I ask.

'I wasn't going to tell you… but I thought you might come here… You seemed to kind of jump when I mentioned that photo… You deserve to know... God, this was where he… where he…'

I fetch her a glass of water from the kitchen. It takes me longer than seems polite, looking for the right cupboard. When I return, she sips hesitantly at it, as though it's poisoned, then sets it down on the coffee table. She looks at the open video box I've placed there, confusion netting her forehead.

'Last week,' I explain, 'when I saw that video case, it was just a box, an innocent little object I wouldn't even have contemplated opening. I'd forgotten that was where he used to keep his drugs. My father *was* killed, but not by you. It was heroin, wasn't it?'

She nods.

'Why have you been avoiding that detective? He's been at my mother's house, my father's funeral… It's surely *you* he wants to speak to?'

'Of course. *I* introduced your dad to H. He smoked it with *me*. But…' Her defence comes out in a wracking series of sobs. 'I didn't know he was going to start taking it on his own. Jesus Christ. I came over and found him with the needle still in his arm. His arm was blue. The look on his face was… horrible. Like he was… just shocked. Frozen. He was slumped at his desk. We *never* injected together. Not once.

We only smoked it, I swear. I panicked when I saw him and tidied away what I could – the needle and spoon, everything.'

'Of course...' I'm talking to myself, assembling the week's events in my mind. 'Injecting once, just one time, would leave a *tiny* needle mark, one that probably wouldn't be seen. There'd be no chance of knowing how he died without an autopsy. But a *blue arm*... An inquest, with that evidence, would be unnecessary; the cause of death is as obvious as a knife protruding from a man's heart. The police weren't being slack, they know *how* he died – overdose, pure and simple, death by misadventure – but nothing's been helped by you keeping quiet. The *why* has been missing. The mystery of the lack of evidence around the body. And your fingerprints must be *all over* the flat.'

Sophia looks at me without expression, her face a death-mask of exhaustion. I didn't spot the fact that she was a user in the churchyard, but it seems so obvious now. 'But... how did *you* know? I mean...' She points towards the video box. 'He kept his stuff in that old thing, yes. But, it's empty. I cleared it away. I cleared *everything* away.'

'Smell it,' I say, holding up the case. 'That smell is unmistakable. To an addict.'

She begins a low wail into a cushion. 'What made him inject?' she asks herself. 'The stupid, stupid *idiot*.'

I settle on the sofa beside her. She becomes rigid and looks uneasy, but the sobbing slows. 'It's not your fault. My father was killed by a contaminant in whatever cheap shit he got hold of. Shame you disposed of the evidence. I could've run tests, found out exactly what it was. We might even have been able to trace the supplier.' The toxin in his blood, which the coroner let slip about, was probably strychnine or quinine. Poor bastard. I think of my overdose, its abruptness, how I was saved only by Ryan's presence. My father was alone.

I watch her cry, her pretty face ruined by running mascara. She looks to my hands and the photo of my parents I've been holding all this time.

The doorbell rings.

'I'm not here!' she hyperventilates. 'I'm not here!'

I pull open the door to find the detective. He stands stiffly, somehow irritably, like a novice journalist sick of the constant death-knocks his once-seemingly glamorous occupation demands. 'Mr Marr. Can we talk?'

I'm speaking to his rosacea. 'It's not really a good moment. I was just going through some of my father's things. We saw him off today. It's an emotional time.'

'I'm aware of that, sir.'

'Have you got information for me about how he died?'

I can see the professionalism tearing at the humane, in the flicker of the eyelid, the swallowing of the throat. 'It's not something I can discuss with you at the moment, sir. I'm looking for a Miss Sophia Henderson.'

'I've no idea who that might be. Sorry.'

'Forgive me, sir, but I watched her enter this property about five minutes ago.' He now embodies the oleaginous calmness of a politician under fire. Though his smile is uncomfortable, it remains firm; I can tell that the chink of sympathy I witnessed will not appear again. 'I would hate to have to explain to you the penalty for aiding and abetting a suspect. Like all of us, on this of all days, I'm sure you'd want this matter dealt with as calmly and as quickly as possible.'

I let him in.

Sophia's terror has dissolved into acceptance and she waits on the sofa, condemned. While her manner appears relaxed, the hands by her side grip the cushions with whitening knuckles.

'You know how he died, right?' she asks him. 'Am I under arrest?'

'We just want to talk to you, so we can put an end to this.' His eyes are on me though, patiently judging what my reaction might tell him about what he can or can't say. He seems to make up his mind. 'But, yes, we know. We know.'

The last of my father's lovers is led wordlessly from his flat.

CHAPTER TWENTY

The door chimes as I enter.

A pale woman in her fifties, dove-white wings at her temples, enquires, 'Can I help you?' with forced solemnity. It's evidently hours past closing time; she wears her coat and a fatigued expression. Kirkby Funeral Consultants is a lower-lit establishment than I remember.

'Just you tonight?'

She doesn't consider this worthy of reply.

'Could you give these to your colleague for me?' I pass over a bouquet of roses, carnations and chrysanthemums. 'They're to say sorry. Well, actually, to say thank you. I was here a week ago and she was very helpful, but I went somewhere else in the end. No particular reason. Somewhere closer.'

She lays them across the desk, suspicion warping her lips as she reads my name off the little card.

'She probably won't remember me,' I add.

'Which one?'

'Sorry?'

'Which colleague?'

'Anna.'

'You mean *Tanya*?'

'That's her.'

She bends to sniff the flowers, warily, as though expecting them to bite her mouth off. Their fragrance reassures her enough to smile and the consequent dimples, crescents etched into her soft cheeks as severely as the dead upon her company's headstones, are worrying in their familiarity.

'I'll make sure my daughter gets them,' she purrs. 'Thanks.'

I exit at speed.

Outside, the dying sun glints off cars, rooftops, shop awnings, and the sky is a multicoloured fan of colours, as brilliant as barium salts upon introduction to a naked flame. I duck back into the taxi and ask the driver to take me to Southgate. I remove the photo from my pocket, an image my father couldn't bear to burn, and once more survey the smiling faces and try to equate them with my limited understanding of love, based on films and novels and that brief, sunny hour in Central Park.

London has grown heavy in the last ten minutes and the hot ferocity of a thunderstorm seems imminent. Sure enough, the heavens rip as we pass Bounds Green and the first spots of rain gun at the windscreen.

On Mariana's quiet road, I check that a light burns in her living room.

'Would you mind waiting?' I ask the driver as I pay. 'I might still need you. If you see me go in, feel free to drive on.'

I scurry through the warm rainfall, then knock.

A shadow flits behind the glass, the fish-eyed spy hole. There's a long pause before the door opens five inches.

She hovers in the doorway, barring me from her home. She's never looked so cagey, so hurt, so off-guard, so ugly. And I've never felt such deep affection for anyone in my life.

'How was the funeral?' she asks, eyes vacant. It's difficult at the best of times to know how this woman feels but, right now, she's unfathomable. She wears jeans, a black hooded top and a pair of oversized Homer Simpson slippers.

'It was okay. But I made a tit out of myself.'

A flash of lightning cracks the sky then, seconds later, a rifle shot of thunder as the storm rolls closer. She opens her door a fraction wider, to regard the miserable conditions, and I notice her suitcase hasn't made it further than the hall. Beside it, a couple of small, blank canvasses poke out of an art store's carrier bag. She tries to hide them from my vision, her body twisting across them.

'How are you feeling?' There's definitely a *touch* of concern in her voice, but it occurs to me she's asking *Are you high?* rather than casting for platitudes about my health.

'Fine,' I say, shrugging my arms through the increasing downpour. No doubt it looks like the usual performance, the whole 'I hate my father' act. I backpedal and explain about his death, its no-longer mysterious circumstances. 'Honestly, I've seen the worst that stuff can do. I've changed, I promise you. I didn't inject in New York. That was Leah's syringe. I have... *lapsed*... since – and I'm telling you this because I don't want any more skeletons in any closets – but it will *never* happen again. Don't ask me why I invited Leah back to your parents' apartment. I think I was worried for her. Nothing happened, believe me. But I wasn't thinking properly, I admit that. I'm so, so sorry.'

My hair's a viscous mixture of wax and rain and I can feel strands crawling down my forehead like some restless arachnid. My shirt's plastered to my chest. There doesn't appear to be even the outside chance she'll offer me a towel. Even in the action of being pushed away one hopes for, at least, contact – the flat hand on the chest; the hot foot sending the colder body out of bed – but here I am with no chance of a parting kiss, a valedictory handshake. She couldn't make it more obvious that I'm an unwelcome presence.

'I know I acted in a terrible way and... Look, I haven't turned up on your doorstep to try and make you change your mind about me, or take advantage of you, okay? And that's not what I was doing in New York either. I really like you, Mariana. More than like you...'

This is torture. I'll say my piece and go. The taxi's still waiting.

'In fact, I think I...'

When she shifts her weight to another absurdly slippered foot, I catch a glimpse of what she's really been concealing all this time. A split-second sighting of a jacket hanging on her banister. Tasteless red and blue leather, white tubing on the sleeves.

A heartbeat thumps in the veins above my ears.

'Aaron...?'

I slip past Mariana, who gives out a little shriek then charges after me.

She doesn't charge far. I find Aaron in the front room, standing by a bookcase. There's no banter from him, no 'All's fair in love and war, mate,' he just stares at Mariana as a guilty complicity bleaches tension across his face. When he finally scrapes together the bollocks to look at me, so unfocused is his gaze he simultaneously manages to avoid eye-contact. A few hours ago, I practically told Aaron I loved Mariana. What kind of friend does this to another, on the day of his father's funeral?

'What are *you* doing here?' I spit.

He runs his hand along the bookcase, a nervous mock-inspection of dust, then arranges three shells in a perfect, pointless line upon her shelf. 'Before you go all indignant on me, Lucas: it's not how it looks. Mariana told me...' As the pair of them make fleeting eye-contact, he seems to think better of revealing whatever he was going to. Probably the false assumption that I'm shooting up again. 'All she wanted to do was talk to someone. About you. I thought you'd probably take it the wrong way so I didn't tell you I was coming here.' His voice is somewhere between defiant and matter-of-fact. He's disappointed in me.

I squelch after him as he crosses between us and into the hall.

'You dick,' he says, quietly enough so Mariana can't hear. 'She likes you, this one.' There's a thin, rueful smile when he says, 'I told her what you said to me at the church.' He wraps his coloured leathers across his back. 'Anyway, I'll leave you both to it.'

My old friend opens the door and strides into the rain.

Inside her lounge of harmless furnishings, books and photos, Mariana looks terrified. Testosterone, our near-confrontation, still hangs as heavy as the storm Aaron's entered. We don't speak to each other for a long sixty seconds.

'Leah and I didn't…'

She holds up her right hand. 'I don't want to hear anything about that girl.'

I take a step towards her. 'You're such a… wonderful, strong, beautiful person.'

'I know. Keep going.'

'You've changed my world view in so many ways. I look at you and, honestly, I *do* believe in intelligent design.'

She can't help but laugh.

'I need you in my life, Mariana. I messed up, I know.'

Emotion gnaws at her lip as she cups my chin and, for a moment, I think she's going to plant me a kiss. What she's really doing, it seems, is looking into my eyes for traces of deceit. She leads me to the doorstep with her hand on my elbow, the way one aids a blind man.

'It's been a long day. Let's do something in a few days, perhaps. Give us both time to think. I'll call you.'

When I turn, halfway down the path, she's already closed the door without a sound.

Aaron's taken my bloody taxi.

Still, the rain isn't falling as hard now, as I trudge home, and night's arrived. Parts of the sky have even cleared and, looking up past a London firmament streaked and bloated by rain clouds, torn and unzipped by vapour trails, I can make out the fascinations of my childhood: the belt of Orion, Betelgeuse and Rigel, Aldebaran and the Pleiades, and, just below and to the right, the bright Mira star in the Cetus constellation.

I meant what I said to Mariana. Tonight, as the moon arcs higher, I can almost understand why some people see God in beauty.

Soaked, I seek asylum in a phone box until the last of the rain clears completely. Across the street, a familiar advert also hides behind the Perspex of a bus shelter. This time, animal rights protesters haven't transformed the angelic spawn into a devil-child.

I feed fifty pence into the miraculously working phone.

'Hello, I'm trying to get hold of Daniel King. I think he's been trying to call me. He's an... um... inmate.'

There's a long pause.

When a voice next comes on the line, it certainly isn't Daniel. 'Hello? I'm afraid Daniel's on his way to another institution.' Her voice fights against echoing acoustics. 'May I ask who's calling?'

Once I've explained who I am and how I've missed his calls, I'm informed that he's been relocated to a Category B prison in Lewes and am given the new number to try tomorrow. I tell her I might even make the journey down there in person.

'He'd like that,' is all she says in response.

There's plenty of money left after the call and I type in a more familiar number.

'Lucas?'

It's Ryan who answers. I tell him how good he was at the service, how proud I am to call him my brother. Naturally, this is met with silence.

It's been well documented that members of my family are unable to communicate with each other, that secrets are kept as a matter of course, so it's with mixed feelings that I keep the truth of our father's death from him. In order for our father to remain a hero in Ryan's eyes, I keep the secrets going.

'Do you want me to get Mum?' he asks. 'I think I can drag her away.'

'From what?'

'Granny and Granddad are here, and so are a few others.' I can make out, in the background, the tinkle of teaspoons, the low mumble of my grandfather's diminishing baritone holding court at their post-wake gathering.

Above it, I hear my mother call in a tired voice, 'Is that Junior?'

'She's on her way,' Ryan tells me.

'You know what? I don't want to interrupt. Just tell her... Tell her I'll call her later.'

He mumbles something to our mother, then returns to the phone.

'I guess I'll see you soon then, Lucas.'

'Yeah. Just one thing: Does Mum often refer to me as Junior? I haven't heard her call me that for over fifteen years.'

'From time to time. I'll tell her not to if you...'

'No, it's fine. It's fine. You know what? It's fine. Well, I'll see you. And thanks. You know what for.'

I leave the box and walk on. Once again, I take the photo of Lucas Senior and my real mother from my pocket, then tear it neatly in two, placing one smiling face back in my pocket and discarding the other, in little pieces, into the puddling rain.

EPILOGUE

I'm brought back by a shrieking of unresponsive brakes, the punishing wrench of straining metal. The other driver manages to jerk his van from us at the last second as we flail and switchback across the ice. Beneath my hands, the steering suddenly freewheels. We slalom down the hill until I manage to handbrake the Jeep and bring us to rest in a gliding slice across the middle of the road. The van carries on and scrunches into the trees on the left-hand side. No one even has time to scream.

I turn to look at my family. They're all belted and safe, but look startled. Apart from my son, naturally, who's delighted.

'Mum? You okay?'

'Fine.'

'Ryan?'

'Yeah. I'm good.'

I look at my wife.

'Mouth?'

'You bloody idiot,' she says.

Ryan's already out the car, making his way across to help the other driver. I disentangle myself from the seatbelt and go over to join him.

The front of the van is folded round a tree in an ugly concertina of steel and broken glass. We help the dazed man out. There's some cutting to his face where the windshield sprayed over him, but nothing serious.

'What happened?' he asks. He's about fifty, I'd guess.

'I hit some ice and came right at you. Sorry.'

He looks over his van, anger straining in his neck, but sees my child and the two women coming to join us and controls himself. Mum's got her mobile out and is trying to work out how to ring the emergency services.

'Don't bother,' the man says.

The snow is falling heavily now and we'll all be buried at this rate. The vehicles will have to be abandoned here, and no tow truck or AA van is going to get through this.

We begin to swap insurance details, but he's inappropriately dressed for the weather and suggests a local pub at the bottom of the hill. A short trek, he says.

We start the trudge down. It might just be because he's nearer her generation but he sidles up to my mother straight away to ask whether he's met her before somewhere. If he's expecting anything more he's going to be disappointed. She's all but given up on men since Clint's affair.

My son jumps between me and Mariana, giggling delightedly as he stomps his Thomas the Tank Engine boots into the snow, sticking out his tongue to catch the falling flakes.

Everyone tells me he looks like me, to the point where I actually believe they're not just saying it because it's one of those things people are supposed to. There's very little of Mariana in him, not yet anyway. Maybe it's nature's way of making me feel more secure about my genes. Who needs to live for the moment when posterity stares back at you every morning over the Coco Pops? He's just turned three.

The going is slow as the snow gusts in great, rushing walls across us.

'Where's this pub?' Ryan asks.

'Just a bit further,' our newcomer replies.

Our son runs to his Uncle Ryan, who hauls him onto his back and treads cautiously over the squeaking snow. Mariana and I hold hands, but don't speak. Clairvoyance blossomed between us long ago, and the day remains a sombre one.

Dad's still in the air, and my insurance premium is about to shoot up.

Would Dad and I be friends if he was still alive? I don't know. But I feel closer to him now than ever before. And I'm not ashamed to admit that I sometimes speak to him.

I still carry that photo in my wallet, slightly creased, and I've seldom thought about the woman who used to stand next to him in the image. I don't need to. Relations with my existing relations are much healthier now.

With Mariana, too, things couldn't be better.

She forgave me in the end, obviously. Though she made me sweat for it, I wasn't going to let her go. I've had chances to be unfaithful, as in those early days, but I never felt like following such opportunities up. Truth be told, I wouldn't dare. She intimidates me too much. I think a lot of men fall for women, whether they know it or not, who they fear a little. Perhaps that's the point. To keep our base instincts in check.

We arrive at a pub called The Three Compasses, warm with laughter, low-ceilinged and covered in nautical charts and images. There's the smell of a log fire. The pub dog pads over to see if we've got anything for him, sniffs at our pockets then slopes away. My family retreat to a booth and I accompany the man I've just nearly killed to the bar and buy him a pint. After we've exchanged details he scurries to a seat on the far side and I survey the unknown ales. I still don't drink, although I'll allow myself a glass of champagne at Mariana's private view next week, the first – we hope – of many exhibitions of her work.

Out of sight from my family, I remove my old diary from my coat pocket. I haven't read it since the days immediately after my father died and I don't intend to now; I learned last time that as a historical document it succeeded on an emotional level but sorely failed on an empirical one. Ever since we set today as the day we were going to scatter Dad's ashes, I had in the back of my mind the idea that I would dispose of this too, but the minute we got up on the Downs

I knew it would have been impossible to bury it in that hard, frozen earth.

I turn to the last page. *Hello, older me, if you're reading this. I hope you got away in the end.* It's tempting to scribble something underneath that final line, to end my chronicle on a more positive note, but I replace it in my pocket and head back to the table with the menus.

When food arrives, my son sits on my right knee and devours the chips I blow on to cool for him. Solipsist and content, the world stops for him as the rest of us concentrate our conversation on the accident and what's perceived as my skilful management of the ice. I don't tell them the truth of the matter. That my instinct to hammer at the brakes sent us straight into the path of the man who now sits, blood drying upon his forehead, at the other side of the pub.

'My life flashed before my eyes,' I half-joke.

Sometime during our meal, a kid comes over with a cricket bat and begs Ryan to sign it, which he does with his usual embarrassed grace. It no longer amazes me that people recognise him, but I've no idea where they pull out these things to autograph from.

I inaugurate the toast.

'To Dad,' I say.

'Happy birthday,' Ryan adds. He would have been sixty.

The snow is falling heavily outside the window. It gathers on the panes beside me, melting silently against the heat, and sliding down in slow, solidifying clumps. Where the white sky lands on budding, spring branches it manages to form impossibly tall and crisp stalagmites, occasionally knocked off by the local children hurling snowballs and building a surprised-looking snowman on the lawn outside.

It looks like my family's going to be entombed inside this warm, friendly place for quite some time yet.

'What are you smiling about?' Mariana whispers.

'Nothing. Excuse me.'

On my way to the bar to pay for the meals, I stop at the

fireside. The dog is sprawled luxuriantly before it, soaking up its smoky, ashy warmth.

With utmost discretion, I once again remove the diary and, for the very last time, flick through it before casting it into the crackling fire. The cover begins to smoke, and then the edges catch as the pages curl slowly upwards and the book burns. The sides of the diary turn black, a blackness which blisters towards the centre before, finally, only the Letraset words remain. And then my name, too, is enveloped in purifying flame, and the cinders are already dancing their way up the chimney to mingle with the weaving snowflakes and the cold, open sky above.

ACKNOWLEDGEMENTS

Not that it matters, but I almost abandoned this novel.

Following a family bereavement, continuing with the book felt disrespectful in some way. However, after a time, I came back to it and saw that not only had the breathing space revealed exactly what was needed in order to fix certain logistical issues inherent in the original draft, but that I shouldn't get too hung up on authorial worries such as fiction versus fictionalisation. Every novel out there plays with those boundaries.

Why am I telling you this? Good question. Not everyone who reads novels wants to write them but everyone who wants to write novels must read, so if you happen to be one of those poor souls, and you're struggling, maybe you'll indulge me this one unsolicited piece of advice I learned the hard way: put your novel aside. Put it aside for a long time. You'll know exactly what it's worth when you pick it up again.

No one writes a book in a vacuum. Thanks therefore to the usual suspects. To Matt. To Tony. To Sam. To everyone – staff and students – from the London City MA. To Tom, Lauren, Lucy and Allison at Legend. To my editor, Rob, who, once again, pushed me via late-night emails and line edits to shine this collection of words ever brighter. To my agent, Louise, who must have lost count of the number of versions of *Blame* she's had to wade through.

And finally, as always, thanks to Patricia. If I tried to do it without you, I couldn't.

COME AND VISIT US AT
WWW.LEGENDPRESS.CO.UK

FOLLOW US
@LEGEND_PRESS